About the Author

Vanessa Carnevale is an author based in Melbourne, Australia, where she lives with her husband and two children. She loves travel, tea and flowers, and often dreams of escaping to the country.

You can connect with Vanessa at www.vanessacarnevale.com

The
Memories
of Us

VANESSA CARNEVALE

avon.

Published by AVON
A Division of HarperCollins*Publishers* Ltd
1 London Bridge Street
London SE1 9GF

www.harpercollins.co.uk

First published in Great Britain by HarperCollins*Publishers* 2018
3

A catalogue copy of this book is
available from the British Library.

ISBN: 978-0-00-829506-6

This novel is entirely a work of fiction.
The names, characters and incidents portrayed in it are the work
of the author's imagination. Any resemblance to actual persons,
living or dead, events or localities is entirely coincidental.

Printed and bound in UK by CPI Group (UK) Ltd, Croydon CR0 4YY

MIX
Paper from
responsible sources
FSC® C007454

This book is produced from independently certified FSC™ paper
to ensure responsible forest management.

For more information visit: www.harpercollins.co.uk/green

For my dear friend, Lucy. May the memories of your mother, and the memories that made us, be cherished forever.

PROLOGUE

We have been arguing for six minutes. Blake switches off the radio. We never travel with the radio off. Unless we are arguing of course, something we hardly ever do. He takes one hand from the steering wheel, flicks open a tin of mints with his thumb, tilts back his head and lets one fall into his mouth. He crunches it between his teeth before swallowing. He doesn't offer me one like he usually does. I sink deeper into my seat and stare at the tin lying in the console between us. The car seems quieter than it did before.

'How are we going to handle this, Gracie? What do you want to do?' he says finally, the sharp scent of mint permeating the space between us. His brow creases in a way that makes me want to reach over and smooth it out. Make things better. Only now would be a terrible time to do that. I check my watch. Another eight minutes and we'll be off the freeway and at the restaurant. We're already late. We are never late. Except for today because we are arguing and the radio is turned off and I don't know how I'm going to tell my fiancé the truth.

'I don't know,' I say through gritted teeth. Only I do know. And it's going to throw our lives into total disarray.

'You don't know?' he says, tossing me a glance. He resets the cruise control, lets his window down, and undoes the button on his collar. A rush of cold air enters the car.

'Can you put the window up?' I say, the annoyance in my voice evident as I try to hold my hair in place.

He presses the window switch and looks over at me. 'If *you* don't know what you want, then how should *I* know?'

'Keep your eyes on the road. Let's talk about it later. I don't want to ruin Scarlett's birthday.' I clasp the flowers I'm holding for my best friend closer to my chest, a classic spray of creamy white Claire Austin roses, the same blooms I manage to source for her every year.

'Don't change the subject,' he says. 'You were the one who brought this up, and I think it's time we work out once and for all how we want things to go. So, let me ask you again so we can put this to bed—'

Deep breaths, Gracie. Deep breaths.

There will never be a perfect time to tell him how I'm feeling. I fumble with my engagement ring and form the words I've been too afraid to admit out loud. 'Okay, so if you want to know the truth, I don't want to m—'

The sound of Blake slamming the brakes robs the breath from my chest and seals our fate. We slide towards the truck that's pulled out in front of us on the freeway and then we are spinning into a lane we shouldn't be in. Blake calls my name. He sees what's coming before me. I scream. Two dozen flower stems lurch from the safe crevice of my arm. They hit the dashboard before I do, the force of the impact showering the car with petals as I'm tossed in one direction and then the other.

And then, the world goes silent.

ONE

When I open my eyes, the first thing I notice are the dinner-plate dahlias on the table at the foot of my bed. They're café au laits. They struggle in cold soil and you plant the tubers when the soil temperature picks up and there's no more risk of frost.

My eyes flutter closed again. I can't seem to form any words to answer the woman who is patting my thigh. She keeps squeezing my hand, repeating the name, 'Gracie.'

'Open your eyes, Gracie. Can you hear me, Gracie?'

I want to tell her she's in the wrong room, that she has the wrong person, but I can't seem to find the energy to.

She squeezes my hand once more.

This time I find the strength to squeeze back.

'Good girl. Open your eyes now, sweetheart.'

I hear footsteps. A male voice. Hushed whispers. Pages flicking. A pen clicking. There is beeping that I hadn't noticed till now, and a steady hum. The room smells sterile. I open my eyes and the room slowly comes into focus. My eyelids feel so heavy.

The woman is wearing a blue shirt with white trim around the collar and her name badge tells me she's a nurse. Her name is Bea. Which means the man standing beside her with a stethoscope around his neck is a … doctor. Which means I'm in a … hospital.

'Hello, Gracie, I'm Dr Cleave. How's that head of yours feeling?'

My arm feels like lead, but I manage to lift it and run my fingers over the bandage that's wrapped around my head. Did I fall? I must have fallen. But when? Where? My heart starts to beat faster. Bea glances at the monitor by my bed and adjusts the pulse oximeter on my finger.

'Gracie,' I whisper, repeating the name that doesn't seem to fit me. I search for another name for myself, but nothing comes.

Dr Cleave narrows his eyes, appearing slightly concerned. 'Can you tell me your full name?' he asks.

I take a moment to think about it, but there is blankness in that space where my name should be.

'Not to worry,' says Dr Cleave, after an abnormally long silence, which makes me worry more.

'How did I … get here?' I can't seem to remember yesterday, or last month, or last year.

'You're in the hospital. You were in a car accident and you've been intubated in the ICU for three days. You're going to feel a little tired, but that's to be expected,' he says.

I try to sit up, but it requires too much effort and I collapse back into the pillows. Everything in my body aches.

'Take it easy, sweetheart,' says Bea, resting a hand on my shoulder. She readjusts the hospital gown so it covers my collarbone. 'Are you warm enough?' she asks, rubbing my forearm. I'm not, yet I nod anyway.

My mouth feels dry. I go to speak, but only a croak comes out. I try again. 'Car accident?' I say, looking at the doctor.

'That's right. You hit your head and you've got a few bumps and bruises. You're going to be fine, though. Are you in pain?'

I pat the bandage.

'Let me get onto that for you,' says Bea. She leaves the room and Dr Cleave moves closer. He fiddles with the stethoscope around his neck.

'By any chance, do you remember anything about the accident?' he asks casually.

I frown, trying to summon my past, but it's like reaching into a vast crater. There's nothing *to* remember.

'No. Nothing,' I reply.

'That's okay,' he says in a voice so reassuring, I almost believe him. He pulls a torch from his coat pocket and shines it into my eyes. I wish he wouldn't do that. 'Now, I'm sure you're wondering about Blake. He was pretty lucky to come out of the accident with only a few stitches and contusions.' He clicks off the light and tucks it away. I blink, trying to regain focus.

There's a knock on the door and a woman enters the room. I can tell she's not a nurse because she's wearing a tailored red coat, a felted wool beret and is carrying an umbrella. Her bow-shaped lips form a smile when she sees me.

'Gracie,' she says, relief in her voice. She hovers in the doorway, seemingly unsure of whether to stay or go.

'Come in,' says Dr Cleave.

'I'm Scarlett,' she introduces herself to him. 'Did she just wake up?' She removes the beret from her head, letting a mass of caramel-coloured curls fall around her shoulders.

Dr Cleave nods. 'I need to ask her a few questions.'

'Should I come back later?' She points to the door.

'No need, I'll be done soon,' says Dr Cleave, glancing over my chart.

I can't stop staring at the woman—Scarlett, who is now sitting beside the bed and holding my hand. I think I am supposed to know who she is. She obviously knows *me*. Why don't I know *her*?

Dr Cleave slides out a pencil from behind his ear. 'I'm going to ask you a few more questions, but I don't want you to worry if you can't answer them all, okay?'

I swallow nervously and nod, feeling the colour drain from my face.

'Can you tell me when your birthday is?'

December? No. March. September? I look up at the ceiling, my eyes darting left and right. Surely I must know the answer. Why don't I know the answer?

'Gracie?' says Dr Cleave, trying to grab my attention.

'I … uh, I don't know.'

How can I not know my birthday? What month are we even in now? It's raining outside. Scarlett is wearing a coat. Okay, it must be winter. I was in a car accident. I hit my head. I'm in the hospital. My name is … Gracie.

'How about your address?'

Oh God, I don't know my address, either.

I stare blankly at him. I want to tell him but can't. It's on the tip of my tongue, and then … it's not. And I can't tell if it's slipped away or if it was never there in the first place. I glance at Scarlett, who is in the chair near my bed, her mouth ajar. She closes it when her eyes meet mine and resumes fumbling with the hat on her lap.

Dr Cleave continues. 'Favourite colour?'

I shrug. 'Purple?' My voice is barely audible.

He looks at me over his glasses before pushing them up his nose. 'Really?'

'Pink?' I say, feeling hopeless.

I squeeze my eyes closed for a second as I draw a long, deep breath. My mind starts to scramble, attempting to search for a recollection of the past, but it's as if my life is like an empty container. I shake it, turn it upside down, except nothing comes out.

Dr Cleave pats my leg. 'I think that's enough for now. I don't want you to worry,' he says, but I can't help noticing the way he's scribbling down notes. 'It's normal for you to feel a bit disorientated like this. I'm going to order a few more tests.'

'Tests?'

'I'm going to order a neuropsych assessment and maybe a couple of scans. You had a significant blow to the head, and while I don't think we have anything to be too concerned about, I'd still like to double-check things, just to be sure.'

'Okay,' I reply quietly.

'I'm going to have a word with Scarlett, and I'll be back a little later. I want you to rest up for now. Do you have any questions in the meantime?'

'I don't think so.' I allow my eyes to momentarily drift shut before opening them again.

'I should let Blake know she's awake,' says Scarlett, who is still sitting beside me. She's stroking the back of my hand with her thumb. I pull away and ball my hand into a fist.

'What's wrong?' she says, her deep-blue eyes trying to meet mine. I don't know how to tell her that I have no idea who she is. I look the other way, avoiding eye contact with her.

Dr Cleave peers over his clipboard, and glances at the hand I've pulled away from Scarlett. He clicks his pen, tucks it in his coat pocket and turns around to leave the room.

Scarlett stands up to follow him.

'Actually ... I do have a question,' I say, directing my words to Dr Cleave. My voice wobbles. 'Who's Blake?'

Scarlett lets out a noise, like a whimper, only louder.

Dr Cleave flips back around, failing to hide the look of disquiet on his face.

'You don't know who Blake is?' he asks, tilting his head.

'Should I?'

Dr Cleave glances at Scarlett, who interjects, 'Gracie, Blake's your fiancé.'

'That's ... impossible,' I reply.

Isn't it?

'You're supposed to be getting married in three months. You've known each other for ...' She looks at the ceiling, as if she's trying to work it out. 'Fourteen years,' she says finally.

'That can't be ... I'm not ...'

Engaged?

'It's okay,' says Dr Cleave, trying to reassure me. 'We'll get Blake in and I'm sure that'll help—'

'I can't ... I don't ... just wait,' I say, trying to make sense of all this. I press my hand against my forehead. *Think, Gracie. Think.* Maybe if they give me a chance to think about it all, I'll be able to remember.

Scarlett places a hand on my wrist.

'Gracie,' she says. 'Look at me.'

I swallow past the lump that's formed in my throat.

'I know you're scared, and I know you're freaking out, but we'll help you to remember.'

My heart starts to hammer.

But what if I never do?

When Scarlett returns to my room after chatting with Dr Cleave, she's carrying a fresh arrangement of flowers. They're not just any flowers. They're tulips. Rembrandts. Like the painter. Butter-coloured petals variegated with bright-red flames.

'The perfect way to brighten up your hospital room,' she says, her lips forming a smile as she carries them over to the round table in the corner. She starts arranging them into a vase that's much too small. She needs to cut the stems shorter.

'It's too early for tulips,' I whisper. 'Tulips don't bloom in winter.'

Scarlett pauses with a stem in her hand. 'What did you say?' she asks, narrowing her gaze.

'Neither do dahlias. They must be imported,' I murmur.

Why do I know this? How can I know this but nothing else, like my birthday? Or my favourite colour? Or *Blake*?

My *fiancé*. The fiancé who, according to Scarlett, I am supposed to be marrying in *three months' time*. The fiancé I am supposed to be spending the rest of my life with but *can't remember*.

'Dr Cleave said he's going to run those extra tests as soon as possible. We're just waiting for Blake to arrive.' She wrings her hands together. 'I told him you're having some trouble recalling things, but I didn't exactly tell him you couldn't remember who he is.' She scrunches her face. 'I think it's better if Dr Cleave tells him, don't you?'

I bite down on my lip but don't answer her.

'Anyway, he left with Noah and went home this morning for a shower and change of clothes. We practically had to force him out of here. He didn't leave your side for days and then the moment he leaves, you wake up ...'

Scarlett continues rambling on, which appears to be more out of nervousness than anything else. 'Noah will pop in after work. Oh, I called Ava from your office to let her know what happened, but I need the number for—'

'Where are my parents?' I cut into her blather.

Scarlett almost knocks over the flowers. She tilts her head and blinks at me as if she hasn't heard me properly. Her brow creases but she stands there, frozen, her fingers gripping the vase.

'My mum? Dad? Brother? Sister?' I press.

Scarlett's eyes widen with each passing second until she regains her composure and sucks in a breath as she approaches the bed. She speaks softly, the way a mother might break bad news to a child in the most honest and gentle way possible. 'You never knew your dad. You're an only child and your mum ... well ...'

I search her eyes for answers, holding my breath, waiting for her to explain.

'Your mum passed away twelve months ago. Her name was Lainey and she ... it was her heart. It was sudden and she hadn't been diagnosed before it happened.'

This can't be true. None of it can be true. How can I not *know* any of this? I don't even remember my own *mother*? Scarlett reaches for my hand, but I pull it away before she can touch me.

'Why do you keep doing that?' She raises a hand to her lips as understanding dawns. 'Oh my God. You don't know me either, do you? You have no idea who I am.' She takes a step back. 'Gracie,' she says, her voice fractured, filled with disbelief. 'We've known each other for years. You don't remember anything about me … us … the past?'

I'm scared to answer her, scared about what this all means.

'I'm sorry,' I say, my voice hoarse.

She cups her mouth, tears forming in her eyes—eyes that are blinking at me in shock. 'I don't believe it.' She snivels. She takes a tissue from the bedside table and blows her nose, turning her back to me. She stands in front of the window, staring out to the carpark. Raindrops slide down the glass pane, the focal point of Scarlett's attention as she takes the time to process this. Finally, she glances over her shoulder at me. I register the crestfallen expression on her face and wince. I don't mean to hurt her like this and I don't know how to make this easier for her.

She starts tearing the tissue she's holding into tiny pieces.

'What if my memory never comes back?' I say quietly.

She approaches the bed. 'You don't have to worry about a thing. We'll tell you everything you forgot. Everything that made you who you are, and everything you would have never wanted to forget.' She sits down and cups my face. 'Okay?' she says, smiling through her tears.

'Um, okay,' I say, agreeing. My head feels full.

Scarlett rubs the moisture from under her eyes and inhales sharply, as if she's hitting a reset button.

She scrunches the pieces of tissue into one hand and tosses them into the bin beside the bed. 'Okay so, where to start?' she says, sitting up straighter. 'Do you know where you were going before you had the accident?'

I look blankly at her. I don't really want to hear this. I want some time alone. To sleep. To think.

'Of course you don't,' she says before I have a chance to answer her. 'It was my birthday, and we were going out for dinner. There were about twenty of us. You baked my cake for me,' she says, smiling. I can tell she's trying to inject some lightness into our conversation to downplay the seriousness of all this, but it doesn't work. She pauses, and I'm almost sure she's waiting for me to nod or show some kind of sign that I recognise what she's telling me; I simply stare back at her.

'You and Blake were running late. You're never late, which is sort of weird,' she says, wrinkling her nose. 'Never mind. Chrissie and Tom were there, Mel and Jack, Erin, Maddie …' Her words trail off and fizzle into the air as her gaze meets mine. 'You don't remember any of these people, do you?' she says finally.

'Um, no.'

'Okay, well, what if I tell you about—'

'My mother,' I interject.

'Gracie,' she says softly. 'Are you saying you don't remember *anything* about your mum, either?'

I don't need to answer her because my expression says it all.

'Oh, love,' she says, closing her eyes momentarily. When she opens them she inhales deeply. 'You were very close, more like sisters than mother and daughter. You used to talk on the phone all the time, at least once a day. And you used to visit her every weekend. You know that much, don't you?' she says hopefully.

'No, I don't. Do I … miss her?' After I ask this question, I realise what a silly one it is. Naturally I must miss her, only I can't seem to tap into any feelings that resemble the heartache of missing someone you love.

'Of course you do,' says Scarlett. 'It's been a difficult year, but you're strong and you're doing okay—slowly coming to peace with things. Nothing could have prepared you for it. She was only fifty-six … no … fifty-eight …' She places a finger on her lips. 'Sorry, I can't remember exactly.'

'What did I love most about her?' I whisper.

She smiles. 'Well, I'd say you probably loved everything about her. She was kind and generous and loving, and she knew how to make you feel better when you were feeling down.'

Something about this answer doesn't sit well with me. It doesn't sound … I don't know … specific? I'd imagine that's the sort of description you'd get about any mother. And I want to know about *my* mother—something unique, something to give me a connection to her. 'Um, what did I love *most* about her?'

Scarlett frowns. 'I just told you.'

I swallow. How do I explain it to Scarlett? 'I … I want to know exactly why she was special to me.'

'She was your mother. That's why she was special to you,' says Scarlett quietly.

I rub my head, which has started to ache. I must look unhappy because Scarlett goes on.

'Well, I know you loved spending time outdoors with her. You also liked baking. Every Christmas Eve you'd bake together.'

'What did we bake?' I ask.

She shrugs. 'Um, shortbread cookies, I think.'

I rub at my head again. She doesn't sound very sure and it isn't the sort of detail I was hoping for.

'It was Christmas,' she adds, looking as though she wants to say more. But right now, all I want is to close my eyes.

'Um, I'm really tired. I think I need to sleep now,' I say, avoiding her gaze as I burrow under the blanket. My eyes drift shut and I let the world fade away, hoping that by the time I open them life might feel a little more familiar.

When I wake up, Scarlett is sitting in the same position she was before. She notices me looking at her and sets down the book she's been reading.

'Are you thirsty?' Before I can nod, her hands are already on the jug of water. She hands me a glass and guides the straw to my mouth.

'Good news. Blake has parked the car and should be up here soon.'

I stop sipping my water and splutter. My body tenses up.

'What's wrong?' she asks.

'I don't feel good about this.'

She shakes her head in confusion.

'About seeing him. I don't remember him. I don't know anything about him—or how we were—what sort of relationship we had.' I desperately want her to understand.

'Why don't you tell me what you want to know and we'll start there?'

'Um, I think I'd rather have the chance to—'

Our conversation is interrupted by a knock on the door.

'I bet that's him. Come in,' she says. 'See, now Blake can tell you everything himself.'

My chest tightens. 'No.'

Scarlett fires me a look of confusion. 'No, what?'

'I don't want any visitors,' I whisper. A surge of adrenaline floods through me. I want to be left alone.

'But it's Blake.'

'No,' I repeat, close to tears.

'Why not, Gracie?'

'Please, I don't know who he is. I don't know how I'm meant to act around him or what I'm supposed to even say.' My eyes plead with her. 'Scarlett, I can't face him right now.'

'But …' Scarlett is unable to hide her shock. 'He's your fiancé.'

The door creaks open.

'Gracie?' says a voice. A voice that is completely foreign to me.

'I mean it. I don't want to see anyone right now.' I draw my knees up to my chest, squeezing my eyes closed, wanting to block everything out.

'Blake, hold on,' says Scarlett, approaching the door. She presses a hand against it.

On the next inhale, my future outside the hospital flashes in front of me—the countless questions, the endless stories, the photographs. The people who have become strangers to me will be desperate to help me fill the gaps, become the person they knew me to be. Blake is going to tell me I loved him and he loved me and I will have no choice but to believe him. And when I leave this hospital I'm going to have to consciously try to fall in love with him.

At this realisation, the world constricts around me and it suddenly becomes harder to breathe. I press my palm against my chest, which seems to be hammering much faster than it should be. I can't seem to stop the rush of thoughts spiralling around in my head. If Blake walks into this room, I will have to look into the eyes of the man I am supposed to marry and tell him I feel nothing for him.

'Gracie,' calls Blake through the doorway.

I shoot a look at Scarlett, pleading with her. 'I don't want to see him. Please just tell him I need some time.' I pin my lip between my teeth and scrunch my eyes closed again.

'Okay, okay,' says Scarlett.

I roll onto my side so that I'm not facing the door, and curl into a ball, bringing the covers up to my chin. I can't seem to get a handle on this feeling of being completely and utterly out of control. Despite my requests, the door opens.

'Gracie? What's going on?' says a male voice from behind me. I close my eyes tighter. I can't answer him. And I still can't seem to control my breathing.

'What's wrong with her?'

'Maybe I should page the nurses,' says Scarlett.

'Gracie, it's me,' he says softly, resting a hand on my arm. He runs his fingers through my hair, moving the loose strands away from my face and then he kisses my cheek, the stubble from his face grazing my skin. The fragrance of his aftershave wafts through the air, and along with that comes a shattering confirmation that I don't recognise it. This aftershave could belong to any man. A series of unintentional moans escape me.

I hear Scarlett whisper to Blake, 'Maybe you should wait outside. Give her a few minutes and I'll explain everything.'

There are footsteps and a moment later the door clicks shut. When Scarlett re-enters the room a minute or so later, she sits on the edge of the bed. 'Breathe, Gracie. Deep breaths,' she commands, rubbing my back. I can't seem to stop shaking. She presses the buzzer for the nurses. 'Open your eyes, I want you to look at me.'

I flick my eyes open. 'I think I'm going to be sick. I don't know what's happening to me.' My face contorts into a grimace. 'I'm scared,' I croak. 'I'm really, really scared.'

Bea enters the room. 'Gracie? What's going on, love? Is everything okay?'

'I don't know what's happening to me … but I can't … I don't want to see him … I don't want to see anyone.'

'I think she's having a panic attack,' says Scarlett.

Bea nods and tells me to breathe, but no matter how hard I try, it still feels like there isn't enough air.

The door clicks open again. 'Gracie!' calls Blake. 'It's just me, I promise you, everything will be okay if you let me in.'

'No,' I say, my eyes pleading with Bea.

'It's okay, honey,' she says, pressing a hand on my shoulder.

She leaves the room and a few seconds later Blake's voice reverberates through the hospital.

'You need to let me see her!' he yells.

'That's not what she wants, she's distressed enough as it is, and we need to respect her wishes,' she says.

'This is ridiculous, I'm her fiancé.'

'She's having an anxiety attack,' Bea says firmly. 'This is not the right time.'

'Let me talk to her, I'll help calm her down.'

'I'm sorry, but she's not in the frame of mind to see you right now. This is all a huge shock for her. It's a lot to take in. She needs time to adjust, to get her head around what's happened. She's frightened and very fragile, not to mention exhausted, and I think it's best to let her accept this first and then—'

'Please let me see her. Five minutes, that's all I'm asking for.'

I cup my hands over my ears. Scarlett rubs my back more furiously. 'Someone needs to tell him I don't remember him,' I say, but it comes out like a drawn-out moan.

'It's okay. It's going to be okay,' says Scarlett, exhaling a long breath.

No matter how convincing she sounds, I don't believe her.

The following days pass like a blur. Scans, sleep, neuropsych assessments filled with questions I can't answer. The constant thrum of monitors and footsteps of nurses coming in and out to check on me. Scarlett humming away from the armchair in the corner of the room, turning the pages of a book, repeatedly telling me that everything is going to be fine when nobody really knows for sure whether it will be.

After he'd run a series of tests, Dr Cleave told me (rather unconvincingly) that there was every possibility my memory loss could be temporary. 'Retrograde amnesia,' he said, confirming the diagnosis. 'You need to be really patient. Life is going to look a little different for you when you go back home. There's a chance your procedural memory has been affected, and we won't know the extent of that immediately. You might find that certain everyday functions are challenging at first. You'll need support, and I encourage you to take things slowly. Lean on those who love you to help get you through this. I know that's going to be hard for someone like you, but it's important you don't try to go through this alone.'

I knew what he meant by that—both he and Scarlett have made it clear they think that me refusing to see Blake or anyone else is a bad idea. While keeping family and friends away isn't an issue, keeping Blake away is turning out to be a bigger kind of problem.

'He's beside himself,' says Scarlett. 'Seeing him might help you remember. He can answer any questions you have, run you through the kinds of things you used to do together—'

'That's not what I want,' I reply, my voice flat. I dig my spoon into a tub of jelly without enthusiasm. I can't seem to stomach anything on my plate let alone the snacks Scarlett has brought me: kale chips, goji berries, a zip-lock bag filled with some kind of assortment of seeds.

Blake has shown up at the hospital every day to try to see me. Today is no exception. It's six pm and on cue, there's a knock on the door.

'Gracie, it's me. Can I come in? I brought your favourite magazines and some photos of our trip to Fiji,' says Blake through the gap in the door.

My body freezes. I push away the tray. I wish everyone would understand that I don't want to have to remember my life, or our life, through his eyes or anyone else's eyes. I want to remember through my eyes.

'What should I do, Gracie? I can't keep turning him away like this,' says Scarlett.

'Ask him what I loved most about my mother.'

'How is this relevant right now?' She frowns at me.

I don't answer her.

She goes to speak but holds back. 'Fine,' she mutters, shaking her head.

'Scarlett, what's going on?' says Blake. 'What's she saying?'

Scarlett glances at me uncomfortably before leaving the room.

'The way she always managed to find a way to smile,' she declares upon re-entering a minute later. 'So, can I let him in now?'

I clench my jaw and take a deep breath, lowering my head against my knees. What Scarlett remembers about my mum, isn't what Blake remembers and isn't necessarily what I would remember. Which means that if I let the people that know me tell me about who I was and what I liked, and who I should be, and what I should feel and how I should feel it, I'll have no way of knowing if that's the truth for me.

'We can't just leave him standing there in the hallway,' she says.

I busy myself by tearing open a packet of chips and sniff them, inhaling their not-quite-so-appealing vegetable scent.

She sighs. 'Fine. Let me take care of it.' She exits the room but leaves the door slightly ajar. I can still make out her voice—only just.

'I'm looking after her, leave it with me. If you don't want her to continue to refuse to see you, you need to listen to what she wants. Because if you go in there right now she might completely push you away. She's confused and she's still in shock. She'll come around with time.'

'What if she doesn't let me back in her life? I don't want to lose her.'

'You won't. She loves you,' she replies, but even I notice the waver in her voice.

I squeeze the packet of chips between my hands, crushing the crisp leaves into tiny pieces. Maybe the one thing we all know for sure, is that I'm already lost.

TWO

I don't recall buying the pastel-blue toaster and kettle in my kitchen. Or the pear-and-vanilla soy candles on the coffee table in my living room. Or the white teapot with gold polka dots and matching teacups in the wall unit. My two-bedroom apartment in Melbourne's South Yarra, a ten-minute walk from the Royal Botanic Gardens, and three blocks from the Yarra River, should feel like a cosy home, yet I can't help feeling like an uninvited guest.

Still clinging tightly to the paper bag from the hospital, I pause by a side table where a set of photo frames are positioned. Part of me wants to satisfy my curiosity about what Blake looks like and what our expressions held in these pictures. I pick up one of the frames and briefly register a black-and-white image of us together. I'm leaning across him, poking out my tongue at the camera. The profile of his face shows a man with smooth cheeks and short dark hair. He's looking at me, smiling.

We *look* happy, but were we *really* happy? How do I know for sure?

One by one, I turn the other photos face down. I can't bring myself to look at them.

Scarlett's eyes are on me, while soapy mountain peaks form in the overflowing kitchen sink.

'Not ready yet,' I say, feeling the need to explain.

'Maybe you should go sit down. I'll bring you some tea.' She turns off the tap and steps in my direction.

I raise a hand to stop her. My left hand, where I'd slipped on my engagement ring earlier this morning—mostly to see whether it might bring back some kind of recollection about my life with Blake. The halo of diamonds catch the light and glisten at me, begging me to remember what it felt like to lay eyes upon them for the very first time. I've sifted through all the possible scenarios of how this ring came to find itself on my finger, but every one feels foreign. Just like everything in this home.

There's a vase of wilted roses on the kitchen bench. A vase I don't remember filling. But I recognise the flowers. Windermeres. They start out as cream double-cupped buds and slowly fade to white. They bloom until late in the season and their scent is fruity—with a delicate hint of citrus.

Turning one of the stems around between my fingers, the petals flutter to the floor. How can I know this but not remember the day my mother sailed away into heaven and out of my sight? I let out a sigh and pluck the rest of the flowers from the vase. A trail of stagnant water drips behind me as I head for the sliding door and toss them over the balcony, expelling a frustrated moan as the petals splatter onto the concrete footpath on the street below.

Scarlett cringes. This isn't easy for her, either.

'You should go lie down. You know what the doctors said. You need to take it easy.'

'Just a minute,' I whisper.

She sighs discreetly and I retreat to the living room, feeling her eyes on me. I'm sure she's wearing the same worried expression that painted her face in the hospital when she registered the news that I didn't know who she was.

Irritation creeps over me as I notice the way the plush throw is draped over the sofa in the living room and the way the remotes are lined up perfectly, one beside the other. I notice the way light pours into the room. It bounces through the antique white plantation shutters onto the decorative mirrors. None of it moves me.

To the right of the living area, there's a closed bedroom door facing me. Scarlett wipes her wet hands on her jeans and patters behind me as I gingerly push it open. 'Gracie, hold on. Maybe you should wait before you …' Her voice trails off. My pulse hammers through my ears. My free hand rises to my temple. There are bridal magazines stacked in a pile beside the bed. Hanging from the curtain rail is an ivory-coloured dress bag. I inch forward to it slowly, nausea washing over me in waves. Pulling down the zipper, I catch a glimpse of the delicate fabric hiding beneath it. What should feel personal and poignant, leaves me cold. What should be known, is not.

I don't remember buying this dress.

I don't remember any of this.

I'm living a life that isn't my own.

Scarlett's eyes, filled with pity, meet mine. Tears brimming, I head for the door, past Scarlett, and retreat to the master bedroom, slamming the door behind me. I drop the paper bag onto the floor and collapse onto the bed. Which side of the bed is mine?

I lay there, on the left side, ignoring Scarlett's knocking, a sound that becomes muted as my attention travels to the book sprawled out on the other side of the bed.

'I need … some time,' I call, my voice cracking. Even I know that time holds no guarantee that any of this will come back to me, though. What if it doesn't?

The knocking ceases. 'I'll be out here if you need me.'

With my face still resting on the pillow, I reach out with my free hand and close the book, revealing the title: *Every Room Tells a Story: A Practical Guide to Home Styling*.

I make a mental note of the things I know, the tiny details that form part of the enormous puzzle that has become my life since the accident.

I'm organised.

I have a flair for interior design.

I'm supposed to be marrying a man named Blake, a man I know absolutely nothing about.

Weighted minutes circle around the clock, and eventually the bruised sky fades to slate, bringing with it a light shower.

'How are you doing in there?' calls Scarlett through the bedroom door.

'I'm fine,' I lie. 'Just tired,' I add, wiping my eyes with the cuff of my sleeve. I chew the inside of my lip, and my eyes start to sting again. I want to be fine. I so desperately want to be fine.

'I'm going to make some lunch soon,' she says, before becoming quiet. There's an ache in her voice that I can't help feeling responsible for. Ten days ago she lost me. Ten days ago I lost everything and everyone.

I run my fingers over the bump on my head and cringe as I apply light pressure to it. I still don't recall the accident, or being in the car. I don't remember where we were heading, or what song was playing on the radio, or whether we travelled in silence. My life is now a case of before and after, and I'm wedged in the middle, not knowing the before, incapable of imagining what's supposed to come after.

No matter how hard I try to drift off to sleep, my mind refuses to cooperate, and unable to rest, circles back to the one question that's been weighing on my mind since Dr Cleave delivered his news to me.

Who am I?

From my bedroom window, I watch a postman on his motorbike cross the street. He stops outside my apartment complex. Scarlett's footsteps echo through the narrow hallway just before the front door opens, and a minute later she slips an envelope under my bedroom door. It rests there on the floorboards, untouched, until the aroma of vegetable soup wafts throughout the apartment and Scarlett makes another attempt at knocking on my door.

This time, she pokes her head into the room and takes a step inside, treading on the letter in the process. She bends down and picks it up.

'I think you should read it,' she says, before setting it on my bedside table. 'He called earlier, you know. To see whether you'd changed your mind about seeing him.'

I fold my hands into my lap, and twirl the ring around my finger. It comes full circle, stares back at me and it's enough to make my lip start trembling. I bite down to stop it. I don't want Scarlett to see me cry. Has she seen me cry before? We've known each other for years. Of course she has.

'That's what I thought. He said to tell you that …'

I raise my hand for her to stop, but she doesn't.

'… he loves you and to take all the time you need.'

Nothing I say can make this situation any easier for either of them, so I nod, confirming I understand, when really I don't understand any of this.

Scarlett waits for me to add something to the conversation and when I don't, she summons a smile and says, 'Come and eat when you're ready,' before closing the door behind her.

There's no return address on the back of the envelope, just a name. Hands trembling, I study Blake's handwriting, its moderately neat font—for a guy, at least—sprawled over the page but contained within the margins.

Dear Gracie,

I know it must be a shock to have almost everything you've ever known ripped away from you so suddenly. There's nothing I want more than to see you again, or hear your voice again, or hold you in my arms again, but if what Scarlett and the doctors are saying is true—that you need space to gather your thoughts and find your bearings—then I'm going to have to miss you for a little while longer.

The doctors told me there's every chance your memory will come back to you, but I figured you might need some help along the way. Maybe you could tell me what you remember, and I'll tell you what I remember, and maybe somewhere, our memories will meet in the middle.

I remember the first time I met you. We were twelve years old. You had on a white cotton dress covered with lemons and you were wearing a daisy chain on your head. You were covered in smudges of dirt, yet I remember thinking you were the most beautiful girl in the world. You'd been trying to capture ladybugs because pests were attacking the roses. You had ten ladybugs in a mason jar and when I asked about them you unscrewed the lid, took one out and opened your palm for me to take it. You flashed me a smile, the kind of smile that told me you and I would be friends for life, and then you said, 'They bring good luck.'

Sometimes, when you're falling asleep, I whisper the word 'ladybug' to you and you smile. It makes me feel like the luckiest man alive.

Don't worry about me. Don't worry about you. Somehow, when you remember, it'll all be okay.

Love,

Blake

I tuck the letter back in its envelope and sink further into the pillow, my eyelids heavy with tears, aching to evoke a part of my life that doesn't feel like my own, and wonder: *If I fell in love with him once, would I fall in love with him again?*

THREE

In the unfamiliar bed that's mine, I wake up in a mess of tangled sheets, my arm embracing a pillow in the place where Blake should be. There's a fleeting moment of comfort in knowing that my body might remember what it felt like to feel close to him while my mind plays catch-up.

I kick off the quilt and try to orient myself as my eyes fixate on the view outside of the terraced homes that throng the street lined with plane trees still persisting to hold onto what remains of their yellowed maple-shaped leaves, even though we're midway through winter. A lone leaf drifts to the footpath and scuttles across the street, where intermittent passers-by head to the nearest tram stop.

Sliding my feet into a pair of slippers, I shuffle to the kitchen, where there's a note from Scarlett letting me know she's headed out to run a few errands and will be back soon to check on me. I open the pantry and start lining up my breakfast options beside each other—a carton of eggs, a loaf of bread, a box of cereal. Nothing seems to appeal until I eye the canister of ground coffee beans. I switch on the machine and stare blankly at it before filling one of the empty compartments with coffee. I push one of the buttons, and wait for the liquid to drip into the glass jug. All that ensues is a grinding noise. I grip my empty mug tighter and try again, pressing the same button, over and over, to no avail. I pour a glass of water into the machine and try again. The digital screen flashes an error message. 'No, no, no,' I say, my voice rising with each push of the button. I press down one last time and finally, defeated, I rip the cord from the power point, disturbing the box of filters tucked away behind the machine. I pull them out from the box, one after the other, until the bench space is covered in them. With the sweep of one arm, I send them to the floor, along with the open coffee canister and my mug, which shatters into countless pieces, pieces that can't be—won't be—glued back together. My body slides to the kitchen floor, and now I am knee deep in coffee grounds, picking up the fragmented pieces of my mug, trying to fit them back together like a jigsaw, even though I know they'll never fit back in the same way they did before. They form the broken words: *Don't forget to live.* I tip my head to the ceiling, close my eyes, and feel my body convulsing into a series of silent sobs as my fists hit the cupboard behind me.

Minutes pass before I finally pull myself off the floor and tidy up the mess with a dustpan and brush. I make a second attempt at making a coffee, this time opting for an instant. Next, I scour the kitchen cupboards for a frying pan and mixing bowl. I find what I'm looking for, close all the cupboards, brush the hair away from my eyes and take the eggs out of the carton. My body stiffens. I know what I *want* to do, but I don't know *how* to do it. I stare at the eggs, mouth agape. How can this be possible? I stand there, unconsciously holding my breath, as I admit to myself that I have no idea how to prepare an omelette. Anger bubbles up inside of me. I can't accept this—won't accept this. I slide my hand across the bench and snatch the recipe book from the wrought-iron stand it's propped on. I furiously search the index. Why can't my attention focus on these words?

Concentrate, Gracie.

I scan the page slowly this time, purposefully. *O* for omelette. *Right there.* Flipping to page twenty-six, I read over the instructions out loud—twice for good measure— and somehow, between flicking my attention from the recipe book to the mixing bowl to the frying pan, I manage not to burn breakfast.

I'm serving up two cheese-and-herb soufflé omelettes with a side of spinach and two glasses of orange juice when Scarlett stumbles through the front door. She wipes her boots on the inside doormat.

'Gosh, it's pouring out there,' she says, lifting the beanie off her head with one hand. She shakes her hair free, allowing her mass of curls to bounce around her shoulders. She enters the kitchen, her left arm full of shopping bags. She wears barely any makeup, her velvety skin, with a hint of colour where it counts, making her lucky enough not to need it. Her jaw drops when she sees me. I swallow a mouthful of omelette and question her with my eyes.

'What's that?' she asks, staring at the plates, her bow-shaped mouth still slightly ajar.

'An omelette,' I reply, uncertain of what I've done wrong.

She sets the bags on the counter and straightens her posture. She rests her hands on her curvy waist. 'But you don't eat eggs.'

'I don't?' I say, glancing at my half-empty plate. 'They're so good though. You should try some,' I add, handing her a fork. 'I made some for you, too.'

She looks at me wide-eyed, her doll eyes blinking.

'What?' I ask, noticing something's off. 'Are you sure you're okay?'

'I'm fine. It's odd, that's all. Unexpected.'

'So why did you buy eggs if you know I don't like them?'

'I didn't. They were already here.' She throws me a look that is enough to remind me.

Of course. Blake.

'Oh,' I reply, exhaling a deep breath. Scarlett heads towards the fridge and starts unpacking the groceries to supplement the ones she'd already shopped for before I came home. 'You were always nagging him to eat healthy. I think he used to bring home junk food just to rile you up.' She holds up a tub of coconut yoghurt. 'I bought you your favourite,' she says, poking out her head from behind the fridge door. 'From the organic grocery store down the road. They asked why you hadn't been in.'

The yoghurt doesn't look familiar. In fact, I couldn't care less about the yoghurt. I'm still thinking about the eggs. And Blake. And how many other things Blake and I might not have in common. I give her a smile of appreciation and inhale sharply.

'You go in every Tuesday for your grocery shop, but you stop by for a chai every morning because you don't drink ...' Scarlett closes the fridge and stares at my steaming cup.

'Coffee?' I raise my eyebrows and take a sip. Her eyes are still trained on me when I put it down. I roll my eyes. 'I know, it's instant. I had a little trouble with the machine.'

A gentle shake of her head tells me she's chosen to ignore the topic at hand. 'I left a list of things for you to get to on the kitchen bench. Once you're ready, that is.'

I scan the list.

Call work to let them know your return date.

Make appointment at the hospital for your check-up.

My heart begins to thump a little harder in my chest. I'm not ready to face the world with the everyday tasks required of me.

'Scarlett?' I say, almost shyly. I'm embarrassed that I don't know how to deal with this list. Work is the last thing on my mind, and the thought of going back to a job when I have no idea what I used to do or how I used to do it, causes me to break out in a sweat. Especially after the effort it's taken me to cook an omelette.

'Yeah?' she replies, staring into the pantry.

'What do I do for work, exactly?' My face scrunches as I brace myself for her answer, the possibilities racing through my head: lawyer, waitress, physiotherapist, town planner, data-entry clerk, chef. God, please don't let me be a *chef.*

Scarlett's shoulders sag. 'You're a stylist. *Country Dwellings* magazine. You work on their photo shoots. You know, arrange the furniture, sort out the props … that kind of thing,' she says. 'Every now and then you do a bit of interior-design consulting on the side.'

My brows knit together as I try to get my head around what Scarlett is telling me.

'Are you … do I like it?' I ask, thinking that I couldn't possibly enjoy it.

She shrugs. 'I think so. Making things look good is what you do.' She waves a hand around the apartment. She's right. It's lovely. Minimal and uncluttered. Fresh and modern yet warm and inviting. 'And as far as work goes, you don't mind the long hours, you love interior design and you've been there long enough. You've been working crazy hours this year, chasing a promotion. You haven't let me hear the end of it. Anyway, I think they're going to let you go back part-time. That's what Ava—your boss—said to Blake last week.'

'Right,' I say, rubbing my forehead as if I'm trying to coax out some kind of recollection about the fact that I have a job people are expecting me to return to.

'You don't have to go back right away,' says Scarlett, sensing my discomfort. 'Maybe wait a week and then see how you feel. By then, you might be ready to see Blake and ...' She huffs out a breath. 'Never mind. Just take your time.'

Now feeling even guiltier about the entire situation, I tip the rest of my coffee down the sink, and scrape what remains of the rubbery omelette into the bin, where it lands with a smack. I head to the bathroom while Scarlett finishes unpacking the groceries. Peering at my reflection in the mirror, I unravel the messy bun on the top of my head and let my hair drop around my shoulders. There are layers. And the kind of blonde highlights only a hair stylist could create. Where do I get my hair done? I run my hands over my legs. Who does my waxing?

As the running water in the shower infuses the bathroom with steam and fogs up the mirror in front of me, I ask myself the more pressing question of whether the blue or yellow toothbrush is mine and try my hardest not to cry.

By the time I've showered and dressed, Scarlett has managed to find the photo albums and has stacked them on the coffee table. She's sitting on the couch, flicking through them with a pensive smile on her face, when she finally looks up and notices me.

I stand there, frozen, looking at the albums and back at Scarlett.

She fiddles with her fingers before speaking. 'I found them in one of the cupboards. They're in order according to year. So, I thought we could go through them and maybe they'd spark some kind of memory for you. There are the photos of the summer we spent in the country a couple of years ago for my wedding and …'

I stare blankly at her.

'You know, the summer Blake proposed?' she says, raising her eyebrows. She continues, and I'm almost sure it's nerves causing her to ramble like this, but it's too much for me to take in right now. I close my eyes, trying to drown out her words. Something about trees and lights and barns and …

'Stop!' I say, more forcefully than I'd intended. I take a deep breath. 'Stop,' I repeat, my voice lower. 'I don't want to know. Not right now. I don't want to know it like this.'

'I don't understand,' she says, her brow creasing. She's looking down at her feet, and closes one of the albums, as if doing that can erase some of her words.

'Me either,' I say, dropping onto the sofa beside her.

'Don't you want to remember?' she asks, turning her body towards me.

I fold my hands in my lap. In the hospital, I'd asked Scarlett to not tell me details about my life until I was ready. I try explaining it to her again. 'Of course … of course I do.

I just … I want to remember on *my* terms. I don't want to remember things because you or anyone else that knows me remembered them a certain way. I don't want to be told stories about how things were and what I felt. I want to *know* it and *feel* it myself. Otherwise, how am I going to know if what I feel is real?'

'Surely if you see Blake again you'll feel it?'

I shake my head. 'Scarlett …' I say softly, looking into her eyes. I know this is going to be painful for her, but I have to make her understand. She blinks at me, her blue eyes wide, waiting for me to speak. 'I have no idea who you are. I don't remember anything about you. I don't remember your birthday, or your shoe size, or the last time we laughed together or cried together or shared a secret together. I don't know where you live or what you do for a living. I don't know if I was a good friend, or a bad friend, or …'

Tears well in her eyes. 'You were the best kind of friend,' she whispers, her face contorting into a grimace as the tears slide down her cheeks.

I nod, maintaining eye contact with her. 'If I told Blake what I told you right now, what would that do to him?'

'He'd be completely heartbroken,' she says through trembling lips.

'Right. So now you know why I don't want to see him at this time. I can't do it, Scarlett. I don't feel anything for him. And I *should* feel something for him. But I don't. And I don't know if I ever will again.'

'That's a problem.'

'Yes,' I agree, handing her a tissue. 'It's a very big problem.'

FOUR

Scarlett hasn't mentioned Blake's name since our conversation the other day. It doesn't change the fact that every morning I wake up scrambling for a memory of the two of us. I've read his letter so many times I could recite it by heart.

Scarlett lets herself in this afternoon, carrying a new supply of groceries. She's taken it upon herself to make sure I have a fully stocked fridge at all times. Unable to take more time off from her teaching job at a local primary school, she returned to work a few days ago. Since she reluctantly agreed to move out of my spare room and back to her home in nearby Windsor with her husband, Noah, she is now checking in on me every day after work.

'Thanks,' I say, as I take a bag from her arms. 'For everything.'

'Noah reminded me to buy you these,' she says, holding up two blocks of chocolate. 'He said you and Blake used to argue over the last piece.'

I turn over one of the packets and read the label. Sour cherry and vanilla. Organic. Handmade. I nod and let out a false laugh, as if I recognise the packaging. It makes me wonder what else Blake and I used to argue over, whether we argued sometimes, or whether we argued at all. Were we arguing when he lost control of the car on the night of the accident?

Scarlett doesn't return the laugh. Instead, she looks at me as if she wants to tell me something but is afraid to. 'He's waiting outside.'

My smile fades. 'Blake?' I ask, my heart skipping a beat.

'Noah. He thought he'd come along in case you changed your mind about seeing ... meeting ...' Her eyes dart right and left as she tries to decide which is more appropriate. '*Seeing* him,' she says, pointing her finger in the air as she finally settles on a word. 'You know what I mean,' she adds.

As much as I want to do the courteous thing and invite Noah inside, I can't, so I stand there awkwardly, watching Scarlett pull out a limp bunch of celery and a bag of carrots from my fridge. She holds them up, demanding answers.

'What?'

'You haven't touched them.'

I shrug my shoulders, hoping she'll let it go.

'You haven't been eating,' she replies, pulling open the crisper to inspect it. 'Gracie! You haven't touched a thing in here!'

It's true. I've mainly been surviving on toast and cereal, as well as the occasional omelette. I can finally make them without consulting the recipe.

She eyes the box of cereal on the bench before her eyes travel to the stack of bowls in the sink. She looks me up and down and narrows her eyes.

'When was the last time you washed your hair?'

My lips twist sideways as I try to figure out how long it's been. *Five days ago? Six, maybe?*

She surveys the overflowing bin.

'Have you even stepped foot out of this apartment since I last checked on you?' she asks with a hint of annoyance in her voice. 'If you want me to leave you to look after yourself, you need to show me you can look after yourself. I promised Blake I'd …'

I close my eyes at the mention of his name, even if he's responsible for saturating most of my thoughts.

'Getting out of the apartment isn't on my priority list right now.' I fold my arms. I don't want to tell her I've been spending my days rotating between bed and the couch. I don't know if I've always been this partial to re-runs of *Escape to the Country*, but at 3.45 pm I'm there, on the sofa, eyes glued to the screen.

Scarlett inhales and fires a disapproving look at me.

'I might not be able to find my way back home,' I retort, and as soon as I say it, I regret it. Scarlett doesn't deserve me making this situation any harder for her than it already is. She has gone above and beyond what any friend would do.

'Sorry, I just … we just … we all just want you to be okay.'

'You want things to be like they were.'

'Yes,' she whispers.

'Well, things are different now. They're not as they were. I don't think they'll ever be the way they were again.'

There's something in my voice I don't recognise. Bitterness. Resentment. Somehow, it all sounds so much worse when I admit my feelings out loud. If things can't ever be the way they were before, then all I have is what is in my life right now. A life stuck in an apartment, with crumpled bedsheets, a fridge full of decaying vegetables, and more empty bowls of cereal than I can count, seems like a terrible prospect for the future. Envisaging anything else seems so impossible, though. Venturing out into Melbourne's busy streets alone frightens me, going back to work isn't an option, and I don't have any hobbies. None that I'm aware of, anyway.

'You don't know that, Gracie.'

'I'm having a hard time right now maintaining your level of optimism. It's kind of hard, considering I couldn't tie my own shoelaces yesterday.'

Scarlett's jaw drops.

'Yeah.' I nod. 'And the day before that? I couldn't work out how to turn on the washing machine. There's this trick, you see, where you have to—'

'I thought the doctors said your procedural memory was okay. Even you said you were okay.'

At my check-up last week, Dr Cleave and his team had reiterated that it might take some time to relearn some of the tasks I used to be able to do with ease. I haven't been completely honest with him or anybody else about not being able to do some of these things.

'Well, obviously, it's not,' I reply, looking down at my feet. I'm wearing the same pair of yoga pants I was wearing three days ago, with oversized bed socks that have slipped down to my ankles. My hair hasn't had a brush through it all day, and a wisp of fresh air hasn't swept through the apartment in days.

Scarlett and I look at each other, and in that moment we both realise that my life has changed in more ways than one.

'Different doesn't mean it has to be harder than it needs to be,' she says softly, almost so I can't hear her.

'For the record, I'm not trying to be difficult. If it's not too much to ask, I'd just like to know whether the blue or yellow toothbrush belongs to me.'

'If you let us in, we could tell you.'

'I don't *want* you to tell me, Scarlett,' I say, the frustration I've been holding onto escalating. 'I want to *know* it and *feel* it and *understand* all the things that make me, *me*. I want to know what it's like to fall in love. I want to know what it feels like to go weak at the knees and have your belly flip-flop when someone you love looks at you or whispers your name. I want to know what it was like to enjoy styling fruit platters and boho furniture because right now, I couldn't think of a more boring job! I'd love to know why I chose to live in an apartment in Melbourne when I can't stand city traffic or concrete footpaths and I'm not interested in art galleries or theatre shows.' I make my way to the pantry and fling the doors open. I start pulling canisters of tea from it, lining them on the bench. Scarlett cringes and takes a step back.

Unintentionally, my voice rises. 'And I'd also love to know why on earth my pantry is stocked with ten different kinds of tea and I have sixteen teapots in the cupboard, when I can't stand the taste of it!' I pause to catch a breath, swallowing down my anger. Scarlett's lip starts to quiver.

'You used to drag me into tea stores, trying to find the perfect herbal tea. We had a thing for tea. It was our thing.'

I push down the guilt, staring blankly back at her. I'm sick of the way I look blankly at her.

'Piermont and Lincoln's on the first Sunday of every month?' she questions me, as if I'm meant to remember.

I shake my head, the words, *I don't remember, but I want to remember*, catching somewhere deep inside my throat.

Scarlett rubs her temples and returns to unpacking the shopping. 'You don't remember that either, do you?' This time she says it like a statement.

'I'm sorry,' I whisper.

Her face contorts into a grimace, tears imminent. She raises a hand for me to not say anything more. I hand her a tissue and she bows her head into it, blowing her nose before she straightens up, gathering her composure again. She unwraps a tart from its brown paper packaging. 'It's feta and asparagus,' she says, switching on the oven. 'Seeing as you're now eating eggs,' she adds, trying to crack a joke.

I don't know what I loved about her before, but one of Scarlett's most endearing qualities is her ability to bounce from sad to hopeful in an instant. As much as I'd like to, I can't seem to find a way to laugh at her joke; another reminder that I'm different now.

'I can do it,' I say, taking the tart from her. 'You get going. You don't want to keep Noah waiting. It's raining out there.'

She releases her grip on the tart.

'Blake asked me to pick up some of his belongings. Is that okay?'

''Course.'

'He wondered if he might be able to come and do that next time. Will that be all right?'

'Um … I guess so. Might be a nice excuse to get me out of the apartment.'

Scarlett doesn't laugh. Her eyes blink at me with disappointment before she hands me the list he's given her. It isn't fair on him. This is his home. I lean against the doorframe of the bedroom and watch Scarlett check off some of the items on the list: t-shirts, a jacket, two pairs of shoes.

'He must hate me,' I say.

'He could never hate you. He's head over heels for you. Why else do you think he's agreed to stay away? Think about the kind of willpower this guy has.'

'So, he does understand?'

She folds the last t-shirt and zips up the overnight bag.

'Nope. He just knows how stubborn you are. Which means he doesn't really have a choice, does he?'

'You honestly think I'm making a mistake?'

Scarlett hauls the bag over her shoulder. 'Yes. I think you are.' She sighs. 'I also don't think this is good for you.'

'What?' I say, following her into the living room.

'Not letting us into your life. We're all worried about you.'

'You don't need to worry about me. You just need to give me some space to figure this out. To let me figure out who I am, and who I was and who I'm meant to be.'

'Tell me what you know so far.'

'Not much. Just a little about my mother … and flowers. I think she loved flowers.'

She smiles. 'Flowers? You both adored flowers,' she says, nodding enthusiastically.

'She taught me what I know about them, but I don't remember a lot,' I tell her. 'Mainly being in a flower field with her … it was spring and …'

Scarlett nods, encouraging me to keep talking. 'Go on …'

'Okay,' I say, exhaling a breath, as I take myself back to that place of comfort.

It was the harvest of my ninth year. 'Flowers start to heal themselves once they've been cut,' said Mum, as she snipped the stem of a rose at the perfect angle, right at the place where it intersected a new leaf line. She said that everything I needed to know about life was in the flowers; they held all the answers to all the questions I might have.

I followed her into the field, my young body tugging an unsteady wagon through the uneven spaces between the rows of sweet peas. She stopped for a moment, tucked her pruning scissors into the pocket of her apron, and waited for me to catch up to her. Then, from behind, she framed my face with her hands and gently turned it towards the sun, just as it was emerging over the verdant hills in the distance. 'That's where all the warmth is, Gracie. The sweet peas know where to look for the light,' she said, tickling my ear with her breath. The scent of my childhood wafted around us in that crisp morning breeze, an olfactory cocktail of blossoming flowers and freshly cut grass. We stood there in silence between the vines of ruffled blooms, the early rays causing the scattered dew drops to glisten; a gentle wake-up call from Mother Nature letting us know there was work to be done on our five-acre plot. Soon the bees would start swarming from their wooden hotels, orienting themselves with the sun, and the tulips would slowly yawn and stretch, opening their petals to greet the first morning light.

She kissed the top of my head and we followed the fragrance of roses to the edge of the plot along the fence line, where she started stripping the first bush of its flowers. She wiped the beads of sweat off her brow with the back of her goatskin glove, and passed a rose to me, as if she were handing me the most precious gift in the world. I ran my fingers along the stem, tracing the curves of the thorns, until I reached the bud.

'They're nature's best healers. They know how to talk to us,' she said, handing me more flowers. When we got home, I sat on an upside-down crate, counting the stems, knowing exactly how many days it took the first one to bloom after the beginning of spring. But I was still left wondering about their secrets; how they knew when to blossom, and how to blossom, and why they blossomed at all.

'That's it. That's all I remember and I have no idea why,' I tell Scarlett with a frown.

'It doesn't matter why. It's progress, Gracie,' says Scarlett with so much hope in her voice I want to believe her. 'You know, we go to the Queen Victoria Market for flowers every …' She stops herself. 'Sorry.' She cringes.

'No, go on.' I can't explain it, but since she's mentioned flowers, I don't want her to stop.

'You and I, Queen Vic Market. Every Saturday morning.'

Got it. Piermont and Lincoln's on the first Sunday of the month. Queen Vic Market every Saturday morning.

'Blake and Noah on the other hand, play golf on Saturday mornings.'

Of course. Typical blokey thing to do, I suppose.

'How's your list coming along?' Scarlett asks, changing the subject. 'Did you call your boss?'

I shuffle awkwardly.

'Gracie?' she says firmly.

'I quit my job.'

'What?! The doctors said that you need as much normality back in your life as possible. Why would you do that?'

'Well, they didn't exactly accept my resignation. Ava said they're going to hold my position for a couple more months in case I change my mind. She said I could even freelance.'

Scarlett shoots me a look of disapproval. 'You never missed a day of work.'

'Well … things have changed. Life's different now.' I glance over to the tower of magazines by the couch. 'I've flicked through pages and pages of those spreads and I can't remember styling a single one. I can't remember any of the prop suppliers I used to use and I don't know a thing about lighting or room sets. Heck, I don't even recognise the route stops on a tram guide! How can I go back to a job not knowing any of this?'

Scarlett rubs her temples, her cheeks filling with air before letting it out steadily. She opens her palms and holds them out, as if she's trying to get a handle on all of this. 'I get it, you're overwhelmed and afraid, but it's going to take time and we all understand that. I think it's a matter of you accepting it. Accepting our help. You can't spend your days flicking through magazines wishing your memory to come back.'

'It's not like I have anything else to do,' I mutter.

She blinks and looks thoughtfully at me. 'Gracie, there's something else I'm worried about.'

I raise my eyebrows, waiting for her to speak. I feel so bad that she's afraid to talk to me, that she's tiptoeing around me like this.

'Have you given any more thought to … the wedding?'

I cross my arms. I don't want to think about Blake or the wedding or the fact that I can't tie my own shoelaces.

'No,' I reply firmly, not wanting to elaborate because I can't admit my intentions to her yet. 'But there is something I've been wondering about.'

'What's that?'

'Was I really as happy as you seem to think I was?'

She looks me square in the eyes. 'Yes, you were happy. In fact, when it comes to Blake, you were lit up from the inside, radiant on the outside, life has never been a better kind of happy.'

I sigh, wishing I had a past to hold onto. Without any semblance of a past there is almost nothing. Aside from Scarlett, all I have is one vague memory of a field full of flowers and a brand-new wedding dress I don't remember buying.

FIVE

Aside from one small detail about loving egg-free coconut-cream cake, days pass with no memories of Blake, or any other significant aspect of my past surfacing. After several failed batches (despite following the recipe *and* using kitchen scales), I've managed to bake my favourite cake with success. Even though Dr Cleave told me that simple tasks could be challenging, I'm still finding it hard to accept. Hence, my six attempts at making coconut-cream cake until I got it right.

On this particular morning, I'm trying to master the fine art of tying shoelaces, with the aim of taking a walk around the Royal Botanic Gardens before lunchtime, when the landline rings. I wait before answering. What if it's Blake calling? I've had my mobile phone, with its countless unread messages from him, switched off and tucked away in a drawer since I returned home from hospital. When I can no longer ignore it, I take a deep breath and answer on the fifth ring.

'Hello, this is Gracie.'

'Oh, Gracie, it's Amanda Chadwick of Chadwick and Nelson Real Estate. I've been trying to get a hold of you for weeks. Your mobile keeps going to voicemail. Anyway, I was wondering if you could come in for a chat. There are a few things we should talk about regarding your mother's property. I've got a busy week in front of me, but does this morning happen to suit? I could fit you in around ten.'

'Uh, yeah, sure … this morning's fine. What's the address?'

She titters. 'Still the same.'

'Right. Okay, well, I'll see you then.' I hesitate. 'Um, what's the street name again?'

After a slight pause, she reels off the address, which I silently repeat in my head several times over. I hang up the phone and contemplate how I'm going to make this appointment. Deciding that I'm going to need to embrace autonomy sooner or later, I look up the address and manage to work out that Amanda's office is only a few tram stops away. As soon as I reach the end of the street, the thought of throwing myself onto a congested tram with other commuters is too overwhelming, so I make the trip by foot, instead. After stopping several times to ask for directions, I eventually make it to Amanda's office, its large frontage visible at the end of a tree-lined street. The trees look unhappy here surrounded by concrete, their naked boughs almost completely free of the weight of their leaves. I reach for a leaf from the nearly bare canopy of an elm, and trace the veins with my thumb. The veins don't meet in the middle.

A receptionist greets me once I step through the door, and a couple of minutes later, Amanda emerges from her office sporting a crisply ironed red shirt, a grey pencil skirt and black patent leather shoes. She flashes me a smile, revealing a mouth of perfectly white teeth. Striding towards me, I'm confronted with the scent of her perfume, a blend of floral tones with a hint of spice. She extends a manicured hand, before gesturing to her office.

'Come right in.' She motions to one of the leather seats in front of her mahogany desk as she reaches into a drawer with her other hand. She pulls out a manila folder, before pushing her glasses up the bridge of her nose. She opens it, revealing a full-page colour advertisement for a property located in the Macedon Ranges. *A perfect family home just a kilometre from the heart of Daylesford.* I twist my head, trying to make out the finer details of the property, a restored 1870s miner's cottage—a white weatherboard, fringed with delicate latticework, with a wraparound porch and grey Colorbond roof on a plot of land surrounded by flowers. Lots of them. I can't take my eyes off them.

Amanda pulls in her chair and starts flicking through the papers in her file. She lifts out a sheet and scans it. 'It's been a while since we last spoke. Now … where to start?' she says, looking up at me. 'So, I finally got a call last week from my colleagues in the country—'

I lean forward. 'When was the last time?' I ask, interrupting her.

She shakes her head with the slightest hint of impatience. 'A few months ago.'

'Sure.' I nod. 'Uh, go on.'

She looks strangely at me and then continues. 'Given the location, the current market and the potential for—'

'I'm not sure I understand.'

She slides her glasses down her nose and peers closely at me. 'I found a buyer for Summerhill, Gracie. They've made an offer that's more than generous seeing as it's ridiculously overpriced in the first place. A young family looking to move from the city.'

I fold my arms across my chest and clear my throat. 'It's no longer up for sale,' I say, trying to act as business-like as possible.

Amanda sits back, purses her lips together and slowly nods, as if she's trying to figure out the real problem here. I pull down my blouse and readjust the woollen vest I'm wearing over the top of it. I really should buy some more comfortable clothes. Everything in my wardrobe feels so stiff and corporate.

'I know where you're coming from, Gracie, but hear me out. I think this is going to be as good as it gets.'

'Tell the buyer it's off the market,' I say, surprised at the firmness in my voice. There's no way I can let this sliver of a memory slip away to a buyer. I know this must be the property I remember—the place I grew up. The place that surely must hold more memories of my mother and me.

Amanda narrows her eyes. 'You've been waiting nearly a year for someone to come along and make an offer on this place. You told me you hadn't set foot there since your mother passed away. Why the sudden change of mind?'

'Memories,' I reply.

Amanda's expression softens as she reaches for my hands. 'I know this must feel like the final goodbye, but the thing is, she's gone.'

'I know. But I need to be close to her.'

Her eyes meet mine.

I swallow uncomfortably. I don't want to have to find a way to explain my reasons for not wanting to sell when I don't understand why I wanted to sell in the first place.

Finally, Amanda gives me a nod and inhales deeply. 'Okay,' she replies in defeat. 'If you change your mind, you know where to find me.'

Relieved, I make my way to the door and pause before letting myself out. 'Could I have a copy of the listing, please?'

She takes the sheet from the folder and hands it to me. 'Gracie, I want you to go home and really think about your decision. If you don't do something soon with it, it'll become harder to sell in the long run. It's only costing you money right now.' She extends a hand and dangles the keys in front of me.

'I promise you I'll think about it,' I reply, nodding as I close my hand around the keys, a hint of hope filling me.

'I know you loved it there.'

I know. I just wish I could remember.

On leaving Amanda's office, I head down the street in what seems to be the direction I've come from, but once I walk several blocks, none of the surroundings seem familiar. In fact, all these homes with their grand façades and luxury cars parked in their driveways seem so similar I can't tell one apart from the other. I fumble through my handbag, a feeling of dread anchoring itself in my stomach. All I manage to find are three lipsticks, mascara, a miniature bottle of perfume, an empty packet of mints and a set of keys. No wallet. No driver's licence. No phone. I close my eyes and groan. 'Stupid,' I mutter.

Pausing on a street corner, I ask a man for directions, but he responds with a thick accent, telling me he's not from around here. I continue down the road, turning into street after street, hoping I can recognise my apartment complex. A glance at my watch tells me I've been walking for over an hour. I wait at a bus stop beside a woman with a toddler. 'Excuse me, by any chance do you know of an apartment complex around here with a white stucco façade and a wrought-iron gate out front?'

'Do you know the street name?' she asks.

I shake my head. 'Um, no, never mind.'

She offers a sympathetic smile and it takes everything I have to hold back the tears.

Dark clouds have gathered above, bringing with them the smell of impending rain. The trees murmur as the wind picks up, and the rain starts to tumble out from the sky with fury. I stand on the street corner on my tiptoes, trying to spot a cab in the sea of traffic, while the tyres of passing cars spray muddy water in my direction. Eventually, I manage to wave down a taxi, and soaked, I take a seat in the back.

'Where are you off to?' asks the driver.

I wipe the moisture off my face and fasten my seatbelt. 'Let me explain,' I tell him.

I tell the driver everything—about the accident, Blake, Scarlett, the apartment, the wedding, the coffee, the omelettes, my shoelaces, the toothbrushes—all of it pours out of me. Harry 'oohs' and 'aahs' and 'wows' and 'my Gods', intermittently handing me tissues over his shoulder. Eighteen minutes later, I blow my nose with as much elegance as a small child, and tell him, 'I think we can go now.'

He nods sympathetically and pulls out into the traffic. We manage to find my apartment thirty-eight minutes and forty-one dollars later.

'Hold on and I'll go up to grab some money for you,' I say, as I unbuckle my seatbelt. I make my way through the front gate and upstairs to the apartment, pulling a fifty-dollar note from my wallet, which is sitting happily on the hallway table. I race down the stairs, and run out to the street. Harry's cab is nowhere to be seen.

SIX

My phone is still flat in my bedside table drawer, and my fridge is still being stocked by my best friend when Dr Cleave finally declares I'm making progress, given the fact I can travel four tram stops, make two route changes and manage to find my way home without needing to take a taxi.

'You should be pleased with how things are coming along,' he tells me, as he closes the folder on his desk. 'How have the appointments with Pete been going? I don't seem to have a report from him yet. I'll need to chase that up.'

'Um, well, I haven't had a chance to see him since that initial session we had.'

Dr Cleave arches an eyebrow. 'I thought you said your appointments were all booked in.'

I chew my lip. 'Well, yes, they were … but …' I shake my head. 'I just don't feel like seeing him.'

Dr Cleave leans back in his chair and folds his hands in his lap. 'Okay, so tell me—how have you been spending your time?'

If I'm not spending the day curled up on the couch or under the bedsheets in my pyjamas, my life consists of little more than walks along the Yarra and to the nearby Botanic Gardens, mainly so I can report back to Scarlett and convince her I'm making an effort. But really, all it feels like I'm doing is waiting. Waiting for the things that have slipped away to come back to me: memories, recollections, reminders. I'm waiting for these things to pop back into my consciousness, with no guarantee they ever will.

Of course I don't mention any of this to Dr Cleave, so I simply say, 'I've been spending a lot of time outdoors. Long walks, that sort of thing.'

He nods approvingly. 'Never underestimate the power of fresh air, sunshine and exercise. Any plans to go back to work?'

'Not really. I think I need a bit more time. More fresh air,' I say, fiddling with my hands. 'My mum had a property in the country—Daylesford, actually. So, I was thinking of spending a bit of time there—I thought the country air might be good for me.' I hold my breath, almost certain he's going to tell me it's not advisable, but his eyes brighten.

'I think that's a great idea. As long as you keep those appointments with Pete. Counselling is very important for your recovery, even if it doesn't feel that way right now.'

My thoughts wander to the listing in my pocket. 'Yes, I think it's a great idea, too.'

As the following days pass, I become increasingly aware that Blake can't wait forever. The apartment is his home, also.

Scarlett visits most evenings after work and finds creative ways to casually hint that I should think about writing back to Blake or at least allowing him to see me. He's been to the apartment twice. Once to pick up his golf clubs and more clothing, and another time to collect some paperwork and other personal items. All arranged via Scarlett. Both times, he left flowers. First paperwhites and then an arrangement of lisianthus. The first note said, *Hope you're doing okay, ladybug.* And the second, *I miss you. I hope you won't need much longer. I don't know how long I'll be able to stay away. Write me?*

'So, did you write him?' asks Scarlett, folding the note. Her patience has been wearing a little thin lately. I don't blame her.

I shake my head in response, unable to tell her what she wants to hear.

'You really need to be a bit more proactive about all of this,' she tells me as she folds the note. 'If you're going to expect Blake to give you the space you're asking for, the least you can do is take some kind of action to at least try to get your memory back,' she says, flicking from TV channel to TV channel. I pinch the remote from her as I drop down onto the sofa with a bag of chips.

'What are you doing?' she says. 'Where did you get them from?'

'I bought them today,' I say, shovelling a handful into my mouth before offering her the bag.

'Good lord,' she whispers to herself. 'Right, this is spiral- ling out of control. This is not the Gracie Ashcroft I knew and this is not the Gracie Ashcroft you are going to become!' she says, snatching the packet from me. 'Do you have no regard for your waistline or your health?' She stomps to the kitchen and tosses the bag into the rubbish. 'These are not organic, nor do they constitute any of the major food groups!'

I look down at my feet, feeling sheepish, like a toddler that's being reprimanded by its mother.

I lick the salt off my lips. 'Well, actually, there is one thing I think I could do to help things along.' I've been giving a lot of thought to Summerhill since my encounters with Amanda and Dr Cleave, and have been waiting for the right time to bring things up with Scarlett.

She takes me by the hand and leads me towards the front door, where she grabs my coat from the stand and pulls a beanie over my head. 'Good,' she says, pressing her palms against my cheeks. 'Blake's coming by in half an hour, and we're going to Piermont and Lincoln's and you're going to tell me all about it over tea.'

Scarlett and I squeeze onto a tram and find two spare seats. 'It's so stuffy in here, don't you think?' She unbuttons her coat and fans her face, her cheeks flushed.

'Scarlett?'

'Mmm,' she replies.

'Tell me about Summerhill?'

She raises her eyebrows in excitement. 'You grew up there. You moved to Melbourne when Blake graduated—'

I raise a hand. 'Don't tell me. Not about him—not yet. Just about the farm.' The way I see it, I'll have a chance to get to know Blake again, eventually, but I'll never have a chance to know my mother again, and perhaps starting at the place I do have a memory of, might lead me to others.

'You put it on the market after your mum passed away. You said it was too painful to hold onto those memories.'

Scarlett becomes silent as the tram doors open and a woman slides into the seat beside her.

I stare into my lap, my stomach twisting at the bitterness of it all. 'And now they're completely gone,' I whisper.

Scarlett orders a pot of oolong to share between us. I think she's overlooked the fact that I'd prefer a strong coffee, but I don't say anything. I watch her pour the steaming liquid into two lemon-coloured teacups rimmed with gold trim, painted with apple blossoms. I gulp mine down quickly, figuring it might not be so bad if I drain my cup in one go.

'I probably should have ordered the peppermint. I don't know why they call it morning sickness when it has the capacity to debilitate you at any given moment of the day,' says Scarlett. She blows a wisp of hair out of her eye and fans her face with her hands.

My back straightens as I register her words. My eyes travel to her belly, which I completely failed to notice before now. A bump. A *baby*.

'How far along are you?' I ask, thinking that she's doing an incredible job of hiding a baby. Maybe it's the oversized winter clothing, or the fact that I have nothing to compare her figure to from before.

She smiles. 'Twenty-four weeks. I've had to go up two bra sizes, you know. It's everything I've ever wanted—to be a mum,' she says dreamily.

I return Scarlett's smile. She's positively radiant.

'I've been waiting for the right time to tell you. I mean, you knew before. You were the first to know after Noah. There's a role for godmother up for grabs. Yours if you want it.' She takes a sip of tea, a hint of a smile playing over the rim of her cup.

'Of course,' I reply softly.

Twenty-four weeks? How could I not have noticed?

'That's what you said last time.'

'Really?'

'Yes. The only difference was that you almost tackled me to the ground and squeezed me so hard I couldn't breathe.' She giggles.

'I'm happy for you. You've got so much to look forward to.'

'And then you said you couldn't wait until it was going to be your turn.'

I pour myself more tea and bring the cup to my mouth, closing my eyes as the tannin-filled liquid travels down my throat, leaving a bitter aftertaste. Was I ready to have a baby? Had Blake and I planned things? Spoken about it?

Scarlett squashes a sandwich into her mouth and pats away the crumbs on her chin with a napkin. She groans. 'I'm starving *all* the time,' she says, her mouth still full. She selects a few triangles and heaps them on my plate. 'These are your favourites.' She pulls her hand back and cringes. 'Sorry!'

'Don't worry about it,' I mutter, pushing away the plate. I've lost my appetite, anyway.

'Tell me about what you mentioned before. The thing you think could help improve things,' she says.

My body tenses. Taking charge of my own life—it all feels impossible. Scarlett's having a *baby* and I'm still trying to piece my life together. My fiancé is at home, the place that once was *our* home, taking care of loose ends; picking up more clothes and things; his things, our things, things from our life together.

'I don't think I can marry him,' I blurt out.

She swallows a mouthful of food and sits there frozen, staring into her teacup as she processes what I've said. Finally, she draws a deep breath and speaks on the exhale. 'I think you're making a mistake. Think about what you're doing. You can't just end it. You need to give him a chance. The wedding isn't for another nine weeks. Surely by then—'

'I don't think you understand.'

Scarlett's cheeks flush and her jaw tightens. Her voice rises, and the group of women sitting at the table adjacent to us turn their heads in our direction. 'Believe me, Gracie, I'm *trying* to understand. I'm the one in the middle here. Do you think it's easy for Blake to stay away from you like this? For me to have to reassure him every single day that he needs to give you the time and space you're asking for in order to get your head around all this? It's not exactly the way most people would go about things.' Her words tumble out furiously, like they've been hiding inside her, wrestling to leap out. She purses her lips and takes a deep breath, regaining her composure. She rubs her temples. 'But then again, that's what we'd expect from you …'

I ignore her last comment and try to explain. I'm tired of having to explain. 'He's a stranger to me. For you, he's my fiancé, but for me … he's …' I don't want to say it. It feels heartless to say it. *Nobody.*

Scarlett gives me a look of total disappointment. The last thing I want to do is hurt anyone, only I can't seem to find a way to make any of this better.

'If you'd reconsider, agree to see him once … get to know him, talk some things over—even if you don't remember him, at the very least, you might find that you *like* him,' she says.

'But what if I don't?'

'That's what you're afraid of, isn't it?'

I chew the inside of my lip and nod.

'This situation is so unfair, not to mention completely absurd. I'll tell you, I think he expects that you'll agree to see him any day now. Don't be surprised if he turns up one day to see you. It's been nearly two weeks since you were discharged and—'

'I'm leaving Melbourne.'

'What?! When?! Oh my God, Gracie, what are you thinking?'

'This is how I'm going to improve things. I'll go to Summerhill and—'

'Your mother's place? But that's two hours away. Everything's boxed up. It's not even ready for you to … Besides, it's listed for sale.'

'Well, it's off the market now.'

'Of course it is,' says Scarlett, the exasperation in her voice apparent. 'You're going to have to see him sometime, you know. You can't simply pretend he doesn't exist. He should be with you, not in my spare room.'

Especially now she's having a *baby*.

'Don't you think I know that?' I whisper, fiddling with the sandwich on my plate. I can feel the women beside us staring.

Scarlett fires a look at one of them, who squirms uncomfortably before looking away.

'When do you plan on seeing him? Or at least talking to him? Can't you at least start with a phone call?'

I straighten up, take in a deep breath and release it slowly. 'I'll write to him.'

'Write to him? As in a *letter*? That's it?' Scarlett stares at me wide-eyed and I know she's trying hard to retain her patience. 'I can't even remember the last time I bought a postage stamp.'

'Neither can I,' I reply. Scarlett misses my joke completely. 'But, yes. I'll write to him. And then … if by the end of spring I don't remember him, I'll agree to see him.'

'But you can't go, you still have hospital appointments, and what if you need help? There are still things you can't do on your own. What if you get lost or—'

'Dr Cleave is only a phone call away. And I'll call you if I need your help.'

Scarlett shakes her head. 'This is absurd. There's no way Blake will agree to this.'

'He has to. If he wants to give this a chance, this is how it's got to be. All I'm asking for is time. Time to find myself. And if I don't remember you, or Blake, or anyone else or any other part of my life, then I'll come back and see him and work out where to go from there.'

'I have a feeling nothing I say is going to make you change your mind.'

'Well, then … looks like you do know me.'

'When do you plan on leaving?'

There's a stirring in my belly, nervous tension mixed with a hint of excitement. 'Saturday. Eight am,' I say, a smile playing on my lips. Before now, the whole idea of going to Summerhill had been just that—an idea. Now it's become something more—an adventure, a promise of hope. 'I've got it all sorted: a train, a bus, and the phone number for a taxi if I get completely lost.' I raise my eyebrows enthusiastically.

Scarlett shakes her head in defeat. 'You've always been so hard to keep up with, you know.'

'I don't know. But that's okay. I'm getting to know.'

By the time Saturday morning comes, the listing of Summerhill is worn around the edges, a tattered piece of paper that resembles one lonely shred of a memory. Before leaving, I drag an empty cardboard box from one of the cupboards to the spare room. Giving the bridal magazines no more than a cursory glance, I pack them away with the two-page 'to-do list' that's sitting on the chest of drawers. I remove my wedding dress from the bag it's hanging in, admire the detail, the lace, the beading, the weight of it. Turning towards the mirror as I hold it against my body, I stand there, imagining what it might be like to wear it, to say 'I do' and fill in the dots later. For a slip of time, I set aside the fear and allow myself to imagine what it might be like to stay. To answer the door and let Blake smile into my eyes—blank eyes, eyes that don't smile back the way they might have before. I picture what it might be like to fold in his embrace as he kisses me on the top of my head and tells me that everything is going to be okay, even though we both know it might not be. What it might be like to lie down in bed with a stranger and squirm under his touch.

My heart begins to race and I struggle to breathe.

I can't do it to him, to me, to us.

Maybe if it's meant to be, some day I'll remember.

I lay the dress on the bed and do my best to fold it as neatly as possible, as if handling it with care and respect might somehow make what I'm doing any less painful. Placing it into the box, I cringe at the sound of the packing tape screeching as I close it up. Then I take the guest list and scan it in the hope that a name, maybe just one name, might trigger a memory of a face, or give me some reason to believe that my memory loss might not be permanent. But as I check the list twice for good measure, I realise that every single person here has become an overnight stranger to me.

Aside from Scarlett's and Noah's, not one name ignites even the slightest recollection of an annoying aunt, or loyal friend or awkward family feud. I brush the hair away from my face, let out a heavy breath, take the stack of blank thankyou cards, and try to find the words to explain to these people why my wedding to Blake won't be going ahead.

I regret to inform you that Blake and I won't be getting married as planned. I've lost something precious to me, and without it, I can't walk down the aisle.
Thank you for your understanding.
Gracie

It takes me over an hour to write the notes, and each one feels more painful than the last. It's a big ask, to expect thirty guests to understand something I can't yet fully comprehend, but I address each one and when I'm finally done, I carry the box to the front door, where I drop down beside it in an exhausted heap. My head rests against its rigid edges, and I know how pathetic this must look—I'm wrapped around a cardboard box, mourning its contents, blinking away tears, contemplating whether to pick up the phone so I can hear Blake's voice and ask him about who I am and who we were, and how we met, and whether we fought sometimes or not at all, but that's not how I want things to be.

I take the folded listing for Summerhill from my pocket, to reassure myself one more time.

Once a thriving flower farm, this five-acre plot with two-bedroom cottage and ample-sized barn is the perfect country escape. Nestled amongst the verdant backdrop of the Macedon Ranges, with Lake Daylesford and Hepburn's coveted mineral springs only a short drive away, this property would make a perfect country home for the right buyer.

The listing goes on to describe the home and its features, but I lose my concentration, circling back to the words: 'Once a thriving flower farm', while the elusive memories of peonies and lavender and cupped roses drift towards me, hovering some distance away, unable to venture as close to me as I would like them to. Summerhill might be the closest I ever get to finding out whether I'll ever regain these memories. In a situation where nothing is easy, this seems at least easier.

There's not much I want to take with me aside from clothes and bare essentials, but before I click the suitcase shut, a grey cotton t-shirt that's been lying over the armchair in the corner of the bedroom catches my attention. It's drenched in the reassuring masculine smell that I now know belongs to Blake. A fresh, woody, marine kind of scent.

It takes another hour to write Blake a letter. My pen scratches the surface of the paper, trying to form sentences that seem coherent in my mind but jumbled by the time I try to get them into written form. With my stomach in knots, and the reality of what it's really like to be dealing with a traumatic brain injury at the age of twenty-six hitting me, I almost give up.

Dear Blake,

I wish I could tell you that I think things will be okay, but I'd be lying if I told you that. I don't even know if your toothbrush is the yellow one or the blue one, but one thing I know for sure right now is this: I can't marry you.

I don't remember much to be able to meet you in the middle. I have no way of knowing whether everything in my life is all I ever wanted. If I fell in love with you once, would I fall in love with you again? Neither of us can possibly know the answer to that question, and I need some time to get to know myself again before I'm ready to find out. Before I can let you in, I need to work out who I really am.

I don't remember much about my mother, but she left me a property in the Macedon Ranges. Apparently I grew up there, but I'm guessing you already know that.

Please don't come to Summerhill for me. Not now. Not yet. I need some time alone to figure this out, to try to remember my life on my terms so I can truly know who I was and what I wanted from life before it was ripped away from me.

When I remember, if I remember, I'll come back to you.

Gracie

P.S. I took a punt and chose the yellow toothbrush.

P.P.S. ~~*I'm sorry*~~*. I'm really sorry.*

I fold my note, with my handwriting that resembles that of a nine-year-old, and run my tongue against the bitter film of glue on the back of the envelope, trying to hold back the tears that are aching to emerge, like a swelling river about to burst at the slightest hint of rain.

For Scarlett, I leave a note beside a box of herbal tea.

Thank you for being the best kind of friend. I'll call you when I'm settled. But in the meantime, please trust me so I can learn to trust myself.
Love, Gracie

My engagement ring stays behind, right beside the letter I leave for Blake. With its countless unread messages, I replace my phone with a new SIM. This is the phone whose battery died weeks ago and I can't help thinking something else died along with it.

I take Blake's grey t-shirt with me.

SEVEN

Woodend, a small country village in the centre of the Victorian Macedon Ranges, comes into view after an hour's train ride from Melbourne's Southern Cross station. As I stroll down the quiet street to the nearest bus stop, the scent of freshly baked pastries wafts from the bakery but is quickly overpowered by the smell of coffee from the café next door.

'Just in time, love,' says the bus driver, as I haul my suitcase up the steps.

'Are you heading to Daylesford?' I ask.

'Sure am.'

'Could you let me know once we've arrived?' I request, before taking a seat. He salutes in response, before telling me we should be there in around forty-five minutes.

The bus rattles away as we pass through a large avenue lined with English oaks, and travel past frost-dusted paddocks and restored homesteads. Puffs of smoke billow from chimneys while a light fog slowly lifts in the distance.

Eventually, we reach the heart of Daylesford, which has come to life under the mid-morning sun. 'This'll be your stop,' calls the bus driver, opening the doors for me. I thank him and tug my luggage off the step, pulling it behind me over the bumpy asphalt, while I try to work out which direction to step in. I tap the door, which opens for me almost immediately. 'Um, by any chance would you happen to know where Summerhill is? It used to be a flower farm.'

The driver rubs his chin and points ahead. 'You'll need to walk all the way down there and turn right once you reach the directional signs for the lake. Once you're there, ask for more directions. It shouldn't be far off.'

An eclectic array of shops throng the main street—a large bakehouse, a bookstore, various gift shops, upmarket clothing stores, and a wine bar whose entry is manned by two wooden barrels with fistfuls of paper daisies cascading over their edges. Couples of varying ages spill in and out of the cafés on either side of the road, emerging with takeaway cups of steaming coffee. It's no wonder everyone looks relaxed here. Originally a gold-mining town, the spot is now a haven for day-spa retreats, pampering and romantic weekend getaways.

At the end of the main street, the shops peter out, replaced by picket fences and Victorian-style cottages, including B&Bs sporting 'No Vacancy' signs, even though it's midwinter. I continue down the road, following the directions pointing me to Lake Daylesford.

Further ahead lies a roadside stand where the street widens. A man wearing fingerless gloves, an oversized coat and a tweed cap is selling roasted chestnuts, the smoky aroma reminding me that I skipped breakfast completely. I breathe in the earthy scent of eucalyptus and sprawling countryside and wait as the man shovels a scoop-full of chestnuts into a brown paper cone and hands them to a customer, while another one, a male, probably around my age, leans against the stall, popping chestnuts into his mouth as he chats to the vendor. He watches me approach, lifts his eyebrows and smiles at me.

'That'll be four dollars,' says the vendor to a customer. 'And for you, Miss, what'll it be?'

'I'm just looking for directions,' I say, digging into my pocket for the property listing.

'The lake's that way,' he says, nodding to his left.

'Well, actually, I'm looking for 495 Darlinghurst Way? Otherwise known as Summerhill.'

The guy standing beside the stall perks to attention. 'You want to know where Summerhill is?' His eyes meet mine, where they settle for a second.

'Uh, yeah. I'm pretty sure it's close by, but …' I flick my eyes to the piece of paper. 'Well, I'm not entirely sure.'

'Nobody lives there, so—'

'I live there,' I say, wondering if he's noticed the hint of irritation in my voice.

'It's a little hard to find.'

He waits for me to reply, but when I don't respond, he continues. 'But if you look beyond those gum trees, you'll see it right up there,' he says, pointing across the road to a cottage on the hill directly in front of the chestnut stall.

The trees, with their hundred-year-old limbs, obscure the house almost completely. I squint, trying to get a better view.

'I hope your electricity's running.' He pops a chestnut into his mouth. 'Cold snap,' he says, raising his eyebrows.

He rolls up the collar of his grey herringbone coat and I can feel his eyes lingering on me as I hand the vendor some change in exchange for a paper cone.

'Everything is in order,' I mutter. I can't believe I've stupidly overlooked this detail. Maybe Scarlett was right about this not being a good idea. She'd asked me not to leave until she had a chance to help me sort out a few things and now I know this is what she meant. Raising the handle of the suitcase, I take a few steps towards the road and call out over my shoulder, 'Thanks for the directions.'

Before I have a chance to get very far, the guy's beside me, his jog slowing to a walk. 'Hey, uh, I'm sorry if I said something to upset you.'

I'm not in the mood to explain that the only person I'm really irritated with is myself. My silence does little to shrug him off.

He flashes me a smile, which I ignore, even if it is of the slightly charming variety. I take another step forward, but he extends a hand just as I move, knocking the paper cone out of my hand.

'I'm Flynn,' he says, as my chestnuts spill to the ground. He runs a hand through the natural waves of his unruly blond hair. 'Uh, not usually this clumsy, I can assure you.' He looks down at the chestnuts, then back at me, his mouth twisting into an amused smile.

Despite his handsome looks—large marine-blue eyes, a strong jaw line, light scruff, and two smile-enhancing dimples that make it almost impossible to not smile back, I'm starting to find this guy increasingly exasperating. I eye off my lunch, which is now scattered around my feet. My stomach growls.

'Nice meeting you, Flynn,' I reply, just before I cross the road.

I tug my suitcase up the gravel-lined driveway, my heart sinking with each step. The garden beds out front are in dire need of attention, the dormant roses desperately needing a winter prune. Bare branches of wisteria snake over one side of the white weatherboard façade, tendrils curling through the fretwork, and the overstuffed letterbox is spewing yellowed, soggy newspapers, which I dislodge and tuck under one arm before ramming my hip against the gate to open it.

I'm overwhelmed by a woody, musty smell the moment I push open the sage-green front door, but despite the cold and minimal furnishings of the cottage, there's an element of warmth here. It feels as if my mother could emerge from the kitchen at any moment; oven mitts on, pulling a steaming hot apple pie from the oil-fired Rayburn. A pair of kitchen scales sits beside a stack of recipe books that have gathered a layer of dust. There's a modest-sized living room with a double-sided fireplace and an armchair positioned in a reading nook, the wall partially covered with bookshelves. Are any of the books mine? Did my mother ever hold me on her lap and read to me when I was a child?

Most of the contents of the cottage have long ago been boxed up, and according to Scarlett, were sold off or donated to charity last spring. But some things remain, like the furniture, drawers filled with kitchen utensils and crockery, some linen, and most of the appliances. After spending some time exploring the two-bedroom cottage, taking in my new surroundings, dusting surfaces and nudging windows open to allow some fresh air inside, I venture outside to explore.

There's a large wooden barn with a gable rooftop and sliding door located around a hundred metres away from the cottage itself. A silver Volkswagen is parked in front of it, a car I didn't notice on my arrival. I approach with caution and call out before poking my head inside.

'Hello?'

'I was wondering when you might turn up. Want to give me a hand?' says a male voice.

I raise a hand to my chest as my breath catches. I flip around to face him.

Is that the guy from the roadside stand? What was his name? Flynn?

'What?' I say, glaring at him.

He points to the car. 'Brought you some firewood. Figured you might need it.' He grabs two logs from the boot of the car and stacks them in a pile.

'Never mind you're trespassing.'

'Don't go too far out of your way to show your appreciation.' He wipes his brow and continues piling up the wood.

I cross my arms. 'I don't need your help.'

'Do you know how to build a fire?' he asks, tilting his head to the side.

He smiles at me and now I'm staring incredulously at him. 'You've got a nerve.'

'Just trying to help. Can't have my neighbour freeze overnight.'

Neighbours? This guy?

'I don't intend to.'

'Well, give me a hand and then I'll be out of your way.'

'I have heating.'

'Not unless you light a fire you don't,' he says, stacking another several logs on top of each other.

I cross my arms. 'How would you know that I don't have heating?' I say, challenging him.

'Because I checked your meter box, and your outside lights aren't working.' I clench my jaw. It's Saturday, which means that if he's right, the electricity and gas company won't be able to connect the services until at least Monday.

He takes off his coat, tosses it into the boot and rolls up the sleeves of his jumper. 'You going to just stand there watching?'

'I'm not—'

'You are.'

'No, I'm …' I stop myself from finishing my sentence, because I can see my reaction is amusing him and this is exactly what he's looking for.

He hands me a couple of logs, which I take hold of and pile up on the stack. The weather here is much cooler than Melbourne's, and deep down I know that if I don't want to freeze tonight I'll need to get the fire going. And like it or not, Flynn's saved me a trip into town for firewood.

'We make a great team,' he says, laughing.

'You don't even know my name,' I reply, reaching for more wood.

He raises his eyebrows and waits for me to tell him. I try to resist rolling my eyes. 'Gracie,' I mumble, extending a hand. 'Gracie Ashcroft.'

He shakes my hand and turns away to reach for the last two logs. 'Bring some in, we'll get the fire going, then I'll leave you be.'

I stand there, hand on hip, contemplating whether I should let him into my house. He is, after all, a stranger. Then again, practically everyone in my life is a stranger.

His voice softens. 'Give me ten minutes,' he says. 'Really. It's going to be a cold night. I don't expect a dinner invitation or anything.'

I shake my head in defeat and extend my arms for him to hand me the logs. By now it's started pelting down. A roll of thunder hurtles through the sky. We stand there, under the doorframe of the barn, the wind whipping against us, water pooling at our feet as we contemplate what to do. The rain shows no sign of relenting.

'Should we make a run for it?' Flynn calls out.

'I think so,' I yell over the rain.

We race to the house, feet stomping through puddles, arriving at the front door soaking wet. We enter and I plonk the wood down beside the fireplace, clothes dripping. I rub my hands together and peel off my jumper. Flynn wipes the moisture off his face, kneels down and gets to work, emptying a box of fire starters he brought with him. He glances up at me. 'You're soaking wet and it's freezing in here. You should go get changed.'

'I'm not cold,' I reply, trying to keep my teeth from chattering. Flynn rolls his eyes.

I head towards my bedroom, and call out, 'How long have you been living next door?'

'A little while,' he replies.

When I emerge from my bedroom, my body enveloped by a couple of extra layers than usual, Flynn's waiting for me by the front door. 'I left some wood in a bucket for you to top up later,' he says.

'Thanks,' I say. 'Um … how much do I owe you?'

He questions me with his eyes.

'For the firewood.'

'You don't owe me anything,' he says, adjusting his scarf. He puffs some air into his hands before rubbing them together. 'Think of it as a peace offering for the chestnut debacle. Now that we're friends, feel free to invite me over for a drink sometime.' He opens the door and steps outside. 'Once you've got electricity, that is.'

'Who says we're ...' I stop myself, because as I stand there in silence, the outside air sweeping through the front door making me shudder with cold, I think to myself that unbeknown to Flynn, aside from Scarlett, he's the only friend I have.

EIGHT

Ever since I arrived in Summerhill, Scarlett's been calling every morning at the same time, and I'm fairly sure it's because she knows I'd happily sleep past brunch, otherwise. Aside from venturing into town to stock the fridge and pantry with essentials—like milk, bread and butter—I've spent most of my time here mulling around doing nothing, but Scarlett doesn't know this of course. Dragging myself out of bed and into the kitchen, I snatch up the phone before it rings out.

'Morning, stranger,' says Scarlett.

'Are you trying to be funny?' I ask, in spite of myself. I drop two slices of bread in the toaster and switch on the kettle.

Scarlett groans. 'Sorry,' she says. 'Just called to check on you before I leave for work.' She says this every morning.

'Have you heard from Blake? I mean, has he written to you? Because he told me he was going to.'

'Yes and no,' I reply, picking up the letter that arrived yesterday afternoon. I tap it against the kitchen table and sigh a little louder than I'd intended.

'What does that mean?'

'It means that I don't know if I should *open* his letter.'

'Why the heck wouldn't you, Gracie?!'

I close my eyes in a futile attempt to drown out Scarlett's rambling—all the usual things about how I'm eventually going to need to meet him, and that it wouldn't be fair to not even read his letters.

'It's just … hard. I'm trying to settle in and I don't want to be more confused than I already am.'

'He moved out,' she says, after a pause.

'That's good,' I say, pouring myself an orange juice. 'He needs to … move on.' There's another long pause. I cringe, knowing my words haven't quite come out the way I meant them to. My juice spills over the edge of the glass.

'I'm going to pretend I don't know what you mean by that,' Scarlett says quietly. 'Or that you don't mean what I think you mean.'

Even I'm taken aback by what I've just said. Is that the way I really feel about things? Is this over before I even give it the opportunity to have a chance? Do I *want* it to be over? And, if it is over, if the accident swept my life away along with the man that was at the forefront of it, will the future hold something equally as wonderful as what I'm told we had?

The juice trickles over the edge of the bench and down the cupboards onto the floor. I cradle the phone in my neck and reach for a sponge to mop it up. 'I should go. I've got a few things to take care of today,' I say, wanting to avoid any further discussion about Blake.

'I think you're in denial,' she says.

'That's ridiculous,' I scoff. 'I'm trying to figure things out.'

'Uh, yeah, by avoiding the problem completely.'

'That's not what I'm doing. I just want to do this my way.'

'By pretending he doesn't even exist?!'

'I can't help that he doesn't feel real to me.'

'I know,' she says. 'Sorry, I shouldn't have … I don't really know how to let you make the mistake I think you're making.'

'You're just trying to be a good friend,' I say, letting out a sigh. 'I wish I was a better one.'

'You are. You always have been. Your stubborn streak seems to have gotten a little worse since the accident, though …' Her voice trails off. 'Oh my God, look at the time. I need to get to work. Speak to you tomorrow,' she says. 'Promise me you'll open the letter?'

'I promise,' I say, before saying goodbye.

I manage to burn two pieces of toast before I finally bring myself to tear open Blake's letter.

Dear Gracie,

When Scarlett told me you were leaving, the first thing I did was go home to try to stop you from going. But I could tell you were gone before I found your note. There weren't any fresh flowers in the apartment.

Life without you in it the way I want you to be in it is one of the hardest things I've ever had to deal with. All I want to do is look into your eyes and frame your beautiful face with my hands and feel the brush of your lips against mine. I want to hold you and tell you that everything was okay, and is okay, and will be okay, even if you can't remember who we were and what we had.

I remember the moment I fell in love with you like it was yesterday. You were sitting under a tree and you were humming to your favourite song. You were sitting on a bed of wildflowers, surrounded by bluebells, with a bottle of pink lemonade held upright between your knees. You were threading a daisy chain, with your tongue poking out of the corner of your mouth. We always argued about that, actually—you're convinced they were dandelions.

Anyway, I picked a bunch of them and handed them to you one by one. When you were done, you put the chain on your head and you took the leftover flowers and you shaped them into a heart on the grass. You looked up at me and smiled, and that's when I knew—that was the exact moment you fell right back in love with me, too. We were sixteen years old.

Here are some things you should know:

The yellow toothbrush is mine.

You sleep with your socks on.

You set your alarm for 5.45 am every morning and then you go for a run.

You and I were the closest thing to perfect I ever knew in my life.

I understand you don't want me to come to Summerhill. I wish you didn't feel this way, but as hard as it is, I understand why you do. I know you'd fall in love with me

again if you had the chance. Somehow, I'm going to find
a way to show you that.
    Love,
    Blake

I chose the wrong toothbrush.

Suddenly, the world goes quiet. Without giving it any thought, I pick up the phone and dial Blake's number, before hanging up.

Realisation hits me—I just remembered his number.

I pick up the phone and dial it again. He answers.

'Hello, hello?'

I want to speak, but nothing comes out.

'Gracie? Is that you?'

My breath catches in my chest. I hang up.

The toaster pops with my replacement bread.

A burnt odour fills the kitchen.

I reach for the tissue box, wipe my eyes clean, and butter the toast anyway.

There are no fresh flowers in the cottage.

I fold Blake's note, stuff the last piece of burnt toast in my mouth, and force myself to change out of my pyjamas. I'm plumping the pillows on my bed when a thought, a knowing, a sense of having been here, done this before, overcomes me.

You should never leave the house with a sink full of dirty dishes or an unmade bed.

Hovering in my mind is a memory of my mother. I'm tugging on the corner of the sheets, helping her smooth them out. Sunlight streams through the window as we pull and fold perfect hospital corners. She declares our work done and I follow her into the kitchen, where she rinses the breakfast dishes, places them on the rack and winks at me.

'Come on, poppet. It's the first day of spring, and we've got work to do. The sweet peas are waiting for you.' She tickles my nose with her finger and kisses my forehead. She smells of honey and vanilla. Taking my hand in hers, we exit the kitchen. At the front door, she takes an apron and throws it over her head before crouching down. My hands rest on one of her shoulders as she holds a gumboot in place and guides one of my feet into it and then the other.

She smiles at me. Green eyes, like mine, the same shape, only bigger. She's so *pretty*. Long hair falls around her shoulders. Light brown, with a hint of blonde—natural highlights from the sun. Her arm wraps around my waist and squeezes gently as she brings my body closer to hers, resting her head against my shoulder. I close my eyes and inhale her scent. Everything feels so safe and perfect.

The moment I open my eyes she's gone, like a moving cloud in the sky, there one minute, evaporated the next— just like my memory.

I slip on my coat, slide my feet into a pair of leather boots and wrap a scarf around my neck. Outside, I venture down the slope towards the main road. My feet crunch the empty chestnut shells past the stall, where the vendor introduces himself as Charlie. He pours a bag of chestnuts onto a roasting pan perforated with holes, and then takes a knife and begins cutting slits in them. 'I see you've moved into the cottage up there.'

'That's right.'

'It's been vacant for a while. Have you got everything sorted?'

'I'm getting there.' I smile.

'Well, if you ever need anything, you know where to find me. Wednesday to Saturday, for the next few weeks at least.'

'And then?'

'And then, I'll have to find something else to do. We never quite know what the future will hold, do we?'

'I guess not.' I shrug.

'Locals that have been living around these parts longer than me tell me it was a flower farm once, you know,' he says, motioning to Summerhill. 'Shame really, because it was apparently the biggest and best farm for miles around. Everyone loves locally grown and sustainable flowers. It's a movement. A bit like the craze for organic stuff right now.'

I nod. 'So I've heard.'

'Chestnuts?' he says, handing me a paper cone.

I raise a hand. 'No thanks. I'm actually allergic.' I gasp and take a step back, stunned at how something I didn't know before seems so clear now.

Charlie's eyes widen.

'Just mildly,' I add. 'I swell up to enormous proportions.'

'Ooh,' he says, pulling them away. 'But I thought the other day you—' He raises his eyebrows.

'I only just found out,' I say, trying to act less surprised than he is.

'Well, at least you know now.'

'Yes, I do. And I suppose that's a good thing.'

'I suppose it is.'

'I better go. Looks like it might rain later,' I say, looking up at the sky.

'Or the sun might come out. You can never really tell.'

At the top of the main street, the roads are cordoned off from traffic to make way for the local market. Here I'm greeted by vendors who are still setting up their stalls, stretching open pop-up marquees, and opening A-frame boards showcasing perfectly formed rainbow chalk letters. A woman shoves ice-cream sticks into pots of handmade creams, while another puts a handful of them into a container beside a tub of raw honey.

'Morning!' says a man as he opens an umbrella. He blows a puff of air into his cupped hands and then rubs them together. The aroma of fresh coffee brings my attention to his stand.

'Is it too early?' I ask him.

'Never too early for coffee,' he replies.

While I wait, a woman with a wooden flower cart ambles past me, pushing her array of pastel-coloured flowers. The cart squeaks under the weight of the galvanised steel buckets of blooms. The vendor hands me a steaming hot paper cup and I hurriedly follow the creaking and groaning until the woman stops, positioning her cart under a large oak tree on the opposite street corner.

Apricot-coloured flowers positioned at the back of her cart catch my eye. Their names don't come to me straightaway, but I stand there, conjuring up an image of myself sitting on a wooden kitchen table, my bare legs, scored with scratches, crossed. With fingers caked in dirt, I lift a bulb from a container and wedge it into a glass vase beside its companions. My little hands reach for a jug of water, carefully pouring just the right amount of liquid into the vase in order to force the bulbs to bloom. And then, as the scent of the waxy florets drifts past me, I'm reacquainted with their name and exactly how I used to trick these flowers into thinking it was winter, compelling them to flower early. Instead of a chemistry set, my mother set me loose with hyacinth bulbs, a vase and a jug of water. Six weeks later, I'd run out to the porch, declaring my experiment a success.

I stand there, desperately willing the memory of my mother's reaction to drift into my consciousness, but even as the deep, intoxicating floral scent wraps around me, there isn't anything else there: no sound of her voice as she sings her praise and delight, no words to hold onto, no facial expression to comfort me.

My thoughts are interrupted by the flower seller's voice. 'What will it be today?' Her appearance throws me for a second as I take in her peculiar choice of fashion. She's dressed in black leather boots with scuffed toes, a pair of leggings, and is wearing an apron, green like an olive, over the top of a loud patchwork dress, embellished with embroidered motifs. On her head, she's wearing a cable-knit beanie pulled over her ears with a large pom-pom dangling from it. Captivated by her eccentricity, I take a few seconds to study her, before turning my attention away from her. I don't want her to notice me staring.

I scan the cart for flowers to take home. She follows my gaze as I eye off the hyacinths. Apricot Passions. 'They smell sweet while they last,' she says, lifting one from the bucket and shaking the excess water off the stem. She pierces me with her hooded blue eyes, and holds the flower close to my face so that I can inhale. Her eyes, marked with crow's feet, open wider, filled with intrigue. 'These ones lean towards the light.'

'I'll take them.'

She nods and reaches for a sheet of tissue paper to wrap them in.

'And the daffs …' I say. I eye the rest of the flowers on her cart. An assortment of in- and out-of-season blooms, as well as what are no doubt imported roses—too perfect and packaged to be locally grown. In what feels like slow motion, I continue pointing to various other flowers—chrysanthemums, tulips, paperwhites, banksias and filler foliage like seeded eucalyptus and woody pear. The flower seller wraps each bunch with care, as if she were bundling a baby in a blanket.

'Special occasion?' she asks.

A smile, laced with a hint of hope, forms on my lips. 'Yes. I think you could say that.'

NINE

I spend the next hour circling in and around crowds at the bustling market, and am edging my way towards a stall of fresh produce, trying to call to mind a way to cook the rainbow-coloured stalks of silverbeet, when someone taps me on the shoulder.

'Fancy seeing you here,' says Flynn, smiling. He smells of fresh aftershave and is wearing a grey coat and jeans, with a navy rib-knit scarf around his neck. He eyes the vegetables in my basket. 'Decided to stock the fridge, have we?'

'How observant.' I laugh, rolling my eyes. 'Now I just need to figure out what to do with them.'

'I could help you with that.'

'Oh, you definitely seem to be the helping sort,' I reply with a hint of sarcasm. I pick up a broccoli to admire its tiny yellow flowers before adding it to my basket. I grab a few oranges, some imperfectly shaped carrots, their tops still on, a bunch of kale and some pumpkin. Flynn offers to take the basket for me while I pay for the produce, and when I turn around, a brown-and-white Cavalier King Charles, with long ears he hasn't grown into, jumps up at me, wagging his tail.

'Easy, boy,' says Flynn. 'Looks like he's excited to see you.'

'What's his name?' I ask, crouching down to pat him.

'Parrot.'

'Parrot?' I titter, looking up at Flynn as Parrot licks my face. I wipe my cheek with the cuff of my sleeve.

Flynn shrugs. 'It makes him unforgettable. And he's also super loyal and trustworthy.'

I nuzzle my face against Parrot's. 'Well, he's very cute, too.'

'Sit,' commands Flynn, and Parrot obeys, but looks up at me with his innocent eyes, his tail thumping against the ground, as if to tell me we're not done yet with the affection.

'I think he likes me,' I say, nodding Parrot's way.

'Seems like it. He's totally smitten,' says Flynn, but the way he looks at me, the way he doesn't look at Parrot but directly at me, makes me wonder whether I should be blushing. Parrot yawns.

'I fixed your front gate this morning,' he says, changing the subject. 'Noticed it was stuck when I came to visit earlier. Did you forget about our deal?'

'Our deal?'

'You know, the firewood. I was going to charge you, but since we're neighbours I suggested a drink might work instead.'

'I've been busy,' I reply, as we nudge our way past marketgoers. 'Besides, don't you have better things to be doing with your time than assisting random neighbours? Don't you have … I don't know, a job or something?'

'Nope, actually I don't. I'm between jobs.' He looks up at the sky and squints. 'Well, kind of between jobs.' Flynn stops at one of the stands, and hands a note to the vendor in exchange for a stick of fairy floss.

'Kind of between jobs?'

He shrugs his shoulders. 'Exactly,' he says, shoving a wad of fairy floss into his mouth. The way he says it makes me think there's more to it than he's letting on.

'Aren't you a little old for fairy floss?'

He pretends to give my question some thought before replying, 'Nope.'

'All that sugar is so bad for you.'

'I know,' he says, swallowing down a mouthful. 'I just can't seem to let go of sweet things.' He pulls off a wad and offers it to me. 'Go on …' he says playfully.

I laugh, and wave his hand away. 'Thanks, but I'll pass. I'll stick to the veggies for now.'

We make our way across the street, where I stop in front of a bakery. Three arched panes of glass, the frames painted in midnight blue, provide a glimpse to an interesting display of bread loaves protruding from a rustic wooden barrow surrounded by artificial sunflowers.

'I just need to pop in there,' I say.

'I'll wait here,' says Flynn, leaning against a lamp post that some white flowers cascade down on. I snap one of the buds off the stem and bring it to my nose. 'Clematis,' I whisper to myself.

'What's that?'

'Nothing,' I dismiss. 'Oh, and you don't have to wait for me. I can manage on my own.'

'It's a twenty-minute walk. I could use the company. And I do make good company. Promise,' he says earnestly, as he finishes off the last of his fairy floss.

Even if I won't admit it, I'm alone here in Daylesford and Flynn, as forward as he is, does make good company. I hand him the flowers I've been carrying and step inside the bakehouse to the melodic sound of bells jingling.

The delicious aroma of artisan baked bread is comforting. A round woman wearing a burgundy-and-white-striped apron, with a dusting of flour on her pink cheeks, finishes serving the customers ahead of me before greeting me with a smile.

'Morning! Cold out there, isn't it?'

'It sure is.'

'What can I get you?'

I scan the labels on the baskets behind her. 'I'll have a loaf of the wholemeal sourdough, please.'

'Lucky last.' She places the loaf in a brown paper bag and squints to get a better look at me. 'You look familiar. You from around here?'

'Um, well, yes and no. It's been a while since I last visited. I live not too far from town. A property called Summerhill.'

'Well, I'm Mae,' she says.

'Gracie,' I reply.

Her eyes brighten. 'Summerhill,' she muses. 'That's where they used to sell the flowers. I've such fond memories of that place. Such a shame they don't grow them anymore. We used to sell sweet pea posies in baskets out front of the shop on weekends. They reminded me of my mum. Bless her cotton socks, she's now up there with the angels. Every time I see a sweet pea, I can almost feel her with me. You know, those flowers from Summerhill lasted weeks in the vase. Not like the ones they're importing now from Kenya and India. Some of them just don't smell the same. Or at all.' She hands me the paper bag with the loaf of bread, then winks at me. 'It's like the flowers know when they're tended with a bit of love. They know when something's missing. Just like a loaf of bread that's missing a special ingredient. Like salt. You always need a pinch of salt in your bread. Know what I mean?'

I nod. 'Yes,' I reply. I know exactly what she means.

'Anything else?'

'That'll be all, thanks,' I reply, glancing thoughtfully out the window to Flynn and the armful of flowers he's holding for me.

'Since you don't have a job, what are your plans here?' I ask Flynn, as I munch on an apple on our way back to Summerhill.

'I think you could say that I'm waiting to see where life leads me,' he says, squinting up at the clouds. He goes silent for a heartbeat before turning his attention back to me. 'You?'

'I'm sort of doing the same, I suppose.'

Flynn waits for me to say more, to expand on the little information I've given him, but it's hard for me to give someone a glimpse into my life when I don't yet seem to fit into any kind of routine.

'You're full of secrets, Gracie Ashcroft,' he says. He tosses his apple core into a paddock and shifts the basket of vegetables he's carrying for me into another hand to check his phone, which is ringing. He tucks it back into his pocket.

'Don't mind me, you can answer it.'

'It's no-one important. So, you were saying …'

'Oh, I don't have secrets—I'm just not ready to let you in,' I tease.

'Well, maybe I'll just need to knock a little harder.'

I briefly smile to myself but don't answer him. Flynn lets a beat pass before speaking again.

'You must have come here for a reason,' he says casually, kicking a loose stone down the road.

'Maybe,' I reply, my attention on the pebble.

Flynn doesn't say a word, just keeps walking, the pebble grazing the road, as if he's lost in his own thoughts. So I join him, losing myself in mine. We meander along, the quiet settling between us. It's not a heavy quiet, or an awkward quiet, but a peaceful kind of quiet, broken only by the sound of magpies and the rumble of cars passing us by every so often. Flynn's pebble veers in my direction. I kick it with my right foot, and it skims the ground in his direction. He kicks it back, and we continue, taking it in turns.

'Have you ever made a decision to follow something in your life, knowing that it might not necessarily turn out to be the right thing to do?' I ask finally.

'And here's me thinking I'd have to knock really hard,' murmurs Flynn, a grin forming on his lips.

I put my hand on my hip and frown at him, pretending to be annoyed with him.

He shrugs off a laugh. 'I thought it was going to be much harder,' he says, before his expression turns serious. 'What exactly did you do?' he asks, his voice low.

'I called off a wedding,' I tell him. Saying it out loud makes it feel more real and somehow it sounds so much worse to me than it did before. 'I lost him and he lost me, and I think we both lost a really good, beautiful thing, but I can't be sure. Every morning I wake up, I can't help wondering whether I made the right decision. I've hurt him and he didn't deserve to be hurt like this. The thing is … even if I change my mind, I don't think things will ever be the same.'

Flynn blinks at me, taking it in. He shrugs. 'Maybe you just need to give it some time.'

'I wish it was that simple.'

By now we've almost reached Summerhill. Charlie waves at us from across the road.

'Charlie!' calls Flynn, waving back.

'What are your plans for the rest of the day?' I ask, pausing at the driveway entrance.

Flynn's mouth twists into a suspicious smile. 'Why do you ask?'

'Because I like your company, Flynn. And one day, I'm going to tell you my secret.' I waggle a finger at him. 'But until then, I'm going to try to figure yours out because I think there's more to you than you let on.'

His phone starts ringing again.

'You going to answer that?' I say, raising an eyebrow. 'Or is it no-one important?'

He puts his phone on silent and shifts his attention back to me. 'What are you thinking?'

'I'm thinking you might want to come over for a late lunch and maybe even a drink.'

'Lunch?' he says, tilting his head to the side.

'Yes, and I'm thinking of something a lot healthier than fairy floss. I'll need your help though, because I have no idea how to cook silverbeet.'

'This stuff?' he says, pulling the rainbow stalks from the basket. 'I know a great recipe for a Japanese-style oshitashi.'

'Well, that sounds healthy enough.'

He laughs. 'I did just eat an apple.'

'That hardly counts.'

'I'll jog off the calories tomorrow.'

You wake up at 5.45 am and go for a run.

'You like to jog?' I ask.

'Yep,' he says. 'You?'

'Mmm, I *think* so.'

Flynn looks curiously at me.

'Well, I haven't been jogging since I got here. But I think I'm going to start again soon.' By now we've reached the front gate. I push it open, expecting it to creak and groan as it usually does. I stand there, moving it back and forth. 'Well, look at that …'

Flynn laughs. 'Interesting.'

'You're something else.'

'Couldn't help myself. I'm finding it hard to stay away.'

'We're just friends,' I warn, making my way to the front door.

'I know,' he says. 'Strictly just friends.'

TEN

The hellebores, with their stamens still intact, have crashed. They last longer in the vase if harvested when ripe, as opposed to when they look their most beautiful. Demanding patience, it's only once their stamens have dropped and their seed pods have started to develop that they'll show their appreciation by happily remaining on show for a while longer as a cut flower. There are more secrets I know about the flowers, and I've been sitting here, under the early-morning bluish-purple hues of light filtering through the house, my blunt pencil scratching away at the faded pages of an old notebook, unearthing details one by one. Like the way daffodil blooms should be cut in the early-morning hours, once the dew has settled and the stems are at their sturdiest. Or how a determined gust of wind, in one cruel act of fate, can sweep through a spring garden and destroy every last petal, snapping even the most robust of stems, halting the blooming process altogether. And roses, they sometimes ball. Life unfolds perfectly for them, but with too much cold and rain, they fail to open. While their tight shells might appear papery and withered, inside lie their beautiful petals, intact, all along. Eventually, the sun comes up, and once I finish documenting every flower I bought yesterday, I head back to town for more.

It turns out that the flower seller's name is Matilda. 'You can call me Tilly,' she says. Her voice crackles like a steady fire in the middle of winter. 'That's what everyone's been calling me since I moved here.' She pulls the leaves from a rose stem, removes the thorns with a stripper and drops it into a bucket filled with water.

'How long have you lived around here?' I ask.

'I've been around these parts longer than you've been alive.' She continues stripping more stems, hardly open to carrying a conversation, but I continue.

'I used to live here when I was younger. About a kilometre from here, actually. On the flower farm. Well, it was a flower farm. It's called Summerhill. You might know it?' I pause and watch her slowly turn to face me. She furrows her brow, the creases so deep, of the variety you'd expect to see from someone who's worked every single day of their life under the sun.

She sizes me up and down and then clicks her tongue. 'You Lainey's Gracie?' she asks finally.

I nod. 'Yes,' I reply eagerly.

'You're all grown up now,' she mumbles, with a slight shake of her head.

'So, my mum ... did you know her?'

'Did I know her?' She chuckles, tipping her head back to the sky. 'Oh, I knew her all right.' She moves away from me and starts selecting flowers from the buckets on her stand, arranging them into a posy. I'm mesmerised by the way she deftly picks each stem and gathers it in between her thumb and forefinger, twisting the posy around so it retains its symmetrical shape as it grows larger and more colourful. She does this almost without looking.

'I don't remember you.' I'm almost hovering over her shoulder.

'I wouldn't expect you to. It's been a very long time since we saw each other,' she says, shaking her head. 'Last time I saw you, you were swinging off rubber tyres for fun and were about this high.' She motions to her hip. 'You have her eyes,' she muses.

'How did you know her?'

She tugs on a roll of grosgrain suspended from the stand, and pulls down a length of a blue ribbon before cutting it with a pair of scissors.

'It doesn't matter how I knew her. Fact is, I knew her.' She wraps a band around the posy and slips it into a paper sleeve before tying a bow around it.

'Was she a friend? My mother? She loved flowers, too.'

Tilly gives me the kind of expression that warns me not to ask more questions.

'I came for more flowers,' I say, changing the subject. I figure I'll press her more about this conversation some other day.

'Another special occasion, I imagine.' She walks to the front of the cart to deposit the bouquet of tulips into a bucket, but I stop her.

'I'll take them. And the gerberas, too. Is this Queen Anne's lace?' I ask, pointing to a stem bursting with tiny white florets.

'That depends,' she says. 'Some call it wild carrot, some call it a wildflower and some just call it a weed.'

'It's too pretty to be a weed,' I reply, taking a bunch and admiring the cluster of flowers.

'It's their unseen beauty that makes the flowers special. They've got the power to change the circumstances of someone's life. What can't be seen is what makes them beautiful.'

I snap to attention at her words. Words that seem familiar, though I can't pinpoint why. 'How do you know that?'

'Anyone who knows the secrets of the flowers knows that,' she scoffs.

'Too bad if you don't know what you're looking for,' I say, directing the words more to myself than her.

She rests her hand on her hip and speaks with an air of frustration. 'You give them a place to grow, they'll show you all they need to. You of all people should know this.'

She bundles up my flowers, snips the thread of twine holding them together, and extends an arm to hand them back to me, but I stand there, staring past her to the homeware and gift store across the street that's captured my attention.

'That'll be sixteen dollars,' she says, her voice like a distant echo. Eyes still trained on the store, I thrust a twenty-dollar note in her direction, accept the flowers, and before she can reach into her empty tea tin for change, I've turned my back and am heading across the street.

When I make my way back to the road that leads to Summerhill, pushing a wheelbarrow stacked with pots, a watering can, a pair of gumboots and a decked-out tool belt with pruning shears and flower snips, I can almost swear Tilly's nodding at me from a distance. I wonder if she's noticed the copy of *A Novice's Guide to Flower Farming* that's balancing on top of it all.

The tingle of crisp air makes the stroll home a pleasant one. I wave hello to Charlie, where he's scooping chestnuts into cones for a family that's stopped by the side of the road. He eyes my wheelbarrow and shakes his head in amusement as I pass the stand, doing my best to not let its contents topple over as I cross the bumpy road. Manoeuvring the wheelbarrow up the driveway, almost losing my footing in the process, I pause at the front fence when I notice a pair of legs protruding from beneath the porch swing in the front yard. *Flynn's* legs.

Nudging open the gate, I approach the porch swing, wondering what he could possibly be doing lying underneath it.

'Just make yourself right at home,' I say, towering above him. I park my new gardening supplies and book beside the swing.

He pokes his head out from underneath the bench and flashes a grin. 'A coffee would be great,' he says.

With an armload of flowers still under my left arm, I unlock the front door and push it open with my foot.

Flynn continues whistling as he shifts back under the swing, a screwdriver in hand. 'They parrot tulips?'

I stop in my tracks and check the flowers I'm holding. Sure enough, these frilly and flamboyant blooms with flushes of pink, cream and green are parrot tulips.

'How'd you know that?' I ask, turning around to narrow my gaze.

He takes a screw out of his mouth, his eyes not quite meeting mine. 'Any guy worth holding onto should know that kind of stuff. To be honest though, I prefer regular tulips. Less showy, still beautiful, and the thing that makes them most attractive is that they have no idea how beautiful they actually are.' His eyes lock onto mine, holding my gaze for a second or so, before turning his attention back to the swing. I'm left speechless, feeling a slow rush of heat pricking my cheeks until I'm almost certain they are flushing pink.

'You should get those into some water.'

I clear my throat. 'Excuse me?'

'The flowers,' he says. 'Don't forget to snip the stems. They'll last longer in the vase.' He attempts to keep a straight face.

'Has anyone ever told you how irritating you are?'

'It's one of the most endearing things about me,' he calls. I catch him smirking to himself. He's clearly enjoying this.

I take a deep breath, annoyed with myself that I don't have a smart comeback. 'How do you like your coffee?' I reply, but before he can answer me, I've shut the front door behind me.

'All fixed,' calls Flynn a few minutes later, poking his head through the kitchen door. 'Is the coffee ready?'

I finish spooning some coffee into a couple of mugs. 'Almost.' I add a dash of milk to both and watch Flynn's facial expression as his eyes travel over the numerous vases I have in the kitchen and living room, before fixating on the fresh blooms I've left on the kitchen table, still wrapped. He looks thoughtfully at them. I'm not sure how to explain why my cottage is filled with so many flowers, but he doesn't question it.

'When you're ready, come check out the swing. It's as good as new,' he says.

I meet him outside, carrying two coffee mugs with me, trying not to spill them as I step over Flynn's tool bag. 'How'd you know it was broken?' I ask, as I hand him a cup. 'Did you want any sugar?'

'No thanks. I tried to sit on it,' he says, as if it's obvious.

'I know you said you're between jobs, but don't you have better things to do with your time?'

'If you're going to drill me with questions like this, you should at least sit down,' he says, shifting from the middle of the swing to the side. As much as Flynn irritates me, there's something likeable about him, so I sit, curling my hands around the pleasantly warm mug. The temperature has dropped since I arrived home and the sky now has a grey tinge to it.

'I wanted to see how you were doing,' he replies casually. 'It can be pretty lonely out here in winter.'

I stare into my coffee. 'Mmm-hmm.'

'There's a decent amount of work to do out here,' Flynn muses, his left foot playing with a pebble. Parrot's lying on my feet, which I don't mind because I can barely feel my toes inside my boots.

I take another long sip of coffee before I answer him. 'Yeah, it's not in the best shape.'

Flynn reaches over to the wheelbarrow and picks up the book I purchased in town. 'Flower growing, hey?' He flicks through it, before finally looking up at me.

I don't know how to respond. It's not the question that grates against me, but the answer I'm searching for. I don't know what I'm doing with this book or with all these flowers. All I know is that they're the only things that offer the loosest thread of connection to my old life.

'I don't know … the flowers, they interest me. I like the way they make me feel.' I take another sip of coffee. 'I've been learning a bit more about myself since I got here, actually.'

'Like what?' asks Flynn.

'I stay away from sugar, and can't cook to save myself. As it turns out, I'm an early riser. I like to jog, and even though I haven't been lately, I think I'm going to start again. Tomorrow, as a matter of fact.'

'I'll join you,' he says brightly. 'Meet me at the field gate tomorrow morning.'

'Okay. Six am too early?' I say, smiling into my mug. I'm almost sure the cold early mornings will be a turn-off for him.

'Nope,' he says, a satisfied expression playing on his lips.

'Cold dark mornings don't bother you?'

'Nope,' he says coolly.

I give a half-supressed laugh. We'll see about that. 'So, what brought you here, specifically?' I ask, my teeth starting to chatter. 'Are you starting a new job out here?'

Flynn's silent for a moment. 'I'm not entirely sure yet.' He checks his watch. 'I'd better get going. The temperature has dropped. I'll let you move inside.' He stands up.

'But you haven't even finished your coffee.' His mug is still on the table beside me. He hasn't touched it.

'Not a huge fan of instant,' he says, making his way to the front gate. 'Should have asked you for a hot chocolate.' He whistles for Parrot to follow. 'See you tomorrow,' he says, holding back a smile. He'd be insanely attractive under the right circumstances, if he weren't so sure of himself, not to mention, *annoying*.

As I carry the two mugs towards the front door, I notice the fresh stack of firewood piled up beside it. And then my body floods with the oddest sensation. I think it's my chest expanding. Before I can turn around to thank him, he's closed the front fence behind him.

ELEVEN

It's 5.45 am and I'm lying in bed, listening to the persistent ringing of an alarm clock that's desperately trying to nudge me closer to who I once was. Except my life is still like a jigsaw puzzle—incomplete, fragments missing, with no clear picture of what might be eventually pieced together at all. I watch the digits on the clock flip over, while my mind scrambles for information from the past, just like it does every other morning.

Nope, still nothing.

From my bedroom window lies a view of a hauntingly beautiful landscape, where a layer of silver has dusted the grass in the fields. From here, Flynn's cottage next door is visible. Its bluestone façade is partially obscured by the branches of an oak that's positioned by a low stone wall separating our properties. The outside light is on, thick plumes of smoke billowing from the chimney. Parrot is lying patiently on the front porch by the stack of firewood near the front door.

I stoke the two-sided fireplace that's almost spent, the smoky aroma filtering through the bedroom. After changing and tucking my laces into my shoes, I head into the kitchen to pour myself an orange juice. Making my way to the door with a piece of almost-burnt toast in my mouth, I scoop my hair into a high ponytail. The sudden rush of cold hits me as I open the front door and almost trip over Parrot.

My arms reach out for something to prevent me from falling, coming into contact with a chest. I look up, the piece of toast still hanging from my mouth.

Flynn lets go of me and helps me regain my balance, trying to hold back his laughter.

'What on earth are you doing here?!' I exclaim.

He points at Parrot. 'Following him.'

'He opened the gate by himself, I suppose?' I say dryly.

He shakes his head, trying to act serious. Secretly, I'm enjoying this. 'Well, not exactly. He jumped over the wall,' he says, pointing at the low stone wall. He says it so innocently that I can't help trying to hide an amused smile.

'I thought we said we'd meet at the rear field gate,' I say, biting into my toast.

He cringes slightly, his eyes trained on the piece of charred bread. 'Changed my mind,' he says, raising his eyebrows and pulling his hoodie over his head. He hasn't shaved this morning, and the scruffy look suits him. He eyes me up and down. 'You ready?'

'Almost.' I take a minute to warm up, stretching first one leg and then the other, while taking the last bite of my toast.

The morning smells distinctly like winter—earthy with a hint of eucalyptus in the air.

'Hurry up, then,' he says, making his way to the stone wall. He glances back and winks at me before jumping over it. Parrot follows. I trail close behind, wiping the crumbs off my face with the cuff of my windcheater.

'Where are we going?' I ask, catching up to Flynn. We're now on his side of the field, making our way up a gentle incline.

'I usually jog near the lake. Come, I'll show you.'

We reach the summit on which Flynn's cottage sits and stop to catch our breath. He points to the towering gum trees studded across the rear of both our properties, where the growth thickens into bush. Several horses, surrounded by the early-morning mist, are grazing in the paddocks to our left.

'Snowdrops,' I murmur, making out the patches of white flowers in the rear paddocks. 'It's so beautiful,' I say, watching the puffs of warm air dissipate in front of me as the countryside starts to wake up.

'Yep,' agrees Flynn. 'Come on, then.' He hauls himself over a sloppily erected wooden fence and I do the same, only my top gets caught on a nail.

'Hold on, I'm stuck,' I call, trying to twist my body around to unhook myself from the fence. I can't quite reach far enough, though, and I struggle to maintain my balance without ripping my windcheater.

'Careful there. Sit back down and hold on,' says Flynn, coming closer to me. I do as I'm told and can feel the warmth from his body as he stands in front of me, his chest brushing my knee as he leans behind me and unhooks me from the fence. 'All done.' He extends a hand to help me down. His hand stays wrapped around mine before I wriggle it out of his grasp.

Something in my chest flutters. I clear my throat. 'Uh, thanks,' I reply, straightening up. I take a step away, re-establishing a comfortable distance from him.

Parrot forges ahead of us, and Flynn smiles at me, a hint of playfulness in his eyes. 'Race you there.'

'Oh, come on! Aren't we a little old for running races?'

Flynn clearly doesn't think so because he's turned his back on me and is racing ahead.

'Let's see what you've got!' he calls.

'Oh, no you don't,' I mumble, beginning to sprint to make up lost ground. My chest burns as my lungs work overtime.

Flynn beats me, but only by a fraction of a second. He wipes his face with his forearm as he slows his pace down to a walk. 'Knew you had it in you,' he says, bending over as he regains his breath.

I don't answer him. I'm absorbed in my own thoughts. A little further ahead is a willow tree that has lost its leaves. We reach the tree that seems so familiar to me, and I move towards it, as if in slow motion. My gaze drifts to the words carved into the trunk, and then the world falls silent, as if a blanket has been draped over me. My eyes narrow, searching for some kind of recollection of being here before, but my mind is completely blank. How many times might I have sat under the shade of this tree, its branches cascading over me like a leafy waterfall, toes dipped in the water, sun caressing my skin as I gazed up at the sky through the leafy canopy? I place my palm over its trunk, feeling the texture of the bark as I trace the letters with my fingers. Letters that form the words my mother once told me.

The sweet peas know where to look for the light.

'Gracie?' says Flynn, his eyes flicking to mine. They're filled with concern. 'Are you all right?'

I try to hold back everything I'm feeling by pinning my lip between my teeth, hoping that he won't notice the trembling. I can't find a way to answer him. Another beat of silence passes. I want to tell him that things aren't right, that everything's a mess, that I don't know who I am, I don't know where I belong, and I don't know how to fit Blake back into my life, but I can't seem to form the words.

Flynn clears his throat before he speaks, the way a person does when they're not sure what to say. 'What is it, Gracie?' he asks, his voice low. 'Whatever it is, you can tell me.'

His deep-blue eyes, a shade darker than they were the other day, are filled with sincerity, and for the first time, I momentarily cast away any judgement I previously had about him possibly being the most irritating man I've ever met.

Slowly, I lift my hand away from the tree. 'Do you know what it feels like to forget something or someone you wish you could remember?'

He turns his body towards the tree, where his eyes travel over the words engraved on the trunk. 'Like when you lose someone and those memories start to feel a little duller— like they're fading away and you'll never get them back?' He pulls the hood off his head and runs a hand through his tousled hair before meeting my gaze again.

'My mother died and I don't remember her,' I tell him.

Flynn steps closer and moves a strand of hair behind my ear. He holds my gaze with his. 'Losing someone hurts like hell, doesn't it?'

I nod, swallowing past the lump that's formed in my throat.

Flynn's penetrating gaze manages to speak a thousand words when only a handful would suffice. My eyes mirror back everything he's telling me. In that moment of understanding, and of being understood, there's no need for more words to be exchanged. He blinks at me, his eyes full of empathy, void of judgement, and for a second, life stands still as I momentarily allow myself to wonder what it might be like to look at someone the way you do when you have loved them for years and they know exactly what you're thinking without needing to utter a single word.

And that's when the wave of guilt hits me like a ton of bricks.

TWELVE

It's been almost two weeks since I arrived in Summerhill. Another letter has come from Blake, and I haven't even managed to regain enough equilibrium to respond to his last one. I'm still not sure what I can say, or what I should say, to make being apart any easier for him.

I take a long gulp of coffee that's been sitting on the table long enough to grow lukewarm, and read over his letter again.

Dear Gracie,

I can't pretend that I don't miss you. I miss the way you'd hold my hand and squeeze and I'd squeeze back and then you'd squeeze three times and we both knew you were saying I love you. I miss how that used to feel so much.

I've been checking the letterbox as often as I can, hoping there might be mail from you. Scarlett said you're doing fine, but since she couldn't tell me anything specific about what you'd been up to, I'm guessing you're not doing much at all.

Getting your life back on track must seem like the hardest thing for you right now, but not many people get to have their time over. But you do, so as hard as this is, and as much as you didn't want this, try to make the most of it. Don't box yourself up inside waiting for your memory to come back to you. Life's too short for that. Get outside and explore. Take long walks. Find a way to laugh every day. Find a hobby—something you love. And if you don't know what you love, try new things. I promise you won't get this wrong.

Love,

Blake

P.S. You love old-school comedy—think Jerry Lewis.

I trace a series of question marks onto the window with my forefinger. Answers to the questions I have about my life might be in short supply, but Blake is right—boxing myself up inside, documenting flowers day after day, isn't going to get me anywhere. So, I pull myself out of the sagging fold of the sofa, take a pen and place a tick beside Blake's first suggestion: *Get outside and explore.*

Summerhill spans five acres, and currently, most of the paddock space is covered with waist-high weeds, overgrown grass and bare trees with carpets of soggy leaves at their feet that need to be cleared. As I wander up to the fields, my boots sink into the spongy earth. The moisture from the grass wicks through my jeans as I venture through a row of garden beds, using my hands to separate the rampant weeds that spill over either side of it. Stumbling over some loose netting and fallen stakes that have been disrupted by the wind, I stop to examine the monochromatic and lifeless heap of growth around me. I'm fairly sure that this tangled mess beneath my feet is what used to be a sweet-pea bed. I try consolidating the memory I have of being here as a child with what I'm seeing now. Inhaling the scent of damp earth, I dig my fingers into the ground and watch the clumps of dirt fall from my hands. I envisage the field the way it sits in my memory—in full bloom, bursts of colour surrounding me, stems swaying in the breeze, butterflies flitting from one pollen-filled blossom to another. The images in my mind play around for a while and I bask in that feeling of peacefulness until I'm overcome with a knowing that this place belongs to me as much as I belong to it.

Shaking my hands clean, I head for the gate that leads to a second field, this one bordered on its three sides by an abundance of almost fully bare rosebushes. Long rows of plants that have died back and are now yellow and withered, peek out from the soil. I can't seem to place what they are. They're almost suffocated by the grass that has been left to grow amongst them.

There's so much to be done here and nobody to do it. My eyes travel to the rosebushes. There are at least a hundred of them, maybe more, all of them needing to be reshaped. Holding onto that thought, I pull my coat tighter around me and think, *Why not?*

Inside the barn, dried lavender bunches that were drained of colour long ago hang from the wooden beamed ceiling, which is now laced with thick cobwebs. The air, scented with damp straw, is weighed down by the cold, but as soon as I orient myself in here, my mood starts to lift. Bales of hay are stacked in one corner and a couple of wagons are lined up in the other. A long wooden table with a seated bench is positioned at the far end.

I reach for my new pruning shears and guide the wheelbarrow outside. Once I reach the roses, I start pruning back each bush as far as I can, stripping each one of its remaining leaves and cutting away any dead wood until they're half the size they originally were. Thorns catch against my jacket and graze my cheeks and hands, scoring tiny scratches into my skin. My thoughts wander to the things I want to know about my life. Like whether I cry at sad movies. Do I play sport? Why did I choose to become a stylist? Why not a teacher, or an artist, or a bookkeeper? What are all the things that made me, *me*? And what were the things that made Blake and I, *us*? With a head full of tangled thoughts, my naked hands furiously reach for branch after branch. Why can't I find the answers? I hate that this has happened to me. I never wanted it. I never asked for it. I don't want this to be my life. I want a reason, need a reason, have to find a reason to get up out of bed in the morning. I wipe my nose with the cuff of my sleeve, completely unaware until now, that I've been crying. I throw the pruning shears to the ground, drop to my knees and notice a plaque in front of one of the bushes.

Lainey Ashcroft. Gone, but not forgotten.

My fingers trace the letters and I feel a pang of nausea at the irony of these words. And then, I look up to the sky and ask, 'Why can't I feel you with me?'

Back in the barn, I deposit the full wheelbarrow by the door and take a minute to rest on a square bale of hay, as I try to calm myself down. A sense of familiarity floats around me, alongside the dust motes that bounce around in the morning light. I grab a clump of straw and inhale its scent. As if on cue, a memory slips into my consciousness, as if it's been waiting for the right time to present itself.

I'm wearing a pair of frayed denim shorts, pulling myself up a rope that's suspended from one of the wooden beams in the barn. The air is pleasantly warm, a welcoming breeze brushing my skin. Someone gives me a gentle push from behind. With my bare feet, I try to grasp a lemon from a basket sitting on a bale of hay. The sound of laughter echoes through the barn as the lemon slips from between my feet and lands with a thud on the bed of straw covering the ground.

'Help me down,' I call out, swinging in circles.

I feel the warmth of a pair of hands, male hands, on my waist as I'm lifted down. My legs wrap around his body. My forehead rests against his, and even though I'm securely held, I still feel like I'm floating.

'My turn now, ladybug,' he whispers, right before his lips brush against mine. I close my eyes. He tastes like lemon and ginger beer. I break the kiss with a grin, and a feeling sweeps through me. A tingle, a lightness, a blissful fluttering sensation. Is that *love*?

My heart starts to pound against my chest. The boy I've just remembered is Blake. Holding the weight of a clump of straw in my palm, I sit in silence, desperate for more details, when a voice calls from a distance.

'Knock, knock.'

Slowly, I blink myself back to reality and face Flynn, who's poking his head through the barn door.

'Just thought I'd come say hello,' he says, grinning at me.

It's as if I've been interrupted in the middle of a dream, the kind that you wish you could close your eyes and finish, if only to feel what you'd just felt, or find out what happens next.

'Bad time?' he asks.

'No, I was just thinking of someone,' I say, brushing the excess straw off my hands.

'Anyone special?' he asks, stepping into the barn.

My words almost catch in my throat, because I can't bring myself to say yes, yet I can't bring myself to say no, either. 'I think so.'

Flynn looks up at the ceiling. 'Wow, this place needs a bit of a tidy-up, doesn't it? Those cobwebs are—'

'On my list.'

'So, you got to the roses already?'

'You've been spying on me?'

'You're covered in scratches, and your wheelbarrow over there is full of rose clippings,' he says, nodding in its direction. 'And ...' He reaches over and touches my beanie. I take a slight step back, caught off guard.

'Hold still,' he whispers. 'You've got some ...' He tugs gently at something in my beanie, as I stand there frozen. He's taller than me, though not by much. While he works on removing whatever is in my beanie, I glance up at him discreetly, noticing his five-o'clock shadow. And his jawline, which is defined, yet not too pronounced. He has a serious expression on his face, and he smells nice. Like a minty, ocean-fresh, just-got-out-of-the-shower kind of scent. My breath catches in my chest. A sensation of warmth pumps through my body and my cheeks heat up. I shouldn't be thinking about Flynn getting out of the shower. He catches me staring and offers a lazy half-smile, and I can't help looking away, as if I've been caught doing something I shouldn't be.

He opens up his hand to reveal a palm scattered with rose thorns. I stand there blinking at them for a couple of seconds, thinking that nobody else except Blake should smell this good to me. Besides, Flynn is aggravating. Oh, but his jawline is …

Stop it, Gracie!

'I really don't have time for this,' I say, awkwardly tugging one of the old wheelbarrows from the corner of the barn. The metal grates against the concrete floor.

Flynn looks at the old thing. 'I think you're missing a wheel.' He bends down to inspect it. 'I could fix it for you.'

I cock my head. 'What did you do before you were between jobs?' I say, crossing my arms, wanting to satisfy my curiosity about him.

'I'm a vet.'

'A what?' I take a better look at him, trying to make sense of this unexpected light that has been cast on him. He looks like the outdoors type, and I'm almost certain that underneath his jacket there are muscles, the kind of muscles you only get from working out. I start to blush again. I look down at my toes. This really needs to stop.

A smile forms on his lips. 'A vet,' he repeats. 'You know …
they work in animal hospitals and—'

'Make yourself useful, then,' I reply, pointing to two wagons that seem to have their wheels intact. I shake my head. I could have sworn he might have been a tradesman of some kind. A plumber, a carpenter, or a builder, but not a *vet*.

Flynn surveys me. 'Are you okay? You seem a bit jumpy.'

'I'm fine,' I say, heading towards the crates nestled under the table. With two hands, I manage to tug free the one labelled *Supplies*.

'I think you should wear some—'

'Gloves,' I say, finishing his sentence. There have to be gloves somewhere in here. I scour through the crate and sure enough, a few pairs of stiff gloves are tucked inside. They'll have to do for now. I grab a pair for myself and toss another in Flynn's direction.

He catches them midair.

'Don't forget the wagons,' I say, gesturing to the corner of the barn, but Flynn's already approaching them.

'What are we working on?' he asks, catching up to me as I forge ahead.

I point to the field. 'See those roses up there? I want to finish pruning them by the end of the day.' I adjust the scarf around my neck and pull my beanie over my ears.

'Are you serious?'

'Do I sound like I'm joking?'

'No, ma'am, you look very serious,' he says, his face pretending to be grave. It lasts all of two seconds before he starts to laugh.

'Why are you laughing?' I demand, pinning him with my stare.

'There must be at least a hundred bushes.'

'And I've done about twenty of them so far. Afraid of hard work?' I tease. 'You could always go home.' I smile into my scarf and give him a cheeky sideways glance.

I can tell he's trying not to smile back, but that just makes me chuckle to myself. And when I do, I like the way it feels, because I haven't felt it in … who knows how long. Despite how I was feeling before Flynn arrived, my mood is already lifting.

My wagon catches on a clump of overgrown grass. Flynn gives it a push from behind to help it along. 'I can do this,' I say, tugging harder.

'You know, that stubborn streak might get you into trouble some day. Think about what you would have done if I hadn't turned up here to light your fire the day you arrived.'

'Oh, I'm not stubborn. You were trespassing.'

'You almost refused my help. That makes you stubborn,' says Flynn. 'What are your real plans here, anyway, Gracie?' he asks casually, in a way that shows me he's intrigued, but it catches me off guard all the same.

'I don't want to talk about it,' I reply, surprised at how firm my voice is. Suddenly, my sense of humour has evaporated.

'No problem,' he says. 'I shouldn't have asked.' Flynn takes a deep breath. 'Wow, the wind's got a bite to it today.' He pulls on a glove.

'Sorry—it's just that we don't know each other very well and I don't really want to burden you with all my problems.'

We continue making our way up the incline. By now, we've reached the point where the land levels out and a little further ahead is the row of spent sweet peas, and just beyond them, the roses. We reach the gate and I push it open. Flynn steps through and I follow after him.

'What's your favourite colour?' he says, changing the subject. He reaches for a pair of snips from the wagon. He waggles his eyebrows. 'Getting-to-know-you question,' he adds playfully. 'So, then you can burden me with all the problems you want.'

'What?' I ask, swallowing my discomfort. I know he's asking a harmless question, but the problem isn't the question, the problem is my answer, or lack thereof. I shake my head, trying to think.

'I bet you like purple. I like green,' he says, looking me straight in the eyes.

I bite my lip. 'Green's nice,' I say, noticing the sapphire in his eyes. 'But I prefer blue.'

Flynn smirks.

'Sweet or savoury?' I ask, playing along.

'Sweet tooth all the way.'

'Well, it appears we have very little in common.'

'Bet I can prove you wrong.' He flashes me a cheeky grin. 'Favourite food?'

Does toast count?

'Um, I don't have one,' I reply. 'Aside from maybe spinach and omelettes.'

'Omelettes?' repeats Flynn. He tips his head to the side, tiny creases appearing in his forehead. It's like he doesn't believe me. 'Really?'

'What can I say? I've had lots of practice recently and I happen to make a good omelette.'

He shakes his head. 'You should get out more to good restaurants. There's this place not too far from—'

'Don't even go there,' I warn, pointing my finger at him.

He laughs. 'Beach or snow slopes?'

I let out a sigh. 'If you want to know the truth—I don't really know.' I scratch my head. 'My life's a little … complicated right now.'

'So is mine. Deliciously complicated.'

'I bet I've got you all worked out. Beach,' I declare.

'Nope,' he says. 'Couldn't be further from the truth.'

'Do you prefer to be indoors or outdoors?'

'Definitely outdoors. As much as I love being a vet, I don't like being cooped up in a city vet clinic. I prefer the country air.' He stands straight and inhales before letting out a contented sigh. 'You?'

'Definitely outdoors.'

'Ah, so we do have some things in common.'

'Oh, I'm sure I can find plenty more things to disagree with you on.'

'So far, it's been a pleasure getting to know you, Gracie Ashcroft. I can't wait to find out how much more we don't have in common. So … what do you do for work?'

'I'm a … was a … stylist for *Country Dwellings*,' I reply, trying on the fresh knowledge about myself, but owning these words is like trying on an outfit that's two sizes too small. There's no way it can possibly fit. It feels like I've blurted out a lie. 'But I've … taken some time off.'

'A stylist … That's interesting, because I thought that maybe you were the kind of girl who likes flowers and the outdoors. You seem like the gardening type to me.'

'Why would you think that?'

'We're standing in a paddock in the middle of winter with a couple of wagons and pruning shears in hand, when we could be out walking a loyal and trustworthy dog or riding horses or sipping beer in a country pub. Or, you could be shopping at the local homewares store or whatever it is stylists for *Country Dwellings* like to do.'

'I loved my job,' I mumble and I hope Flynn doesn't notice the doubt in my voice.

'Obviously,' he replies. 'Unless you were doing something you thought you should have been doing for the sake of not doing the actual thing you loved because you didn't think you should have been doing that.'

'Why would anyone do that?'

'Sometimes the past has a funny way of influencing our future,' he says.

But what if you can't remember your past?

'What if you didn't have a past to hold onto?' I say, my voice low.

'Then maybe you'd leave things to fate and destiny.'

By now we've reached the roses. He snips a branch off a bush and tosses it into the wagon.

'So, you think that sometimes you're meant to end up where you end up? That maybe you're meant to end up with the right person, in the right career at exactly the right time?' I pull on my gloves and start working on the bush adjacent to Flynn's.

'Maybe.'

'Well, if you could live your life over, what would you do differently? Would you still be a vet?'

'Almost nothing. And yes, I think I'd still be a vet.'

'Why'd you become a vet?'

'Animals have a way of understanding that people don't. They see what we don't see. And I've been fitting tiny splints on injured sparrows since I was a kid. I figured I'd be good at it. Though I'd be perfectly happy living off the land, tinkering and building if I could do that.'

'But you wouldn't do anything differently if you had your time over?'

'Nope, because everything in life has led me to exactly where I need to be.'

'I don't know if that's true for me.'

Flynn pauses. 'Nobody really knows if that's the truth for anyone. But believing it takes a whole lot of questioning and doubt out of the equation.'

'Well, that's a positive way of looking at things,' I say, considering his words.

He shrugs. 'What other choice is there?'

I lift my arm and unhook the fabric of my sleeve from the thorns it's caught on.

'You can't travel back into the past,' he adds.

'But isn't it our past that shapes our future?'

'To a degree …'

'Exactly,' I say. 'It's our memories that make us who we are.' My skin tingles, tiny goosebumps appearing on my forearms. If memories are the delicate threads that knit our souls together and make us who we are, who can we be without them? I continue pondering this as Flynn and I steadily work on filling the wagons with dead stems, making way for renewed spring growth.

'So, you prefer the country over the city?' I say, once we finish pruning the last bush.

'Let's just say this here is a far cry from the smell of sterile vet rooms and dog vomit,' says Flynn.

'This place must smell heavenly in the spring,' I muse, imagining the field awash with the pastel tones of roses and sweet peas. Something stirs inside of me as the pictures form in my mind.

Flynn removes his glove. 'You didn't tell me what you'd do differently,' he says.

I search his eyes for answers, trying to recall his question.

'If you had your time over.' He tosses his gloves into the wagon.

'I have no idea,' I reply pensively as my gaze rests on the winter landscape enveloping us. I might not know what I would do differently, but I do know that the field surrounding us, drained of colour but dappled with the odd cluster of snowdrops, promises a carpet of possibility.

The following morning, I sit in front of the fire, under the weight of a woollen blanket, twirling a pencil around, trying to find the right words to pen to Blake. I've been avoiding writing to him for more than one reason. Partly because writing a letter takes so much effort, and partly because I still don't know what to say. How to admit to the person who loves you more than anything in the world that they've lost you? Without quite knowing how I fit into my own life, I have no idea how to fit Blake into mine, and with each day that passes here, I'm finding it harder and harder to imagine a place for him to fit into my future.

Dear Blake,

Do you believe in destiny? Because I don't know if I do, or if I ever did before. Aside from one brief memory of us, I don't have any memories of falling or being in love with you and I'm scared I might never remember.

I went for a jog the other morning and I prayed so hard that I might remember what it was like to have loved you through all those years we spent together, but no matter how hard I prayed and waited for another memory to surface, not one ever did.

I like it here at Summerhill. I've been filling the house with flowers and pottering around the garden. I don't have a hobby yet, but I took your advice about getting outside and exploring. I started with the roses and I think I'll tackle the weeds soon, too. It's all a great big mess. A bit like my life, really.

I hope you're doing okay and that even in some small way, you're getting on with your life without me and that the phone calls about the wedding have settled down now.
Gracie

With a heavy sigh, I fold the letter and slide it into an envelope before making my way into town.

I'm in need of more fresh flowers for the house.

Tilly is on the same street corner as yesterday. She has a woollen beanie pulled over her head, covering her ears, and she's humming as she reaches for a Sweet William stem and tucks it into the arrangement she's holding in her left hand. She admires it and then tightens the string around the bouquet before slipping it into a brown paper sleeve.

'Morning, Tilly. I've come for more flowers.'

'Let me guess?' She closes one eye and looks me up and down with the other. She brings a finger to her lips. 'Tulips.'

'How'd you know I was going to say that?' I'm shocked by her accurate guess.

'When you're as old as me, and you've been working the flowers for as long as I have, you just know what's going to suit. Here, hold these,' she says, pushing a bunch of snowdrops into my arms. 'Now close your eyes,' she commands. 'Breathe in.'

I take a deep breath. I'm not sure what Tilly wants me to do or why. I peek through one eye, but she's quick to tell me off.

'Keep 'em closed. I'm not finished with you yet. You need to listen, but not with these,' she says, cupping her hands over my ears. Again, I peek through one eye at her. 'You've got a problem with following instructions?' she scolds. 'Just like your mother, always wanting to give instructions, never taking the time to listen,' she mumbles.

I stifle a laugh.

'Try again,' she says, more firmly this time. 'I want to see if you've got the gift.'

'What gift?' I whisper, my eyes still closed.

'Quiet,' she snaps. 'Breathe.'

Instinctively, I burrow my face into the flowers and inhale.

'That's it,' she commands, her voice hoarse.

I clamp my eyes shut and focus on steadying my breath. She continues her melodic humming, against the symphony of other sounds. People bustling around the morning market; footsteps, laughter, chatter, dogs barking, children laughing, bicycle bells ringing. Tilly gently nudges the flowers closer to my nose. The scent is faintly reminiscent of honey and orange blossom. Inhaling more deeply now, my breath slows to a comfortable rhythm and the sounds naturally fade into the background.

'Keep listening,' Tilly orders in her crackly voice.

The scent of the snowdrops becomes stronger. I can't hear the people around me anymore, but I can *feel* them. In my mind, I can see the blanket of white snowdrops covering a field, heralding the end of winter, their drooping heads a misleading interpretation of how much they can withstand the cold. With their buds encased in their petals, they're filled with warmth inside so they can survive the temperature outside. I'm struck with awe at how beautiful they are. They're magnificent. I'm overcome with an intense feeling of wanting to share them with the people around me. The sounds nearby filter back into my consciousness and I open my eyes, but my attention turns away from Tilly, to the bustling market. An elderly woman is ambling past the stand. She seems so lonely. A young woman standing in front of a café pulls a phone from her pocket and cups her mouth as tears begin to fall from her eyes. A man with sagging shoulders and an expression of desperation, hands out flyers to passers-by. He's lost his dog.

'Words?' says Tilly.

I shake my head, not quite understanding.

'What are the first words that come to you?'

'Hope and strength,' I reply, the words spilling out of me before I can give them any thought.

'Knew you'd have the gift.' She clicks her tongue in satisfaction.

I'm still not entirely sure what she means, but I can't help wondering whether it has something to do with the fact that I'm much more aware of the people around me now than I was before. Reluctantly, I hand the flowers back to her.

'They're yours. God knows it looks like you need them. It's not all about what you can see, you know,' she says. 'It's about the way they make you *feel*.'

'Let me pay you for them, then. How much?'

She waves her hand at me and continues arranging the flowers she's holding onto in a posy. 'Just for the tulips will do.'

I hand her a ten-dollar note, which she stuffs into her tin before handing me a bunch of fringed tulips.

'I've got work to do. Was there anything else you wanted?'

'No, I think I have all I need for now,' I reply. I look down at the flowers cradled in my arm. 'The tulips—why did you choose them for me?'

'Why don't you go home and let me know once you've figured it out?' She gently nudges me towards the street.

The woman who was on the phone has started to walk away and is about to cross the road. I speed up my pace and reach her. She's waiting for the line of cars to pass. 'Excuse me,' I say.

She looks at me, her face stained with tears, her cheeks a blotchy shade of pink and red.

'I thought you might need these,' I say, extending my arms. She throws me an odd look and my body tenses. I glance over at Tilly's stand. She's watching me. 'I think you might need them more than I do,' I add nervously.

'My mum just passed away,' she whispers. She eyes the flowers, and a resurgence of tears begin to flow. 'These were her favourites,' she says, smiling through her tears. My heart starts to beat a little faster and it occurs to me as I let go of the snow-capped blooms that maybe Tilly's right. Maybe it's not only me that needs the flowers. Spring is, after all, right around the corner.

THIRTEEN

That evening, I curl up in bed with my (until now) untouched copy of *A Novice's Guide to Flower Farming*. After reading about soil types and bed preparation, I glance up at the clock and realise I forgot to call Scarlett today. I reach for the phone and dial her number, hoping it's not too late.

She answers on the second ring.

'Gracie! I've been trying to call you all day.'

'I've been busy. I bought more flowers today. Did you know that gerberas should have their stems scalded in hot water before putting them in a vase?'

'No. I didn't,' says Scarlett, and I can tell by the sound of her voice that she thinks I've completely lost it.

'Same with hydrangeas. You can bring them back to life, Scarlett.'

'Right …'

'I know all these things. I remember all these things.'

'Anything else?'

'What do you mean anything else? I'm telling you every-thing. My mother used to let me force the hyacinths to bloom. You can do it by putting the bulbs in a glass jar with some pebbles and …'

'Gracie.'

'Yeah?'

'I'm worried about you.'

'Don't be. I'm fine.'

'All this talk about the flowers, I think that maybe going back to your old routine could help. You haven't even been seeing a therapist or any of the specialists Dr Cleave rec-ommended. Besides, you're all alone out there and what if something happens? What if you get lost or need help with something?'

'I've got a neighbour who can help. I have to tell you about him. He's so completely perplexing, you've no idea. But he's harmless. A helper, really. And he makes good company.'

'A guy?'

'I must admit, he's quite handsome.' As soon as I say it, I regret it. In anticipation of Scarlett's reaction, I suck in a breath. 'Sorry. It was … just an observation.' I run my finger down the stem of the gerbera that's wedged next to the spine of my gardening book, acting like a bookmark.

The line is heavy with silence. I wait; Scarlett doesn't respond.

'How's Blake?' I ask quietly. 'And how are you feeling?'

'Ugh. Still nauseous every day. I've been wanting to visit, but I don't think I can manage the car ride.'

'Don't worry. Just come up when you're ready.'

'As for Blake, I haven't seen or spoken to him, but Noah says he's doing okay.'

'Just okay?'

'Apparently, he's been a little elusive, wanting to be left alone lately. He's still fielding a lot of calls from wedding guests demanding answers—it's been never-ending for the last couple of weeks.'

'Mmm-hmm,' I reply.

'Do you want me to tell you anything about him? There's so much I want to tell you. So many things you need to know. I could tell you a story, or—'

'No,' I reply, cutting her off. 'He told me some things in his letter.' I twirl a loose thread from the quilt around my finger. 'I was happy.'

'Yes, you were. And you will be again.'

'It's late. I should let you go.'

'Get some rest. I'm at a cocktail party. Better get back to it. Noah's presenting an award for a new charity.'

We exchange our goodbyes and I hang up the phone, promising to call back soon. I open up my book and read over the introduction again.

When I look out onto a field of flowers I feel Mother Nature's heartbeat. French lavender swaying in the breeze, wildflowers caressing the pastures, sunflowers turning their faces towards the light. I squint into the sun, feel the earth beneath my toes, and think to myself that there's no place I'd rather be.

I reach for a pair of socks in my bedside table drawer, pull them on, and as my eyelids drift shut, gerbera resting against my chest, my heart gives a gentle nod.

The ceramic pie weights in my palm roll around as I transfer them from one hand to the other, thinking about Tilly, and my mother, the woman who lost her mother yesterday, and of course, Blake. Outside, there's an empty bird feeder in the front yard, that I still haven't got around to filling. There are so many things I should get around to doing here before spring, like mowing the lawn, attacking the weeds ... finding the courage to face my fiancé.

The tulips, now sitting in a vase under the kitchen windowsill, have opened up, their rubbery stamens smiling at the light. As the sunlight fades, the frilly petals will close, the cycle of one day complete.

'What do you want to tell me?' I whisper, as the pie weights clack against each other. 'Why did Tilly choose you?'

Elbows leaning on the table, chin resting on one hand, I sit in a chair, hoping for some kind of answer to come to me, and when it never does, I muster the strength to stand up, releasing the pie weights from my hand. They roll across the table in different directions. One after the other they drop to the ground in a series of thumps. When I bend down to pick them up, the room appears different to me than it did before. Crouching down in this position, I'm struck by how many vases of flowers I've beautified the house with. I take them all in: the china-pink hyacinths brushing shoulders with the milky-white viburnums, the tangerine double-cupped Lady Emma Hamilton roses with their heavenly pear-and-grape fragrance infusing the living area, teemed with branches of crimson Japanese quince and rich lemon-coloured winter jasmine. The tulips, the hellebores, the daffs—they all make my heart feel a little more open, and it dawns on me that working with the flowers—having them around me—brings me joy. It's as if I've unlocked a secret—the realisation that flowers are important to me because they make me feel good. Scarlett had told me she and I used to go shopping for flowers every week at the Queen Vic Market, and now I know why. My love for flowers all started here, in Summerhill, with my mother. Suddenly, I feel closer to her. I might not remember her, but I have come to know part of the bond that binds us together—a reverent and mutual love of flowers.

I bring the vases from the various positions they've assumed around the open-plan cottage to the dining table. I line them all up: juice bottles, milk bottles, mason jars, drinking glasses, and Waterford Crystal vases, all holding the blooms I've been travelling into town and back for over the past several days. Arms crossed, I study each one, and before I can give it another thought, I pull the stems from each vase, slip my feet into my leather boots, close the door behind me, and head straight to the barn.

First, I lay the flowers and filler foliage on the wooden table. Rummaging through a crate labelled *Flower Supplies*, I manage to find some green floral tape, a few rolls of ribbon, wire, pruning scissors and a toolkit. My tongue protrudes out of the corner of my mouth, as I concentrate on the task at hand, a surge of excitement pulsating through me. Between my thumb and forefinger, I create the junction point and cluster the viburnum stems together, balancing each side. Then I add the gerberas, a couple of tulips, and the filler stems of Queen Anne's lace. Not satisfied with how the posy looks, I take the seeded eucalyptus branches and use those, too. As my hands get to work, my mind drifts, time stands still, worries slip away, and I'm flooded with pleasure. It feels like everything in my life is in place. I smile proudly at the posy I'm holding, and with my spare hand I reach for the roll of floral tape before trying to cut it using my teeth.

'Knock, knock.'

I look up and see Flynn standing in the doorway of the barn.

'Looks like you've got your hands full. Here, why don't you let me help,' he says. He takes the tape from my mouth and pulls some length from it. I give him a nod once the length is right and he gives it a snip.

Concentrating, I wind the tape around the stems and adjust the blooms.

'You're a natural. You sure you haven't found your calling here?'

I give Flynn a sideways glance as I reach for some cream ribbon. Holding the edge of the posy in place with my thumb, I tie it around the stems.

'There. All done,' I say, bringing the posy up to my face. 'It's beautiful, isn't it?'

Flynn looks thoughtfully at me. 'Sure is. It looks like a …'

It's only then I realise I've put together the kind of arrangement that a bride might use on her wedding day. A mass of viburnums so soft you're almost afraid to touch them as they might bruise, parrot tulips with ruffles of peach and soft pink reminiscent of a marbled sunset, and clusters of Queen Anne's lace, offering the kind of touch that makes you sigh with delight at how perfect Mother Nature can get it.

I look down at my hands.

I'm holding a bouquet.

I'm supposed to be getting married in just under two months.

I rest the posy on the table, step away, and take a few deep breaths. I'm almost certain that Flynn's noticed the way the colour has drained from my face. His eyes dart from the posy to me and back again, as if he's attempting to figure out the connection between the flowers and my odd behaviour.

'They reminded me of him,' I say, trying to sound as casual as possible. 'Of the wedding …'

Flynn clears his throat. 'Uh, he must have been special to you,' he replies. 'Even if you did call it off.'

'He was. Only I don't remember. I don't remember him, or what we had, or why he was special to me. I don't remember any of it.'

Flynn searches my eyes for answers. 'Nothing at all?' he asks, the shock visible on his face.

'I was in a car accident. When I woke up in hospital I couldn't remember a thing, and I came here with a single memory—of me being here with my mum when I was nine years old. That's it, that's all I have. Just my mum and the flower fields.'

Flynn presses his lips together, waiting for me to continue.

'I was supposed to be getting married in September and I haven't even seen or spoken to my fiancé since I was taken to the hospital.' I start packing up the supplies on the bench, placing the items back into the box they belong in. 'You know what? Maybe coming here was a terrible idea. I think I've made a mistake. I should probably go out, get a job, force myself to return to a "normal" life, like my best friend keeps telling me. The only problem is, I'd need to check with her about what my normal used to look like.'

'Gracie …' Flynn's Adam's apple bobs up and down, but before he can say anything, I continue.

I raise my hands in the air, my voice rising a notch. 'Look at this, I mean it's stupid, right? I've quit my job, called off my wedding, and left my life behind—my fiancé, my best friend, and everything else I can't remember—and I'm here, in a barn, in the middle of winter, spending days playing with stupid flowers as if it's miraculously going to help make things better. I mean, it's ridiculous. There's clearly something wrong with me.'

Flynn steps forward and holds me by the shoulders. He keeps his eyes trained on mine until I make eye contact with him. 'There's nothing wrong with you, Gracie. You're just going through something traumatic. I mean, it's not every day someone loses their entire life like that,' he says.

'But it's completely absurd, isn't it? That I'd up and leave the way I did? I know the accident affected my brain, but this is ludicrous. Even I know that.'

'So tell me. Why did you leave?'

'Because it didn't feel right to stay.'

I swallow past the discomfort. Telling Flynn the truth feels easier than admitting my true feelings to Blake.

'I don't want to fall in love with someone for the sake of it, out of a sense of obligation. So far, my memory hasn't come back and there's a chance I won't ever regain it. I was hoping it would and then things would click back into place and I wouldn't have to worry about having to decide whether I'm prepared to get to know him again.'

Flynn inhales, giving this some thought. 'What if you could give him a chance? Rebuild your life together?'

I shake my head. 'I can't bear the thought of living with a stranger in that way.'

'You wouldn't have to live with him, maybe you could just meet with him.'

'I don't feel ready to do that yet.'

'What about a phone call?'

'Nope.'

'You don't feel anything for him? At all?'

'I wish I did. I really do. But here's the thing—I don't. How can I feel something for someone I don't know?'

Flynn sucks in a breath. 'Wow.'

'I know … it's terrible, isn't it?' I say, cringing.

'It's not the most pleasant situation for him … or for you,' he says.

He picks up a tulip stem and twirls it between his fingers. 'So, what happens if you don't remember him? You tell him it's over?'

'The thing is … I think it's already over. But yes, I'll need to properly tell him it's one hundred per cent over. I want to be sure of my decision before I do that, though.'

Flynn nods silently, acknowledging what I've told him.

'It's a mess, isn't it?'

Flynn swallows, clenches his jaw, and then runs a hand over his cheeks in contemplation, before finally speaking. 'You know what? I have the perfect antidote for this.'

'What's that?'

'Come. I'll show you.' He makes his way out of the barn. 'Grab your coat and lock up.'

For a second I think about saying no, that maybe this isn't a good idea.

He looks back at me over his shoulder. 'We don't have all day, you know.'

A few minutes later I emerge from the cottage, sporting a beanie on my head, gloves on my hands, and cashmere coat, which is buttoned up to the top. 'Okay, so what now?'

'We're going to The Wild Wombat,' he says, his eyes lighting up.

I wrinkle my nose. 'I don't know where that is.'

He jumps over the stone wall and I follow. 'Am I dressed appropriately?' I say, leaping up onto the wall.

He laughs, extending a hand to help me down. 'You look perfect.'

'This is not a date,' I say, as we approach Flynn's car.

''Course not,' he says, opening the door for me.

Taking the driver's seat, he tears open a packet of gum with his teeth. 'Gum?' he says, offering me a stick.

I grin at him. 'Thanks,' I say, popping it into my mouth.

We make our way through Daylesford, taking a slight detour for a scenic drive past the Botanical Gardens.

'I should know this area inside out,' I say, mindlessly staring out the window. 'So pretty,' I murmur.

'It's not too late to get to know your way around,' says Flynn, glancing over at me. 'Starting with The Wild Wombat.'

'A country pub?' I ask, laughing.

'Only the best pub in the entire area.' He pulls into the car park and checks his watch. 'Nice and early. We have all afternoon to drown your worries away.' We exit the car and he bends his arm for me to loop mine through.

I throw him a look of disapproval.

'Oh, come on.'

I slide my arm through his and giggle as he playfully pats my beanie. Flynn pushes open the large wooden door and we step inside the deliciously warm and cosy Wild Wombat. We take a spot on a leather lounge by the fire.

'Beer? Cider? Wine?' he asks, his eyes wide. He's wearing a powder-blue jumper over a check shirt, the colour accentuating his eyes.

'Hmm, I'll try a cider,' I say.

'Apple or pear?'

'Um, I think apple, but maybe …' I look up at the ceiling, trying to decide, but before I can answer, Flynn is already at the counter ordering our drinks. He returns carrying three bottles.

He sets them down on the wooden table in front of us and tucks his wallet into the back of his jeans. Then he leans forward and slides two bottles in my direction. He turns them around so the labels are facing me.

'You don't know what you preferred before, but now you'll know what you like today.'

I take the apple and Flynn clinks his bottle against mine. 'To fresh starts, clean slates and new beginnings,' he says, his gaze penetrating mine.

I take a sip, set down the bottle and then try the pear.

'Which one wins you over?' he asks.

'The one I thought would. The apple.'

He beams a satisfied smile in my direction. 'Good,' he whispers.

'So, what are the things you wish you could remember?' asks Flynn after our second round of drinks.

There's something about Flynn and the way he acts so casually, that there's no pressure from him to remember, that makes me feel like I can talk to him about things without having to be concerned about any judgement from him. When I'm talking to Scarlett I feel so guilty, so swept away by pressure to know all there is to know about how life was before.

'Well, I have no idea whether I had a sense of humour.'

Flynn's eyes light up. 'So, should we test it?'

I nod enthusiastically. I take another sip of cider, the bubbles playing on my tongue, a feeling of comfortable warmth sweeping through me.

Flynn clears his throat. 'Okay, so there's this guy, he walks into a bar, and he says to the lady beside him …'

He pauses, the rim of the bottle resting against his lips.

'What does he say?'

'Hold on.' He stares at the ceiling as if he's trying to recall something.

'Hold on what?' I ask impatiently.

'No, I mean hold on, because I can't think of a joke.'

I start laughing.

'You're not supposed to laugh. It wasn't a joke.'

I laugh harder.

'I don't think that's a reliable test for you. Totally flawed. What else are you curious about?' A barman takes away our empty bottles. 'Could we have another round? And a menu, please?' asks Flynn. 'I'm starving,' he says, lifting his eyebrows. He leans back into the couch.

'It's only four-thirty.'

'Still starving,' he says.

The barman returns with two menus. I glance over it, not really sure what to order.

'Are you happy in your job? I mean, I know you're between jobs, but do you like it? Love it?'

He nods. 'Yeah, I do. I love animals.'

'How did you know you loved it? How did you know that being a vet was something you really wanted to do with your life?'

'My family lived in the city, but over the summer break, we'd move out to the country. Dad would work from home, or commute back and forth, and Mum would spend time baking and gardening. She'd make us breakfast in the morning and the next time she'd see me would be close to dinnertime. Our neighbours had geese and chooks, and I hung around and learned stuff. Eventually, Dad bought me a horse, and when it got sick, that's when I knew. I never got over losing Pepper. If I could stay out here, living in the country, I'd have horses, and cows and geese and maybe even a couple of goats.'

'Why can't you stay?'

He shrugs. 'I have a practice in Melbourne, which I don't know if I'll go back to. Depends if things work out or not, I guess.'

He drains the remaining cider from his bottle.

I stare into the crackling fire. 'Sometimes I wonder whether coming here was the right thing to do.'

'You can't go backwards, Gracie. Only forwards.'

'At least you have memories, though. I've got no memories, and no compass, and no way of knowing whether a decision is right or wrong. Heck, I don't even know whether

I'd like the duck liver parfait or the Lancashire hot pot. How can I go through life like this?'

'You could always go with a side of kale chips and see how you like those.' He grins.

I shake my head. 'Or I could order both,' I say, a smile stretching across my lips.

Flynn smiles back and nods. 'Exactly.' He turns his body a little closer to mine, his eyes piercing me. 'If you could make a list of all the things you would have wanted to know about your life before, what would they be? What's the stuff you really want to know but are too afraid to ask?'

'I want to know all the things that make me who I am,' I say softly. 'I used to work as a stylist for *Country Dwellings*. I spent nearly three weeks in Melbourne after I was discharged from the hospital and all I could think about was that I couldn't stand the city traffic or the suffocating apartment and I couldn't care less about the best light to photograph a throw rug or a bowl of fruit. And like it or not, I'm going to need to find a way to pay the bills soon. There's an apartment in Melbourne that rent needs to be paid on and I can't expect …' It's hard to say his name. 'Blake to pay my share. I'm going to need a job. But I've no idea what to do, and I can't do some of the things I used to be able to do, so I don't think I'm any use to anyone.' Thankfully, before coming to Summerhill, Scarlett had helped me access my savings account, but I can't keep living off those funds.

Flynn nods thoughtfully. 'So, what are you passionate about?'

'Pardon?'

'What makes you feel good? What are you drawn to? What are the things in your life you couldn't live without? What kinds of things give your life meaning?'

'That's the whole problem. I don't know.'

'Well, maybe start there. Apple or pear cider. Duck liver parfait or Lancashire hot pot. Styling for *Country Dwellings* or something else. Whatever it is, it might take you a bit of time to find. Or … the very thing that lights you up and completes your life could be the thing that's right in front of you.' He stands up and goes to order from the menu.

My fingers trace the motif of an apple blossom on the label as I watch Flynn approach the bar. The thing that's right in front of me. That seems impossible. Not to mention totally, absolutely, and forget-the-whole-idea kind of ridiculous.

Three hours later, thanks to the cider and Flynn's bad jokes, we determine that I do have a sense of humour.

'So, now let me tell you about one of my most embarrassing moments,' he says, smiling.

'Go on,' I say, laughing before he even starts telling me.

'I was trying to impress a girl once, when I finally mustered up the courage to ask her out on a date. And just before I got my answer, a swarm of bees came out of nowhere. I'm talking hundreds of them. Buzzing so loud you wouldn't have been able to hear me if I screamed.'

'Oh no …' I say, trying to hold back my laughter.

'Yeah, and I'm allergic. So, I made a run for it, but the only place to go was the waterhole.'

I cup my mouth, suppressing a giggle.

'I made a splash and got the date. She said yes.'

Now I'm laughing so hard I almost hiccup.

Flynn stops himself laughing and then looks intently at me. 'You're beautiful when you smile. You should do that more.'

'Well, maybe you should tell more bad jokes,' I reply, finishing off what's left of my cider. I almost miss my mouth. 'I think I'm done,' I say, feeling gloriously warm and light-headed.

Flynn laughs. I laugh. And then my thoughts circle back to what he just said to me. *You're beautiful when you smile.* And from there, my thoughts travel all the way back to Blake.

'You know, the guy I was supposed to be getting married to. He was my childhood sweetheart. And I can't help feeling like I might be ruining his life.' I wave my bottle in the air, suddenly almost on the verge of tears. 'Does that make sense?' I know it's the alcohol giving me free rein to pour out my heart, but I can't help thinking I've crossed the line when Flynn flinches.

'You don't need to feel guilty. About not marrying the guy. We end up with who we're meant to end up with.'

'I want to believe that, but somehow I don't know if that's true.' I go to take a sip of my cider and when there's no cool gush of liquid, I illogically stare down the neck of the bottle as if it's a telescope. 'Maybe I do need another drink,' I say, looking up at Flynn.

He looks past me, through me, beyond me. 'It has to be true,' he murmurs. And that's when I notice the tiny flicker of doubt in his voice, and the way his perfectly defined jaw appears tighter than it did before. I flop against his chest and close my eyes.

'Okay, let's get you home,' he says, reaching into his pocket for his keys. The fabric of his clothes feels warm and comforting against me. I wish we could sit like this for a while, but Flynn gently moves away and helps me up, guiding me out the door and into the cold. We reach the car, where he fastens my seatbelt for me as I giggle away to myself.

'The other day I remembered that I'm allergic to chestnuts, you know.'

'What?' he says, glancing at me and back to the rear-view mirror as he reverses.

'You saved my life. Well, not saved my life—but you saved me from an allergic reaction of epic proportions. I think meeting you was meant to be.'

I'm not sure what he replies, because by the time the car winds down the bend in the road, I'm already dozing off to sleep.

FOURTEEN

The last thing I need in my life is a complication like Flynn.

When I open the front door the following morning to find him standing there, two steaming paper cups in one hand and a paper bag in the other, I have a feeling my life will become just that. Even more complicated.

Parrot jumps on me. 'Hey, boy,' I say, crouching down to pat him. 'Excuse the bed hair,' I say groggily. My head is throbbing and I don't have any headache tablets in the cottage.

Flynn doesn't seem to notice my dishevelled appearance at all. He follows me into the kitchen and hands me my coffee.

'Perfect,' I murmur.

'Figured you could use one of these this morning, since you didn't turn up for our run, which you agreed to yesterday. Regular for me and an extra-strong coffee for you.'

'Thanks,' I say, unable to recall that part of our conversation. I cringe, thinking about the alcohol. 'You got up to go for a run?'

'Same time every morning. I'm starving,' he says, opening the bag and its contents. He unpacks a carton of eggs, a parcel of bacon, a fresh loaf of bread and some spinach and mushrooms.

'You came to cook breakfast?'

He shrugs his shoulders. 'You okay with that?'

Am I okay with that?

'I suppose it beats burnt toast.' How *do* I feel about Flynn coming to cook me breakfast? The thrumming in my head makes it hard to concentrate on any kind of question that requires deep consideration, so I reach for my coffee and take a sip of that, instead.

Flynn fills a glass with water and then reaches into the bag for a box. He presses out two pills and extends his open palm to me. 'Figured you might not be able to face the day without these,' he says, winking at me. I drain the glass, washing down the tablets, and watch Flynn busying himself in the kitchen, opening and closing drawers, trying to find what he needs. *Okay.* I'm okay with this, I decide. He grins at me from behind the stove, an egg flip in one hand. I readjust my hair into a messy bun on the top of my head. He's wearing an apron he found in one of the drawers. Red polka dots. With ruffles. Which would be completely laughable if my head didn't hurt so much.

'Just to make things clear. The fact that you took me out last night doesn't mean you should be getting any ideas,' I warn, verbalising my thoughts out loud for good measure, only the words sound unconvincing to me. I wonder if Flynn gets the same impression.

'Wouldn't dare,' he says, trying to hold back a smile, and now I'm sure he's not convinced either.

'We're simply—'

'Neighbours,' he says, finishing my sentence.

'Well, actually, I was going to say friends.'

He laughs. 'Friends it is.'

'Even though I find you rather irritating at times.'

'Compliment?'

'Just an observation,' I say, my lips pressed against my cup.

'That's not the impression I got last night,' he says, glancing at me over his shoulder.

'Oh? I don't remember much about last night. I hope I didn't say anything I shouldn't have.'

'Well, no. But you did tell me you found me insanely attractive. That was right after I tucked you into bed.'

'I … uh … what?! I did not!'

'You did.' He laughs.

I cross my arms and look suspiciously at him.

'You don't have to believe me. You just have to ask yourself how you really feel about me.' His lips twist into a smirk before he snatches a piece of bacon from the pan. 'Come on. Let's eat,' he says, chewing on the meat.

He serves up two plates while I'm left wondering whether or not he's telling the truth.

I swallow a forkful of scrambled eggs. 'What?' I ask, when I notice Flynn watching me.

'Nothing,' he says quietly. 'What are your plans for today?'

'I'm going to do something that makes me happy,' I reply, my eyes widening. 'As soon as I shower and let these tablets kick in, that is. You?'

'I need to head back to Melbourne for a couple of nights. I've got some appointments to take care of. Actually, I was wondering whether you'd mind checking on Parrot while I'm away?'

'Not at all. He could stay here, though, with me,' I say, giving him a pat. I slip a piece of bacon his way, which he gulps down without chewing on it.

'I didn't see you do that,' he says.

I wink at Parrot. 'Whatever happens while he's away stays between us,' I whisper.

Flynn smiles. 'All right, well, I'll drop his food by before I leave.'

We finish eating and as we're clearing the table the phone rings. I ignore it.

'You going to answer that?' asks Flynn.

'Oh, it's probably not important,' I say, reaching for my coffee, knowing it's Scarlett.

The phone rings out and several seconds later starts ringing again. 'You really should answer that,' he says.

He's right. Scarlett will be ready to send out a search party for me if I don't pick up the call.

'Hey, Scarlett,' I answer, trying to sound as fresh as possible.

'Where have you been? I've been trying to call you since yesterday afternoon!'

'Sorry, I was out.'

'You were out? Where'd you go?'

'To a pub.'

'A pub?'

'Mmm-hmm.'

'You mean to say you went to a pub *alone*?'

'No, I went to a pub with a friend.' I smile at Flynn.

Flynn stares into his coffee.

'A friend?'

'His name's Flynn. You told me to get out of the house, to get back into the real world, into a routine. I had an invitation to go out and so I did.'

Scarlett's talking so loudly, I'm almost certain Flynn can hear her. I cover the receiver and mouth, 'Sorry.'

'You mean you went out with a guy?'

'Well, he's just a friend, it's not anything …' I look sheepishly at Flynn, who's now pretending not to listen. 'I need to go. We're in the middle of breakfast.'

'You mean he's still there? Oh my God, Gracie, the minute I let you out of my sight! What's Blake going to … What do you mean—'

'I'll call you later,' I cut her off.

I hang up the phone and glance at Flynn, who looks mildly uncomfortable. 'That was my best friend, Scarlett. She thinks you stayed the night.'

He laughs. I laugh. We both laugh as if it's the silliest proposition ever.

Last night definitely wasn't a date.

My cheeks start to burn. I stand up, the screech of the wooden chair against the tiles breaking the silence. Plates in hand, our attention turns to the car that's just pulled up at the letterbox. The colour drains from my face.

'Looks like you've got mail,' says Flynn.

The letter isn't from Blake. The letter is from the bank. The bank that's advising me that the mortgage repayment for the farm is overdue. And now I understand why Amanda tried to tell me that selling to our interested buyer was a good idea. After Flynn leaves, I call the bank to discuss the letter. The bank manager informs me that I've been making payments towards the rent for our apartment in Melbourne plus mortgage repayments on Summerhill. My savings are going to afford me limited time here, maybe four months at the most. This means I'm left with no choice but to somehow find a way to keep the farm, or sell up completely. Both options feel impossible. One of them feels imminent.

I toss the calculator across the kitchen. It hits a photo frame, dislodging it from the wall. I drop my head onto the table, the thump muted by the sound of breaking glass as the photo of me and my mother hits the ground. There is no other place for me to call home. I have no job, I have no past, I have no idea how to navigate the future. Teetering on the edge of a crossroad with no clear path ahead, it's hard to know what to do. The barn needs tidying, the garden needs a complete overhaul, and the fields need clearing. Everything is a mess. My life is a mess. I have no idea what came before and I have no idea what lies ahead, but I know what I want right now.

I want to stay.

I really, really want to stay.

'What am I going to do, Parrot?' Parrot looks up at me with his droopy eyes before he goes back to devouring the bone he's been chewing on. I look out the window to the field. If I sell up now, I won't even have the chance to see the fields in bloom. It's the flowers that are supposed to hold all the answers to all the questions I might have about life. If it's true that they know when to blossom, and how to blossom, then maybe it's up to me to understand why they blossom at all, before I have to leave this all behind. Of course, there are some things I know about the flowers, but I need to learn more. And I think Tilly is the woman to teach me.

FIFTEEN

Tilly has finished trading for the day and is pushing her cart across the street to the sound of intermittent screeches as wheels turn. She moves slowly, as if every step is counted. I wave my hands and shout from across the road. 'Tilly, wait!' I must look so silly waving at her like this. 'Tilly!' I shout again, but she still can't hear me. A woman taps her on the shoulder and she turns around to face me. I cross the street, and without stopping to catch my breath, tell her why I've come here. 'I need your help,' I blurt. 'I need you to teach me what you know about the flowers. How did you know to sell that woman the viburnums? Why not the proteas or the Iceland poppies?' I ask, pointing to a woman who has just left the stand. I brush the loose strands of hair away from my face. I'm still puffed out from running. I've jogged most of the way into town.

She stares at me, as if she's weighing up her response.

'I think you choose them for a reason. It's like you have a special way of knowing exactly what flowers people need most. Am I right?'

'Why do you think I choose them?' she asks smugly.

'I don't know. That's why I'm here.'

'Well ... come back once you've worked it out.'

I swallow my embarrassment.

'And once you figure it out, you might find that you actually don't need me at all. Because the flowers, it's—'

'Their unseen beauty that makes them special.' Goosebumps tingle on my arms at the thought of how true these words feel to me.

'Exactly.' She smiles to herself.

'Who told you that?'

'I think you mean, who told your mama that,' she says, looking at me above the rim of her glasses. She pushes them up over her nose, and I follow her bony finger with my eyes.

'Please. Tell me about her. I need to know.'

'I can't tell you anything about your mama that you don't already know.'

I bite my lip. 'Well, that's not entirely true,' I say.

Tilly squints at me with curiosity. 'Go on.'

'Well, I was in an accident you see ... about six weeks ago. And ... well ... I lost my memory.'

Tilly looks to the flowers and then to me, her face scrunching into a puzzled expression which makes her appear more wrinkled than usual.

'What *do* you remember?'

'Very little. I just have the odd memory here and there of being with my mother on the farm. Details about the flowers. I can tell you that dahlias hate wet feet, and peonies have a short flowering window, tulips grow taller in water, and if you dip a gerbera stem in boiling water they last longer in the vase.'

'And that's it?'

'Well, I can reel off more facts about the flowers, but I don't remember much else,' I admit.

'Come past on Monday morning before ten—the last cottage at the edge of Worthington Way. You'll know it when you see it. I'll have something for you.' She reaches over to her cart and pulls out a small paper bag. 'But in the meantime, take this,' she says, handing it to me.

'What is it?'

'Open it when you get home. Think of it as a prescription.'

I want to ask her what she means by this, but the expression on her face makes me think better of it, so I just reply, 'Thank you.'

Back at the cottage, I potter around the house, mulling over Tilly, the flowers, my mother and my memory. I turn the paper bag Tilly gave me upside down. Packets of sweet pea seeds, enclosed in brown paper envelopes, fall out. On the back, in barely legible scrawl, she's written some instructions, including a warning to sow them where the cold can't reach them. Each packet contains one hundred pea-sized balls. I hold one in the palm of my hand, before enclosing it in there and putting it in my pocket.

I close my eyes and in my mind hear my mother's voice, like a gentle wave, bringing truth and knowing to the shore.

The sweet peas know where to look for the light.

Flynn shows up at my front door close to eight o'clock. I wasn't expecting him home until tomorrow and I'm already in my pyjamas.

'Hey,' he says. 'Sorry it's late. I would have called, but my phone went flat.'

'No problem,' I reply, feeling slightly embarrassed about my attire. Flynn doesn't seem to have noticed. Parrot rushes to the door and starts running around in circles. 'Clearly he missed you.'

Flynn crouches down to pat him as I close the front door. He looks tired, worn out, a little ragged.

'How was your time in Melbourne?'

'Fine,' he replies coolly.

'So, what did you do there?'

He shrugs. 'Just had some work to take care of.'

'Sounds all so mysterious,' I say, raising my eyebrows.

Flynn looks at me for a few seconds, as if he wants to tell me something but is holding back.

'What is it?' I ask.

He shakes his head. 'Nothing.'

'Have you eaten?'

'No, but I'm—'

'Let me guess. Starving?'

Flynn follows me into the kitchen. He looks at my plate on the table, where a slice of bread smothered in honey and a few bread crusts remain. 'Is that your dinner?'

I shrug my shoulders. 'Well ... cooking's not my forte and it was just that kind of day. I got it from a local stall three paddocks away. As Linda said herself, "You can't get any better than Central Highlands Honey Co."'

'Gracie, this isn't good for you.' He takes off his jacket and pulls out a chair.

'It's Manuka.'

'You know that's not what I mean.'

'On homemade sourdough.'

He raises an eyebrow, showing me he's not convinced with my justification.

I roll my eyes. 'Omelette or toast?' I ask, throwing him a look that tells him that the appropriateness of my meal choices isn't up for discussion.

He eyes off my chipped yellow ceramic plate and looks up at me. 'Toast,' he says finally, without lowering his gaze. 'With honey. Because it was just that kind of weekend.'

Something in my chest flickers, and suddenly I'm aware of the way my heart is beating a little faster than before.

I slide my plate in front of him.

He smiles. A knowing smile, a smile telling me he gets it. I no longer care that I'm sitting in the kitchen wearing pyjamas, because I'm sitting in the kitchen with Flynn, the friend who seems to understand me the way nobody else does, considering how little I know about myself. And maybe the best kind of friends, the ones you keep for life, are the kind of friends who understand why sometimes the very best meal choice is toast with honey—even if it is a little burnt around the edges.

Flynn eats five slices of toast before declaring he's full. When he's done, I offer to wash up the dishes and prepare a hot drink. In the short amount of time I spend in the kitchen, Flynn manages to fall asleep on the sofa, against the soothing sounds of the crackle from the fire and the splattering of raindrops against the roof and windows. I stand there in contemplation, watching him, trying to decide if I should wake him or leave him be. The most logical thing would be to nudge him awake and send him home, but he's clearly exhausted, so I take a woollen blanket from the hall cupboard and lay it over him.

'Night, Parrot,' I whisper, before switching off the light and retreating down the hall into my bedroom.

I light a candle, prop myself up against the pillows on my bed, the soft glow from the lamp keeping me company in the ticking moments, while the room infuses with the scent of pear and lime and my mind tries to find a solution to my financial situation. I come up with nothing. Sleep is already so elusive, and now with this to worry about, it's all the more difficult. I rest my head on the pillow and close my eyes, when Flynn calls softly from down the hall. 'Gracie, are you still awake?'

'Yeah,' I call. Before I can get up, he pokes his head through the bedroom door.

I sit up. 'You fell asleep. So I thought I'd let you rest.'

'You look tired. It's late and I should let you get some sleep,' he says.

'I find it hard to nod off. It's okay once I fall asleep, but it's the getting to sleep that's hard. I toss and turn and think about … I think too much. Usually, I read for a bit and …'

He steps into the soft light of the room. 'Lie down,' he says, his voice low.

'Excuse me?'

He moves slowly, the room falling silent. I'm fixated on him—the way he reaches for one of the books from the bed, stacks the rest of them carefully on the bedside table, and sits down beside me. We are so close, I can feel the warmth radiating from his body. He doesn't say a word but meets my eyes, holding my gaze for longer than he ever has before. My heart rate quickens and a jolt of excitement tingles through me. Flynn makes himself comfortable, propping himself up against the oversized pillows on the bed, before reaching for Blake's t-shirt between us. He holds it in his palm, feeling the weight of it in his hand. I swallow uncomfortably. Flynn's on my bed and Blake is … I don't know where or what Blake is anymore. Flynn moves the t-shirt across, closer to my side of the bed. I shake my head, clearing my throat. 'It's just, uh …'

'No big deal. It's not like it's his underwear.'

Our joint laughter diffuses the awkwardness. Flynn leans back and flicks to the front page of the book. I'm mesmerised by the way the soft lighting accentuates his jawline, the way his lips move when he concentrates, how his five-o'clock shadow suits him. He notices me looking at him, and glances across, a smile playing on his lips—a caring smile, a loving smile, a smile that shows me how safe it is to be with him right now. I smile back and feel his hand close over mine. He squeezes and clears his throat, and when he pulls his hand away, I try to stop myself from reaching out for it again, but can't. My fingers find his, and without lifting his eyes from the book, he takes hold of my hand and starts stroking it with his thumb.

'*Everything You Need to Know About Flower Farming*. I hope this is going to be as good as *David Copperfield*,' he says, breaking the silence.

'What? Really? You've read that?'

'Shhh,' he says bringing a finger to his lips. He starts reading. 'Whenever I'm cradling a freshly harvested bunch of flowers in my arms, I feel like I'm holding the world in them. I was brought up amongst flowers, spending long summer days on the roadside stands, where sellers would roll up bunches of blooms in day-old newspapers, handing them over to customers, knowing they had the power to change the course of someone's day.'

'Hold on,' I say, opening my bedside table drawer. I take out a pair of socks and put them on. 'Okay, you can keep going now.'

He looks at my feet and smiles to himself before turning his attention back to the page. 'There's no greater feeling when you prune a bunch of roses on a Thursday afternoon, at the tail end of winter, with a guy who's more handsome in your bed than in the field.'

'It does not say that,' I say, laughing as I slip myself under the comforter.

He gives a half-supressed laugh and then presses a finger to his lips. 'You don't want to get a second wind.'

I bring the covers to my chin, leaving one arm exposed so Flynn can take my hand in his again. I'm aware of the softness of the bed, the pillow, the light, and Flynn's voice, guiding me steadily into a state of relaxation I haven't experienced since I came out of hospital.

He reads with the same kind of reverence one might give a classic, his voice smooth, rhythmic, soothing. I peek at him over the edge of my comforter, and something in my chest flutters. I inhale, not quite sure what to make of it all.

Turning to my side, I cradle my head in my hands and let myself be lulled to sleep by the sound of Flynn's lulling cadence, which is anything but irritating. As I slip from being awake to almost asleep, to that space where memory plays with the present, and daytime overlaps into night time, and wakefulness meets sleep, he whispers the words, 'Sleep tight, Gracie,' right before I hear him blow out the candle.

There's a body on the side of the bed where Blake should be, but it doesn't belong to Blake. I roll away from Flynn, disturbing his sleep in the process. He flicks his eyes open and smiles lazily at me.

'Why are you still here?' I say, sitting up now.

He also sits up and shrugs. 'I fell asleep.' He extends his arms and stretches. 'I'm starving.'

'What?! How can you be thinking about food right now?'

He runs his hands through his hair and rubs the stubble on his chin. 'I always think about food.'

The alarm buzzes and I lift the comforter off me and stomp towards the other side of the bed to turn it off, stepping over Blake's t-shirt, which is now on the floor. I'm not annoyed with Flynn. I'm annoyed with myself. What would Blake think if he knew about this?

I'd explain that Flynn and I are nothing more than friends. Because that's precisely what we are. *Aren't we?* We both reach for the alarm clock, but Flynn grabs it before I do.

'Let's go for a run,' he says, teasing me with a smile. He shifts the alarm clock from one hand to another like a ball.

'Give that here.' He raises it higher so I can't reach it.

Flynn switches off the alarm and sets the clock down.

'You shouldn't have stayed the night,' I say.

'But I did, and I'm here and it's done, and today's a new day.'

I look at him, dumbfounded. 'How can you say that?'

'Can't go backwards, Gracie. Only forwards.' He slips on his shoes and heads for the door. 'Meet you in fifteen minutes. Loser cooks breakfast.'

'I shouldn't have let you stay,' I say, but he doesn't hear me because he's already out the door.

The front door clicks shut behind him. Flopping back onto the bed—Flynn's side of the bed—I let out a groan and stare at the vaulted ceiling. My mind travels to the way his clear blue eyes greeted me in those moments separating sleep from wakefulness, and I can't help wishing I knew whether Blake's eyes might have met mine in the same way. I pick up Blake's t-shirt, bringing it to my face, inhaling, searching for a hint of his signature scent, but even that has faded now.

Flynn and I parted ways after our run this morning, agreeing to meet back at my place after showering. He turns up, freshly shaven and showered, the scent of lemongrass soap on his skin, and his hair still damp. I finish drying off my hair, join him in the kitchen and toss him the ruffled apron from a drawer. 'Since you lost the race,' I tease. I smile to myself as he puts on the apron without making any mention of the polka dots or ruffles. I switch on the kettle and open up the windows. Somehow, the thoughts that were tormenting me this morning don't seem so bothersome thanks to the post-run endorphins.

Flynn outdoes himself in the kitchen, cooking the eggs sunny side up, the way I've learned to like them. He heaps a pile of spinach and mushrooms onto our plates and takes off the apron.

'Is that a car?' I ask, listening to the distant rumble of a motor travelling up the gravel driveway.

'Sounds like it. Um, I think I left my phone in your room,' he says.

'Go ahead,' I say, before making my way to the front door. Parrot beats me there and starts barking and twirling around in circles. Moments later, there's a knock on the front door.

It's Scarlett, standing there with a smile on her face, suitcase by her side.

'Surprise!' She wraps her arms around me, the bulge of her belly pressing against me as she squeezes the breath out of me. I'm unsure of how we used to interact together, but I squeeze her back.

She beams at me, her eyes filled with happiness. 'I had a couple of extra days off and I finally went two whole days without feeling sick, so I thought I'd take advantage and come up to see you.'

'Well, I'm glad you're here,' I say, smiling.

'You scared me you know, when we spoke last week and you had that guy at home. I thought you might have gone and found yourself a new man.'

I bite my lip. 'Nope, nothing like that,' I reply, letting out a deep breath. Blood rushes to my cheeks. Closing the door behind her, I usher her inside.

'Wow, it's been a while since I was last here,' she says, looking around, taking in the surroundings. That's the moment Flynn steps out of my bedroom and begins walking down the hallway. Scarlett's face drops as her eyes meet his. She leans on the handle of her roller suitcase and looks as if she's about to lose her footing.

Flynn, noticing her reaction, stiffens. 'Uh, hello,' he says, smiling at her.

Scarlett turns to face me, her mouth ajar, questioning me with her eyes.

'I didn't know you—' she begins, but I cut her off.

'Scarlett, this is my neighbour, Flynn. Flynn, this is my best friend, Scarlett.' I glance at her suitcase. 'She's staying the night—I think.'

Flynn extends a hand. 'Nice to meet you,' he says. He seems a little caught off guard by her obvious discomfort at seeing him walking out of my bedroom.

Scarlett nods silently. She suddenly appears frozen and strangely uncomfortable. 'Uh, I'm Scarlett,' she says, sticking out a rigid hand, which Flynn shakes. I've never seen Scarlett appear so stiff and awkward.

'Are you feeling all right?' I ask, noticing the way her face has turned a concerning shade of white.

'No, actually … I'm not,' she says while still looking at Flynn.

'I'll get her a glass of water,' says Flynn, glancing at me.

'It's not what you think—we're just friends,' I mumble, taking the suitcase from her and wheeling it into the living room. My voice pitch wavers and a sudden rush of guilt pricks me. It's as if I've been caught doing something I shouldn't be.

Flynn returns from the kitchen and hands Scarlett the glass of water, which she accepts, mouthing little more than a 'thank you'.

'All right, well, I better get going, I might see you round,' says Flynn. He tucks his phone into the back pocket of his jeans.

'What about breakfast?' I say, feeling awful about the whole situation. Flynn seems so uncomfortable.

'Actually, I should go … leave you to spend some time together,' he says. 'Parrot, let's go.' He whistles and Parrot scampers in from the living room to his side. Flynn smiles at me, meeting my eyes. There's a reassuring softness in them—one that I haven't noticed until now. 'I'll see you soon,' he says quietly. He turns to Scarlett. 'Enjoy your time together.'

Scarlett nods without looking at him.

I close the door behind him and turn to Scarlett. 'What's going on?'

'What's he doing here?'

'He's my neighbour. And I know it doesn't seem that way, but honestly, nothing happened between us—we're just friends.'

'But he was in your bedroom. What's going on between you two? Did he stay the night?'

I take a deep breath and cringe, my face scrunching up. 'Mmm … well, yes, but there's nothing to it. Like I said, we're really just friends.'

The more I say it, the more I wonder whether I actually believe it.

Scarlett doesn't mention Flynn's name for the rest of the weekend, but it doesn't stop me from thinking about him. His car is gone again, and didn't return last night, either. It's none of my business where Flynn spent last night, but it plays on my mind all the same.

'I didn't think you drank herbal tea anymore,' says Scarlett, as I bring a cup to my mouth.

We're nestled in the corner of The Daylesford Convent, which has been lovingly restored and repurposed as a café and art gallery. A tower of cut sandwiches and slices of carrot cake sit between us, as we make the most of the last hour we have together before Scarlett has to drive back to Melbourne. After a full day of pampering at the local day spa in Hepburn Springs, this feels like a perfect end to our weekend.

My forehead wrinkles. 'I don't,' I say, setting down the cup. The cup I poured without giving things a second thought. It's oddly frustrating to think that some of my old habits and preferences for things have a way of popping up unexpectedly.

'You seem a bit distracted,' says Scarlett, taking a sip of her tea.

'I was just thinking about … Blake.' *Err, Flynn.* My cheeks heat up.

'Spring will be here in a couple of weeks,' she says quietly.

I purse my lips and nod silently.

'A lot can happen between now and the *end* of spring,' I reply, reaching for a sandwich. I open it up, examine the tuna and cucumber, close it, and reach for a different one.

'You prefer the herbed cream cheese,' says Scarlett. She sighs. 'I know you don't want to know details about your life, but I'm finding it really hard to not tell you all the things I want to, Gracie. Especially now.'

She takes a bite of her sandwich, a slow bite, a thoughtful bite, one that makes me feel like she thinks I don't realise how much could actually happen over the next few months.

'I feel like I'm making progress,' I say, looking down at my plate. 'I actually prefer the salmon.'

Scarlett chews her lip. 'I don't know if that's quite enough to get your life back on track.'

'Scarlett, I need your advice,' I say finally.

'You know, it's usually me asking you for the advice.'

'Really?'

'You never liked being told anything. You had this free spirit, you know. We'd call you a crazy little ember, because you had so much energy and passion, and you never let life get on top of you. When your mum passed away though ...' She pauses, as if she's unsure of whether to continue.

'It's okay. Go on,' I say, swallowing a piece of sandwich.

'You changed. It's like you lost your way, your direction. You started reassessing all these things in your life ...' She continues, dropping a sugar cube into her teacup, following it with a splash of milk. 'You and your mother were close—really close. She was almost ready to retire the farm before she passed away. She wanted you to take over.'

'Wow.' My mind wanders to Tilly. What else might Tilly know about all of this?

'When do you think you'll be ready to come back?' asks Scarlett, veering slightly off topic. 'To Melbourne, I mean? I'd love to show you the nursery. Noah's gone all out with the Scandinavian baby furniture and ...' She sighs again. 'We really miss you, Gracie. So do all the people who know you—your future in-laws, your—'

'Stop,' I say firmly, momentarily closing my eyes. 'Just let me get through spring.' I set down my fork. Sooner or later I'm going to have to stop ignoring the fact that my life has a thousand loose ends needing to be tied up.

'Fine,' Scarlett whispers.

I clear my throat. 'I can trust you, can't I?' I push away my tea—elderberry and mint, which isn't as bad as I thought it might have been—and fold my hands in my lap.

Scarlett blinks earnestly at me. 'Of course you can,' she says, her voice low. She shifts in her seat and folds her napkin.

'I can't stop thinking about him. I know I said we were just friends, but I can't help wondering if Flynn ...'

She covers her mouth with her hand. 'Oh God, Gracie. Don't put me in this position. Please.' Scarlett shoves aside her plate. 'I need to go to the bathroom,' she says.

'I have nobody else to talk to about it,' I say, looking up at her.

How stupid of me to open up to Scarlett about this, of all people.

'This whole pregnancy thing—day and night, dancing baby on the bladder,' she says, her words spilling out as if she can't hold them back.

'I know you'll probably want to tell Blake about Flynn, but … I think it's best that you don't … for now. Until I can work out exactly where things stand between us and how long I'll be staying.'

She clumsily pushes her chair in. 'I don't want to see you get hurt, Gracie. I don't want to see either of you get hurt.'

Scarlett goes to the bathroom, and when she returns we leave the tearoom, and the silence that has weaved its way between us doesn't go unnoticed as we stroll through the main street. We admire pieces in local antique shops, where we unearth treasures like a silver baby rattle, and other vintage finds like a damask fabric-covered armchair I almost can't resist bringing home with me.

'There's so much I want to tell you, Gracie. About Blake, about your life, about all of it,' says Scarlett casually, as if she can't quite say it if she's looking me in the eye. 'No matter what happens over the next couple of months, I want you to know that.'

'I'll be ready for you to tell me more soon. But in the meantime, tell me about your baby. Tell me about all your hopes for this little person.'

'Well, so far, all I can tell you is that I've never felt so enormous as I do right now. As far as hopes go, all I desperately want is for her to be happy and healthy.'

'That's what we all want, isn't it?' I reply.

'Yes. Of course it is.'

'It's a girl?' I hesitate before extending a hand to Scarlett's belly. She nods, encouraging me. I place my hand against the fabric of her blouse, feeling the warmth beneath. Scarlett places her hand over mine. 'Don't beat yourself up,' she says quietly.

I pull away, unable to maintain eye contact with her. Am I that transparent? And are my feelings about Flynn that obvious?

'This armchair is gorgeous. It would look so good in the living room,' I say, changing the subject.

'Perhaps you should think about redecorating,' says Scarlett. 'It might help.'

I tap the rattle against my palm. 'Maybe, but I think I have something else in mind,' I say thoughtfully.

I reach into my pocket for the round seed, Tilly's seed, and show it to her.

'What is it?' she asks, uncertain.

'A seed that's going to bloom into a sweet pea,' I say, raising my eyebrows. 'But I like to think of it as a key. A key to unlocking a part of my life I feel ready for.'

She takes it from me and rolls it around in her palm. 'I think gardening will be great for you,' she says. 'In a few weeks the weather should be warming up, and getting outdoors should help clear your head. Besides, you're a natural when it comes to flowers.'

SIXTEEN

Tilly's house, enclosed by a small cottage garden at the end of a narrow road lined with trees, wasn't difficult to find, just like she promised. Her flower cart, stacked with empty buckets, is retired in the front yard under a large jacaranda waiting to blossom.

I knock once and the door immediately groans open. Tilly's hair is pulled into a bun and she's wearing an apron, an oven mitt still on one hand.

'Come on in,' she says.

I follow her, closing the door behind me as she limps down the corridor to the kitchen. The house smells like a bakery— deliciously warm and sweet, apples caramelising on the stovetop, ribbons of steam laced with the scent of cinnamon, brown sugar and raisins rising up and causing the window to fog. She switches off the gas and pulls a steaming loaf tin from the wall oven, the aroma filling the compact kitchen.

'You didn't need to make any effort.'

'Who said anything about it being an effort?' She sets the tin on a cooling rack. 'Now, we should get down to business. What did you do with the gift I gave you?'

'Um, nothing, I wasn't sure when to plant them exactly.'

'Sit,' she commands impatiently, nodding at one of the kitchen chairs.

I pull out a wooden chair from the table. A white cat pounces to the floor.

'What's a girl to do? Swat you over the head with what's obvious to me but not obvious to you?' She turns the tin upside down on the wire rack and starts tapping it with a wooden spoon.

'I'm sorry, Tilly, but I've no idea what you mean.'

She flips around to face me. 'Why did you come to Summerhill, Gracie? What is it you think you're looking for?'

'I wouldn't know. Because I don't remember anything that came before.'

'Well, that sounds like you're in a perfect position to start afresh, don't you think?' She takes two teacups from the cupboard. 'Tea?'

'I don't drink tea, aside from chai. Water will be fine,' I reply, twisting the cuff of my sleeve around my thumb. I still have my coat and scarf on.

She tsks under her breath and carries a teapot over anyway, setting it on top of a crocheted doily.

'Well, then?' she asks, peering at me tetchily.

'I don't know, Tilly. I don't know what I'm doing here. All I know is that I don't belong anywhere else.'

Tilly raises an eyebrow. 'You came to my flower stand eight times in seven days.'

'Yes.'

'And somehow, even if not by choice, you've been given a clean slate, a way to create a life you want that's free from all the baggage and the drama that most people spend their whole lives trying to escape.'

'But what to do with it, Tilly?'

'Well, it's darn obvious, isn't it?'

'What is?'

Tilly reaches for a pair of glasses on the table and slides them on. She sits down and reaches a knobbly hand for an envelope. She pulls out a handful of photographs and flicks through them before selecting one and passing it to me.

'This here is some of what you don't remember.' Staring back at me is an image of Summerhill.

'Is this you?' I bring the grainy photograph closer, as I try to make out Tilly's features. The sun has facilitated the creases and sunspots she wears on her face now, but the resemblance to the younger, more slender woman in the photograph is unmistakeable. She's standing by a flower cart, the same cart she uses today. 'Who's the little girl?' I ask, pointing to a child wearing a blue dress. She's holding an armful of yellow tulips, a small white dog by her side.

There's a pause.

'Tilly?'

Tilly peers at me over her glasses. It's then I notice the way that despite her tough exterior, there's something soft-natured about her, about the way she speaks without really needing to utter words. My heart beats a little faster, knowing what she's trying to tell me. I flick through the other photographs, all of Summerhill. One of them captures the peony field in full bloom, a strawberry milkshake of colour in long rows. Lady Alexandra Duffs. Madame Jos Odiers. Sarah Bernhardts. Bowl of Creams. I know these flowers. I know them all.

My voice catches in my throat. 'It was ... me, with you, on the farm?'

Tilly sighs. 'I thought you looked familiar the moment I saw you. You have her eyes,' she says, taking one of the photos. She runs a finger over the image of my mother.

'Nobody grew flowers with the same kind of attention she did. I wasn't going to let anybody have that farm. But there was something special about your mother, Gracie. She loved the flowers and the flowers loved her. And she knew what you and I both know. Flowers can unlock memories, provide a window to hope, or a message of love. They bring joy. They're ...'

'Nature's best healers,' I whisper, blinking at her.

A trace of satisfaction forms on her lips. 'That's the gift,' she says. 'And you, just like your mother, have it.'

'You sold her your farm?'

Tilly's eyes glaze over, as words steeped with nostalgia pour out of her. 'You were only three years old when she turned up at the farm, asking for a job. Giles, my husband, thought it was crazy, opening up the spare room to a young mother and child, but we didn't have any grandkids yet, so I thought, why not? You took to those fields like a dear little wildflower. In the afternoons, you'd hear me pushing the cart up the incline, those bells gently ringing, letting you know I was on my way, and you'd race out the back field, and come back with an armload of flowers to restock the buckets. We even had one with your name on it.' She points to a photo and sure enough, there's a bucket labelled *Gracie's Selection*.

'So what happened? Why did you sell the farm?'

'Giles got sick. The doctors said the sea air would do him good, and he'd always loved the seaside, so we moved out to the Mornington Peninsula. The flowers never grew the way they did here, though. You were nine years old when we left. Your mother said you didn't stop crying for two weeks. And Giles—well, he's been gone fifteen years, now. I lost my daughter, Elsie, far too soon as well. She married young and had already moved away to France by the time you and your mother came to stay—she passed away four years after Giles.'

'I'm sorry,' I say.

She sighs heavily.

'So, what brought you back?'

'I knew I should have come back sooner. Sometimes we do what we think we should do, not what we really want to do. I had a thriving little flower shop on the coast—but I always preferred being mobile. My father built that cart when I was just a young girl.' She smiles to herself. 'Always fancied myself a little Eliza Doolittle. Selling flowers is what my mum did, and what hers did before, too. All the way back to before they migrated to Australia when they stocked their carts at Covent Garden and infused the grubby streets of London with their violet posies. They used to speak with the flowers back then. You could declare love with tulips, cure a broken heart with cranberry, or show appreciation with a bellflower.' She points to an arrangement of dainty white bell-like flowers in a vase. 'See these flowers here? Lily of the valley. These would be a way of showing a return to happiness.' She tugs on a sprig of rosemary that's tucked among the green foliage in the vase and inhales its fragrance. 'And this represents remembrance. My great-grandmother would have told you that it would have helped bring back your memory.'

I nod slowly, accepting the sprig from her.

'The way I like to work with the flowers, though—is to feel them. Feelings are more powerful than words and I've seen firsthand the way flowers can change people's moods and even the way they see life.'

I take it all in, my hand gripping tightly to the photograph. 'What brought you back here to Daylesford?'

'I came back after your mother's funeral. I'd been staying with a friend of mine in Apollo Bay when she passed, so I got your message three weeks late. By the time I came back, you'd put the place on the market. I'd been away so long I hardly recognised it anymore. Didn't realise how much I'd missed it. So … I decided to move back. In those years I was away, I only saw your mother a handful of times. I missed her a lot. She came to visit once or twice … said you'd ended up with a fellow named Blake. As she always knew you would.'

I try not to fidget. 'It's not … we're not … it's … there's nothing …'

'I think what you mean to say is that you don't remember him.'

'I wish I did. But I don't. So, I think it's best that I …' My thoughts immediately turn to Flynn. 'Move on …'

'I'll take a guess that deep down, somewhere inside, you know what's best. And if you're meant to be together, life will find a way for you to be together. And if you're not …'

She shrugs. 'Then you'll end up with someone else. But the worst thing you can do is go backwards. Because the past has a sneaky way of always holding onto your back collar. Never wants you to move forward, if you know what I mean?'

'I think so.'

She pours herself a cup of tea, the cup wobbling as she brings it to her mouth.

We're interrupted by a knock at the front door.

'It's just me, Tilly!' calls a male voice.

A plump face with rosy cheeks appears through the gap in the door. 'Just the usual delivery, shall I leave them out the back?'

'Thank you, Ellis.'

He opens the door fully and steps inside. 'Nice to see you got some company today, Tilly. Is this your granddaughter?'

'No, Ellis, this is Gracie. She's from Summerhill.'

'Nice to meet you,' he says, standing proud. Ellis, a short, round man, probably in his late fifties, with beady eyes and a kind smile, extends a rough palm and gives my hand a vigorous shake.

'Summerhill. Now that was quite the farm. That's where they used to do those Open Paddock Days, do you remember, Tilly?'

''Course I remember.'

'They'd put them drink stands out, with the red-and-white umbrellas and the little ones would sit on them wooden crates charging two dollars for a glass of lemonade. The girls would sell those flower crowns, and the local jazz band would come up and we'd all sit on the bales of hay having a good old time. Francine and Will would park the vintage caravan in the paddock, where they'd sell scones and ginger beer. And at the end of the day everyone went home with an armful of peonies, happy as can be.'

Tilly blinks slowly, a satisfied smile forming on her face, as she no doubt is recalling the pictures of these scenes in her mind. She nods at me. 'This is Lainey's daughter, Ellis. She's all grown up now.'

'There's a resemblance there, isn't there, Tilly? Just like her mum. Now, I thought Summerhill was for sale?' he muses, looking up at the ceiling. He scratches the bald patch on his head.

'It was, yes,' I reply.

'Yeah, well, a hundred thousand dollars overpriced is what I heard. Hope you don't mind me saying so,' he says.

Tilly interjects by explaining that Ellis saves her a trip to the Melbourne wholesale flower markets by delivering her order twice a week. 'I can't seem to grow enough in the greenhouse. Not at my age, anyway.'

I smile at Ellis. 'It's fine,' I reply, not taking offence. It seems Ellis lacks a filter, but I can't help finding him amusing.

'So, is it still on the market?' he asks.

'Well, not exactly. But it might have to be soon. The bank's been chasing the repayments and I'm not working at the moment, so …'

Tilly narrows her gaze. 'Now, those seeds I gave you. What are we going to do about them?' she says sharply.

Ellis playfully raises his eyebrows, clearly used to Tilly's brashness. I glance at the photos and back to Tilly, feeling my chest expand. 'Well, maybe you could show me where to plant them? When was the last time you came to Summerhill?'

The following morning, I wait for Flynn beside the field gate and start stretching. We haven't seen each other since Scarlett arrived unannounced, but yesterday I came home from Tilly's to find a note wedged under the door asking me to meet him for a jog this morning. Leaning forward, I touch the grass with my fingertips, releasing a slow breath. I straighten up, and without consciously intending it to, my body moves itself into a pose it seems to recognise.

And then, my body folds and stretches as it begins a series of sun salutations and it's clear to me my body knows exactly what it's doing. My fingertips don't seem to mind as they brush the cold blades of grass that glimmer under the still-dark morning.

I'm folded over, feeling the intense stretch, surrendering my body into the pose, observing the way everything has slowed down, when my mind wanders to Blake's last letter, the one I found in my mailbox yesterday afternoon after I'd returned from Tilly's.

> *Dear Gracie,*
>
> *Yes, I believe in destiny, but sometimes even destiny needs a helping hand.*
>
> *I'm glad you're spending time in the garden. Keep doing what you're doing, and some day, hopefully soon, I'll be able to show you what it's like to fall in love.*
>
> *Love,*
> *Blake*

I'm still pondering this, when Flynn arrives.

'Hey,' he says.

I peek through my legs and see he's standing behind me.

'Nice view from here.' He bends down and twists his head, flashing me a smile. Straightening up, I turn around to face him, my cheeks probably a flushed shade of rose.

'You don't hold back, do you?' I say. Flynn pins me with his gaze and a sensation surges through me; something pleasant, uncontrollable, dizzying.

Without lifting his gaze, without letting his usual smile creep across his face, he takes a step forward, kisses me on the cheek and whispers into my ear, 'Trust me, you have no idea how beautiful I think you are.'

It takes a moment for me to catch my breath, and even longer for the floating feeling to subside. It's like I'm seeing Flynn for the first time. His eyes, his tousled hair, the way he twists his lips into a shape that almost resembles a smile, but not quite, in anticipation of my reaction. Suddenly, a flash of deja vu jolts through me. Did Blake ever talk to me like this? I'm almost sure he must have. I stare down at my feet, forcing myself to break our gaze.

'I missed you,' he says.

I scrunch my eyes closed, unable to look at him. This isn't Blake, and I shouldn't be experiencing the kind of hammering in my chest that I am right now. I shouldn't be this glad to see Flynn when Blake is somewhere back in the city trying to piece together his own life, waiting for the day I might re-enter it.

Finally, I open my eyes, trying to ignore the wave of guilt.

'Flynn … I … we can't be …'

'I think we already are,' he says softly. Sensing my discomfort, he quickly changes the subject. 'So, did you have a good weekend with Scarlett?'

'It was great, actually. I, uh, noticed you were gone again for the weekend.'

Flynn blows into his hands and rubs his palms together. 'Yeah. I had to go back to the city again.'

I wait for him to elaborate, which he doesn't. 'Are you thinking of moving back there?' I ask, almost holding my breath.

'Nope. Not for now.'

A relief I am unwilling to explore floods through me. 'About Scarlett … sorry if she made you feel uncomfortable the other day. It's just that she knows Blake, and with you staying the night she didn't know what to make of it …' My words trail off. *I* don't even know what to make of it.

'No problem,' he says, in a kind of dismissal. He looks down at my shoes. 'Your shoelaces are undone.'

'Yeah,' I reply, before starting to jog anyway. I don't want Flynn to make a big deal about this and I definitely don't want him to know how much effort it takes me to tie my own shoelaces.

Flynn reaches for the sleeve of my top, forcing me to a stop. He looks down at my laces again, and then back at me, casting me a knowing look, a soft look, a you-can-be-honest-with-me look. I crouch down and attempt to discreetly tuck the laces back into my shoes without making a fuss. When I look up, Flynn almost looks sad. The last thing I want is for him to feel sorry for me.

'They'll just come undone again,' he says.

I shrug. 'Should be fine. Let's go.'

We continue running, the cool air burning my cheeks, and once we slow down again, Flynn's eyes dart back to my feet. My laces are now scraping the ground. Flynn stops jogging. 'Your laces, Gracie.'

I place my hands on my hips, drawing in a few deep breaths. 'It's fine,' I say, trying to shrug him off as I look into the distance to sweeping views of the woodlands. The sun is rising, a bright globe casting light onto the expansive paddocks.

I crouch down again and take the laces in my hands. If I can just remember how to do this correctly once more. I make the first loop, which comes undone. I let go and start over. Conscious of how long it's taking me, I glance up shyly. I bite the inside of my lip. 'Since the accident ...' I clear my throat. 'Never mind,' I say. I hate that something so simple, something that should be so easy, isn't.

'You don't have to explain,' he says softly. He crouches down in front of me, his hands meeting mine as he moves them away. There's a softness in his expression as he loops the ties over each other, before he looks at me, with eyes that tell me he understands. He secures the laces with a double knot so they won't come undone. Then he shifts his weight, and instead of reaching for my other shoelace, he reaches for one of my hands. Without saying a word, he places my hand on one of the laces before placing his hand on mine. And then, he manoeuvres my hand through the motions, until this shoe is tied too.

'Thanks,' I whisper.

'No problem.' He pulls away his gaze and stands up, before extending a hand to help me do the same. I stand, still feeling self-conscious. 'Don't be embarrassed,' he says, his voice low. I look into his eyes, and take in the way they are looking back at me with something more than kindness.

Something I think I want to reciprocate. 'None of this is your fault.'

Flynn is still holding my hand. He gives it a squeeze. One small squeeze, and it's enough to resuscitate something inside of me. As I gaze back into his eyes, I'm struck with an overwhelming urge to let myself be folded into the comfort of his arms. All I want right now is for Flynn to hold me and tell me that everything will be okay, that today and tomorrow and the next day will turn out fine. I swallow the lump that's rapidly forming in my throat as all the things I've been holding onto crash against me. Frustration, confusion, shame, and of course, all the things I shouldn't be feeling for anyone except the man I can't remember.

'Don't cry,' says Flynn, shaking his head. His brow creases, as if something in him hurts too. He pulls me closer to him, and reaches a hand behind my head, guiding me to lean against the firmness of his chest, where I close my eyes and inhale the scent of freshly laundered clothes, and ironically *try* to forget. Because all I can think about is Blake then Flynn, and Blake then Flynn, and Blake then Flynn.

Flynn tilts my head up, and slowly and purposefully draws me into a world where only the two of us exist. 'I really want to kiss you,' he whispers, moving his hand behind my neck, tugging me closer to him. The breath knocks out of me, but I don't pull back. Wreathed in the morning mist that's slowly lifting with the rising of the sun, Flynn presses his lips against mine, holding me tighter, then tighter still. My arms wind around him and any thoughts about Blake fall away like petals dropping from a flower. Flynn's lips brush over mine unhurriedly, as if time has the capacity to stand still, and I find myself surrendering completely. His mouth on mine sends a tingle up my spine and steals my breath. I'm completely lost in this slip of time, returning the kiss, wishing it would never end. Breaking away gently, he looks deeply into my eyes and smiles, pausing briefly before planting his lips on mine again. My heart starts hammering furiously in my chest. Flynn rests his forehead against mine and strokes my face. Everything feels special, right, beautiful. Only it can't feel like this. *Shouldn't* feel like this. My eyes meet his, and as I suddenly realise that my feelings about him have become totally transparent, I pry myself away from him, heart pounding, head spinning, knees wobbling. It feels like a life-defining, everything-is-shifting, I'm-not-in-control-of-this kind of moment.

I cup my mouth with my hands, tears pricking my eyes.

'Gracie,' he says.

I raise a hand in a gesture that tells him I need a few moments to compose myself, while the reality of what's occurred sinks in. I wipe my eyes with the cuffs of my sleeves.

'I know what you're thinking, Gracie, but—'

'I'm complicated, Flynn. This is complicated. It's not a game. Blake doesn't feel real to me, but that doesn't mean I should be moving on like this without him knowing.' I pierce him with my eyes and try to steady my voice. 'So, I think we really need to make sure we both understand that we should just be friends.'

He throws me a look that tells me he's not convinced. 'You're more than that to me.'

I rub my temples. 'You don't understand. I'm stuck in a situation I don't want to be in and I don't entirely know how to resolve. Especially if you're in the middle of it.'

Flynn cringes and then looks at me with an expression so unguarded I can almost feel his pain when he tells me, 'Since we're being so honest here, I should let you know that I'm okay with complicated.'

The real question here is, am I?

'So, what am I supposed to do?! Stop writing to him altogether? What if he shows up here? What if I wake up tomorrow and remember him?'

'I don't know what happens then,' he says through a clenched jaw. 'I don't know what to tell you. Because if I'm honest, the thought of that scares me more than you can imagine.'

'Told you it was complicated.'

He nods. 'Yeah,' he murmurs, looking up at the sky, avoiding eye contact. 'You did.'

I raise a hand and touch his cheek. 'I'm sorry,' I whisper.

His Adam's apple bobs up and down as he swallows and then he zips up his hoodie, shrugging me away. 'We should finish this jog.'

I rub the moisture away from my eyes and look out to the river, past the willow, its branches flowing over. It looks like it's crying too. 'What direction are we heading in?' I say, feeling the weight of the entire situation on my shoulders.

'I'll follow your lead,' he says.

SEVENTEEN

Tilly arrives at Summerhill early on the following Monday morning. She ambles up the driveway, taking languid steps, as if her body is letting her down with each one. She pauses, sitting on the stone wall to rest. It's a sunny morning, one I'm taking advantage of by sitting on the bench in the front garden. I close the book I'm reading about soil conditioning and the best way to grow flowers with sturdy stems suitable for the cut-flower trade, and go out to meet her.

'Tilly!' I call, waving. She raises an arm and waves back at me.

'I'm so glad you made it,' I say, scooping my arm through hers, helping her up. 'I have so much to show you. Should we have some tea first?'

'Thought you didn't drink tea,' she replies, her body stiff until we take a few steps forward, her movements relaxing with each one. She shrugs me away when we reach the gate, which I hold open for her. She gazes intently at the cottage and frowns with disapproval.

'Yes, there's a bit of work to be done,' I admit.

'Go fetch me a pair of gloves,' she says curtly, waving a hand in the air. 'And a pair of snips and some rubbing alcohol.'

'But what about the tea? I just took a tray of scones out of the oven, too,' I say, trying to hide my disappointment. I'd tried so hard to follow the recipe, and had even made a practice batch last night. Flynn had come past in the late afternoon to help me work out how to fire up the Rayburn, and stayed a while to help polish off one too many scones (once I finally managed to make a batch that wasn't too sticky, too rubbery, or too dry) without cream, because I'd managed to curdle it, so we made butter, instead. Neither of us spoke about what happened during our jog the other morning, which is a relief because I've been trying to push our kiss out of my mind, something that is turning out to be almost impossible.

'The tea can wait. If you don't tend to the garden, the garden won't be able to look after you,' says Tilly.

I return from the barn with the wheelbarrow and a pair of gloves and snips for the both of us.

'Now, you see these?' She runs her hand over the dried-out brown stems of a plant. 'You know what they are?'

'Should I?'

'You had a field full of them last time I was up here, so you should know.' She waves a finger at me. 'We're going to have to work on refreshing your memory. These here are peonies. And big billowy peonies, come spring time, are going to be your biggest seller. All the brides want them, and all the people seeking a little more joy want them, too.'

I finish pulling on my gloves. 'I can't work on the field, Tilly. And I won't be selling anything this spring, I'm afraid. I think I'll stick to working on the front garden here, and maybe I'll plant a cutting garden out the back. A small one … and then, once spring is over …' My voice trails off. 'I'll probably have to return to Melbourne.' Face Blake. Deal with the ramifications of calling off a 'wedding that was supposed to be'.

Tilly furrows her brow. 'Nonsense,' she scoffs, pointing a crooked finger at me. 'The flowers need you as much as you need them. And the sooner you see it, the less time we have to worry about you talking nonsense.'

Before I can say a word, she reaches up and takes a snip from my hand, and deftly trims the dry growth from the peony bush. 'See the eyes here?' she says, pointing to a number of pink-coloured buds protruding from the earth. 'They should be covered. You're lucky we've had a mild winter, but you need to get onto that right away.' She moves on to the next plant, and explains how peonies only have a short blooming window; a three-week flush of pink and white blooms before it's gone. 'When I was last here, your mother had over two thousand plants. Luckily, you don't need to pull the tubers up every year like the dahlias. Once every three will suffice, and then you can divide and replant. They hate wet feet, those dahlias. Pretty little things, but higher maintenance. Keeping the possums from munching through them is only the beginning.'

'She had dahlias, too?'

'They were her favourites, after the sweet peas, that is. She would plant sweet peas at every cost. Worked out how to get the sturdiest stems and the maximum yield. Ranunculus too. She had a soft spot for the double blooms, but she was always messing around with the frilled-edge tulips, as well. At the end of the day your mama loved them all.'

'I wish I could remember her.'

'You want to get close to your mother, you'll want to get close to the flowers. Because everything you feel when you're with the flowers, is everything your mother encouraged you to feel about the flowers, about life, and about the way you see the world. You understand?'

'I think so,' I reply.

'Good. So, the sooner you make a start, the better.'

'It's just that after the accident, I find it hard to think ahead, to plan, to work things out … and besides, it would be impossible to do such a physically demanding job alone. The plots in the field are far too big for me to manage.'

Tilly's eyes widen as she lets out a puff of breath. 'I guess it all depends on how much you want it.'

She prunes back the last peony bush in the front garden and grasps the fence in an effort to help herself up. I rush to her side to help her. 'Now, I'm ready for you to show me the fields,' she says, wiping her hands on her apron, looking towards the gate.

Tilly and I pace up to the fields and stop at the first one, a clean slate of expansive paddock. Tilly makes a suggestion that it could be the perfect place for me to try planting some gladioli. 'You've plenty of space, so why not?' she says, her eyes brightening. 'And you know what? While you're at it, some California poppies, and maybe even some zinnias.' I follow her lead as she makes her way further ahead to a patch of overgrowth. 'The dahlia field,' she says, placing her hands on her hips. Her eyes scan the area as if she's seeing something that lies beyond what can be seen. 'Too late to dig them up, but hopefully, with any luck, you'll get a decent crop in summer. You won't want to leave them to overwinter next year, though. If you can get a hold of several hundred more tubers, you'd be able to fit more dahlias over there,' she says, pointing to one side of the field. 'You'd usually want to plant them in November for a nice summer crop, but if you stagger your planting windows and get some new ones tucked into the ground this spring, your plot will be continually flushing.' She shields her eyes from the sun as she gazes out towards the adjoining field. 'Now, see over there,' she says, motioning to the side of the field that's exposed. 'You'll need a wind barrier for the sweet peas there.'

'Do you really think I can do this, Tilly?'

She turns to face me. ''Course you can. You're an Ashcroft. Why on earth couldn't you?'

'It's a huge job.'

''Course it is. All those roses along the border? They're the most sought-after David Austins I know of. You'll have brides knocking each other over by your front gate for arrangements. At the rear of the back field where the bushland starts is going to give you all the filler foliage you'd ever need. Eucalyptus blossoms, tea tree, emu grass—it's a forager's dream.'

'I can't do arrangements.'

'Nonsense,' she says. 'You're already doing them. Just like your mother did. She would be down the end of the driveway every Sunday morning, filling her pockets with enough money to buy you everything you ever needed. This place belongs to you, Gracie, and I don't want to see it miserable like this, do you hear me? Because them flowers need a place to grow. But more than that, there are people waiting for them. And if you don't get a move on, you'll miss the planting windows altogether.'

She leaves me to contemplate things in the middle of the field as she shuffles past me on her way down the path towards the cottage, as if she still owns it. I chew my lip, considering what she's telling me. As well-meaning as Tilly is, this is an impossible job for one person.

'Don't just stand there, get moving, we've plenty more work to do once we get inside,' she calls.

I can't help chuckling to myself as I follow her lead back to the cottage.

Inside, Tilly orders me to fetch a notebook and pen. And as she reels off planting instructions, I take notes, urging her to slow down. She repeats things, at first with a sense of frustration, and then when I share the pages of my almost illegible scrawl with her, she takes a pen and makes her own notes for me, jotting down details about what kind of care each flower needs, and exactly how many weeks I have to get everything done. She motions to the books on gardening I have sprawled over the kitchen table. 'Once you get through those, come back and see me.'

She stands up and points a finger at me. 'Spring's on her way, and she wants you to know it.'

'Thank you,' I reply, feeling the hope in my chest expand.

'You need to fill up the bird feeder out front,' she adds.

Tilly's right. I really need to buy a bag of birdseed. But first, I need to run some numbers.

EIGHTEEN

The worst part about worry is trying to find a solution to a problem when the problem feels too big for an easy solution. After a restless sleep, where I spent most of the night listening to the howling wind, my thoughts tangling around me, there's a knock on the door. Bleary-eyed, I open it. I may have recently showered, but I haven't yet managed a coffee.

I open the door expecting to greet Flynn, but it's Charlie from the chestnut stand. He adjusts his braces and tips his cap. 'Morning, Gracie.'

'Good morning, Charlie,' I say, smiling. He shifts his weight from one foot to the other, appearing a little nervous.

'Would you like to come in?'

He nods and steps inside, taking off his hat as he walks through the door.

'Coffee? Tea?' I ask.

'Tea would be great,' he replies. He follows me into the kitchen, where I put on the kettle and start brewing a batch of tea. For myself, I make a coffee.

'Not working today?' I ask, studying his face. He looks a little more worn out than usual as he fiddles with a button hole of his woollen coat.

'No, not today. My wife, Maggie, she's a tad unwell these days and has been needing me a bit more than usual. In fact, that's why I'm here. Your friend Tilly—the other day she passed by my stand.'

My ears prick up.

Charlie taps his hat against his palm. 'Well, she mentioned you were going to be growing some flowers here—that you were thinking of getting the farm up and going again.'

'She did?' I ask, surprised. I carry the teapot over to the table. 'Sugar?'

'Just one.' Charlie pulls out a chair and sits down. 'She mentioned you'd need help with things.'

I spoon the sugar into his cup before replying. 'That's right, I haven't had a chance to work out that side of things yet, though,' I mumble.

'I should also tell you that I think I have your first customer.'

'Oh?' I reply, intrigued.

'And I'm also looking for a job,' he adds.

'A job?' I study Charlie's face as he takes a sip of tea.

'I'm quite handy on a farm, and now that chestnut season's over …'

I take a few seconds to consider what Charlie's asking me before setting down my mug.

'Charlie, I would love to offer you a job, only I can't. Besides, I wouldn't have funds to pay you. At least not right away. Things are a little tight at the moment.'

'If I'm honest with you, I don't really need the money, Gracie. I work to keep my ticker in shape—to pass the time. Maggie has her good days and her bad days, so work— especially the outdoor kind—gives me a bit of an outlet, if you know what I mean. Gets a little lonely, otherwise.'

'I know exactly what you mean.' I want to ask about Charlie's wife but hold back, letting him speak.

'So, I was thinking … for Maggie—she'd love to spend some time here, once the flowers are in bloom. There's nothing Maggie loves more than fresh flowers. Now, I know it's not much, but we'd personally guarantee you an arrangement a week and I know lots of people in town who'd buy from you. Tilly can't meet the demand for fresh flowers as it is, and locally grown blooms are so hard to find. Even Tilly struggles to supply them. Hers usually are imported, and you can spot them from a mile away—they almost never have a perfume. And what's the point in having a rose with no scent, am I right?'

'You're right—but they're still beautiful to look at,' I reply.

'And sometimes a flower is more than its petals.' He pauses, and sets down his cup. 'So, what do you say, Gracie? Will you let me help you out here on the farm?'

I still feel hesitant. 'I don't want to take advantage of you.'

'You wouldn't be taking advantage of me. You'd be helping me. And I'd be helping you.'

'Let me think about it?' I relax into my chair, considering Charlie's proposal. Could it really work? 'Tilly put you up to it all, though, didn't she?'

'Maybe a little. She said she thought it could be good for me—to spend some time outdoors helping you out. I've always enjoyed a spot of gardening,' he muses.

'Tell me about Maggie,' I say, changing the subject. 'She's unwell?'

Charlie drains the tea from his cup before clumsily setting it back on its saucer. 'Maggie and I have been married for over thirty years, now. After a certain point, I suppose you lose count. She used to run one of the local tearooms. Until she started getting sick, that is. At first, she started forgetting the customers' names—even the regulars. Then their orders. She'd mix things up. Initially, I thought it was stress. So, we took a holiday—we went on a river cruise from Paris to Monte Carlo, but when that didn't help, I knew something was undeniably wrong. Days with Maggie seem longer now, but at the same time, they're over far too quickly.' He looks out the window, past my shoulder, and sighs. 'She doesn't remember a whole lot—only bits and pieces, really. What I really wish is that she would remember the time we had together, especially in those early years. There's no pain quite like the pain of someone you love not being able to remember your name.'

A beat of silence passes while I contemplate these words. 'Alzheimer's?' I ask finally.

Charlie's chocolate-brown eyes are now damp. 'I started losing her three years and twenty-six days ago. It was gradual. Some days are better than others. Some days she remembers me. Other days she wouldn't have the foggiest.'

'It must be very hard for you,' I acknowledge. I plonk my mug on the table. I can't seem to take another sip, my thoughts turning to Blake and how he lost me so suddenly.

'I'd do anything to have her remember me, us, our life together,' murmurs Charlie. 'But there isn't much I can do. That's where I think your farm could help. Maggie used to spend a lot of time visiting the Botanical Gardens with her mother when she was younger and she loved tending to the garden.'

'So, the flowers help?' I ask, the pitch of my voice uneven.

'They won't bring her memory back, but they might bring her a dash of happiness, and we both need a little more of that in our lives.'

I reach for Charlie's hand and give it a squeeze. He places his palm over mine and blinks at me, his eyes filled with hope. 'I know it hurts terribly, Charlie, and that she never wanted it to be this way. She didn't have a choice.' Something uncomfortable lodges itself in my throat. I can't help thinking about my accident and how hard everything must be for Blake right now.

Charlie sucks in a breath and clears his throat before speaking. 'I grieve for her every day and yet … she's still alive,' he says, as he stares blankly out the window.

'I understand,' I whisper.

I release his hand and reach across the table to the stack of gardening books and pull out my notebook. I jot down Maggie's name, draw a line underneath it, and write down the names of flowers I'd like to give especially to her. And then I gaze out the window to the expansive fields outside, and think to myself that I've never felt closer to my mother, or that thing called purpose, than I do right now. 'I'd like to meet her,' I say, digging my hand into the pocket of my jeans. 'I have something for her,' I reply, rolling a seed between my thumb and forefinger. 'Something I think she might like. Something I know will bring her a bit of joy.'

After Charlie and I say our goodbyes, I tie an apron around my waist and head out to the barn, where I fill my wagon with a few gardening supplies before wheeling it up the incline to the fields. Here, I fasten a tool belt around my middle, stretch open a glove, look up to the sky, and pray that somehow my time here in Summerhill will show me who I am and who I'm meant to be. That somehow, enough spring buds might poke their heads out of the soil and give me a way to find whatever it is I'm looking for.

It will take me days to rid the seemingly endless rows of peonies of weeds. I continue working on them until after midday, skipping lunch entirely. My back aches, my legs feel as if they can't hold me upright for much longer, and the knees of my jeans are completely soaked through and caked with mud. Eventually, I pause for a drink of water, and when I assess my progress in the field, squinting in the sun, I take a literal step back. A memory filters into my consciousness.

It was spring, and the peony field was sprinkled with masses of lush green bushes, the surrounding fields were awash with colour—shoulder-high sweet peas climbing up trellises, pink-and-white ruffles basking in the afternoon light, and knee-high rows of tulips of every colour imaginable. My skin felt deliciously warm, baking gently under the sun. The delicate breeze carried with it the scent of grass and flowers and a life filled with endless blessings.

I was with my mum, among the rows of peony plants. 'You can't expect them to bloom in their first year,' she said, her delicate fingers reaching out to inspect the round bud. Tiny ants crawled over it and onto her hand. She'd told me they helped the buds unfurl. The ants were a good thing— they too shared in the magnificent gift Mother Nature afforded us.

'Why not?'

A smile crept over her face. 'Because they need time to get good roots, find their centres, know that they'll be loved and cared for. In a year or two, they'll know that they were meant to be here all along, just like us. And that's when they'll truly blossom—once they know exactly why they're here.'

I laughed, snipped a stem at the base, and tickled her nose with it. 'So, this one must be special. It really wanted to be with us,' I said, inhaling the opulent scent.

'Who do you think needs it, Gracie? Who might be waiting for it? Who needs it more than you?' she said, affectionately touching my nose. Her green eyes sparkled back at me.

'Tilly,' I whispered, as something in my chest expanded. It was a feeling I had felt before, when my mother gazed at me in admiration, or when I nestled my body against hers in bed at night. But this was different. This was bigger. This was everything my mother gave me, and it was in that moment that I knew I could give this to someone else. Through the flowers, my mother had just taught me everything I needed to know about love and compassion. Mum smiled at me, as if we were sharing a secret, a knowing, a truth that nobody else around us might have understood in the same way.

She nodded in encouragement, back across her shoulder to where Tilly was at the outer edge of the field. She was dressed in jeans and a pale-blue checked blouse, with a wide-brimmed hat on her head that fastened with a ribbon under her chin to keep it in place.

'Tilly!' I called, running towards her, the round bud of the not-yet-open peony bouncing against my ankle as my feet pounded through the rows. As I approached her with that single bloom in hand, I knew that nothing would bring Giles back to her, but the blessing I held could possibly bring back the faintest hint of a smile on the lips of the woman who'd become like a second mother to me. Puffed out, I stopped in front of her and held up the drooping peony stem. She crouched down and extended her arms right before I fell into them. I tried to wriggle some distance between us, but she hugged me tight, squeezing the breath out of me. When I was finally able to pull away, I flicked up my gaze. She was smiling through tears that glided down her face. It was the sort of smile that was mixed with grief and love and warmth and sadness. It had the hallmark of appreciation, the infusion of a lifetime of memories, and the easing of pain. And that's when I knew; if there was one reason a flower might bloom, this was it. I had witnessed firsthand the true beauty of the flowers.

The memory, so vivid, departs from my mind, and I'm left standing in the field, squinting at the skyline, holding onto something so precious that my decision to revive Summerhill almost makes itself. But that night, when I reach over for the stack of books on flower farming from my bedside table and line them up beside me on the bed, it feels almost futile. By the time I churn through all these books, spring will have come and gone.

NINETEEN

It turns out Charlie's house is exactly five properties away from Summerhill. The moderately sized cottage with quaint sash windows and a fire-engine-red front door is surrounded by plenty of open space. I step through the front gate, past a number of chickens left to roam freely in the front yard, and notice a woman sitting in the garden. She's wearing a pair of grey pants, a cashmere cardigan, and her blonde hair falls around her face in short layers.

'Lara, is that you?' she asks. Her eyes are hidden behind a pair of large sunglasses and I can't quite tell if she's looking at me or behind me, so I check behind my shoulder just in case, but there's nobody there.

'My name's Gracie,' I say, stepping forward. 'Were you expecting a Lara?'

'Not today,' she replies absently.

'I'm a friend of Charlie's. I live down the road,' I explain, as Charlie steps through the front door and into the garden. He waves at me as he strides over.

'Love, this is Gracie, the young lady I was telling you about. She's thinking about getting the flower farm up and running again. We spoke about the possibility of me giving her a hand with that.'

Maggie nods and extends a hand into the air. Charlie looks at me and nods. My hand meets her frail one, dotted with age spots, adorned with rings that catch the morning light, and she gives it a gentle squeeze.

'Lara comes every other day to keep Maggie company,' says Charlie.

I nod, understanding. 'I brought flowers for you,' I say, handing Maggie a bunch I'd procured from Tilly earlier this morning. She extends both arms out in front of her, and I deposit the flowers in them. She buries her face in them, inhaling deeply. I'd deliberately chosen some of the strongest scented blooms I could find. Earlicheers, a handful of muscari and a few hyacinths.

She lightly runs her fingers over the petals. 'Hyacinths,' she whispers, her voice filled with delight. It's as if she's mesmerised by them.

Charlie glances over at me, a momentary expression of happiness on his face.

'Is she staying for a cuppa?' asks Maggie, rubbing a floret between her fingers.

I exchange a glance with Charlie. 'Actually, there are a few things I'd like to discuss with Charlie about some work I'd like to do on the farm, so a cuppa would be perfect.'

My heart fills with something I can't quite pinpoint. I think it's the desire for something I've been looking for since the accident. *Purpose.*

Charlie flicks on the kettle to prepare our teas and coffees while I chat to Maggie about the flowers. I don't know if she's listening, because she sits as if she's cocooned in her own world. But finally, she looks at me and speaks. 'Dear, why don't you go on home early?'

I look at Charlie, questioning him with my eyes. He sighs discreetly.

'Soon,' I say, going along with it. 'But I brought something else for you,' I say, producing a small gift bag.

She turns over the bag. A seed packet falls out. She looks up at me, somewhat puzzled. 'They're sweet peas. They'll fill the air with a scent that's heavenly, they're beautiful to look at, and if you give them the right place to grow, they'll provide you with a sprinkling of extra joy.'

She smiles for the first time. 'We should plant them, dear,' she says to Charlie as she tears the packet open.

Charlie wipes the corner of his eye before he sets down a mug of coffee in front of me.

And that's when I know that I really must go home and run some numbers.

No matter how many times I try to calculate how it might be possible to make an income from flower farming to afford the bank repayments, the numbers don't add up. I'm in the barn, chewing on a pencil, where the walls are plastered with sheets of butcher's paper—sowing windows, blooming periods and harvesting timelines drawn on each one in thick black marker. As hard as I try to focus on the figures, I still haven't been able to work out how many corms or seeds to order, let alone any yield estimates, which means I can't even work out any potential profit I might be able to make.

I'm tearing a sheet of paper off the wall when Flynn enters the barn. I ball up the wad of paper and toss it away with a frustrated groan. It flies across the room in Flynn's direction and almost hits him. He catches it just in time.

'Hey,' he says. 'Having a bad day?' He steps over the mess of crumpled paper on the floor.

'Sort of.' I press my temples in an effort to relieve the pressure. I have a headache coming on.

He walks closer to me and stands beside me as he considers the paper taped to the wall. I shift my weight from one foot to the other, and stare at the ground. I don't want Flynn, or anyone else for that matter, seeing how hard this task is for me. I should be able to do this, but everything here serves as an undeniable reminder that I'm different, now.

'Can I help?'

'Um, maybe another time. I was about to go for a run.'

'In jeans and a jumper,' he says, turning his body towards mine. He raises an eyebrow. 'Gracie, I know that things right now are a little tough. You don't have to do what you're doing by yourself.'

'And what is it you think I'm doing, exactly?'

His gaze darts from the paper on the wall, to the calculator on the bench, to the floor. A flush of warmth pricks my cheeks. 'Trying to figure something out the hard way,' he says, picking up a crumpled ball. He goes to smooth out the page.

'No,' I reply, trying to snatch it from him. I don't want to admit to Flynn that this is what I want to do when there's every chance I might fail. I haven't even told Scarlett about my plans yet. Ever since she came to visit, and acted the way she did around Flynn, I've avoided telling her too much about what's been happening here or how much time Flynn and I have been spending together.

He cocks his head. 'You don't think you can trust me by now?'

I swallow the discomfort in my throat. 'I do trust you,' I whisper. 'It's just that …' I feel my cheeks burn. 'I should be able to do this on my own.'

'You can't help what happened to you,' he says. Flynn smooths out the paper and takes a moment to register what I've been trying to do—my page of failed calculations testament to how unlikely it is I'll ever be able to manage a farm. Flynn squints as he tries to make out my handwriting, which causes my cheeks to flush with embarrassment again. Quietly, I start to walk towards the door, not wanting to witness his reaction.

'Wait,' he says, reaching out for my arm, without lifting his gaze from the page.

'Is this …? Do you want to make Summerhill a working flower farm again? Is that what you're trying to do here?' he says, lowering his voice.

I look down at my feet and nod.

'All the reading you've been doing lately—it's so you can do this?'

'Well, I thought I would just work on the front garden, but I think I want to do more here.' I grab one of the books from the workbench and sit down on a bale of hay, where Flynn joins me. Sitting beside each other, our shoulders touch and I try to ignore the way that makes my heart beat. My thoughts dart to our kiss the other week.

Focus, Gracie, focus.

Friends. Just friends.

I let out a long breath of air. 'Okay, so this book explains how to set up a polytunnel,' I say, opening the book for him to see. 'And this book here,' I point, 'explains the flower varieties that can be planted now for summer flowering. The peonies and roses—they're already in the ground, so they'll bloom in spring. All they need is a bit of ongoing maintenance.'

Flynn scans the page, while I continue chatting away at him, more out of nervousness than anything else. 'The spent sweet peas in the field need to be mowed down, so I can make way for new ones. So, the first step is to tidy up the fields, condition the soil and prepare new beds.'

Flynn's bottom lip protrudes as he nods in acknowledgement, but his face remains expressionless. 'But before I do any of that, I need to work out whether it's even possible or worthwhile.' I pause, snap the book shut, and finally look Flynn in the eyes. 'And that's turning out to be a bigger problem than I thought,' I say, frowning. I fold my hands into my lap as I await Flynn's response.

He hesitates before speaking, as if he's trying to find the right way to tell me what he wants to say. He clears his throat. I brace myself for his words because I can sense what he's thinking. *This is a bad idea. Terrible. Will never work.*

'Gracie, this is something you need to give a lot of thought to. The irrigation system, composting, not to mention preparing all the beds—we're talking potentially months of work here and not just for one person.'

My shoulders sag and I unconsciously shift farther away from him. 'It's important work, though. For me, for others.

I met Charlie's wife, Maggie, the other day, and you should have seen the way she reacted when I took her flowers. She …' My voice trails off.

Flynn pinches the space between his eyes as he shakes his head. 'That's great. Really great. You make people happy and that's a special quality that you have. But have you thought this through? I mean, *really* thought this through? Maybe you could just … I don't know, sell flowers? Like your friend Tilly.'

'You think it's a crazy idea, is that what you're saying? Growing *and* selling flowers is a silly idea?'

Flynn ignores my question. 'Does this mean that you staying here in Summerhill … is *permanent*?'

'I don't really belong anywhere else. But I don't see how that even matters. How is that even relevant?!'

Flynn's eyes fixate on the wall. I sit there, mute, as he contemplates things, watching him out of the corner of my eye, wondering what he's thinking. He shifts his attention to me. The way he looks at me makes me feel as if he's holding back his true thoughts.

'Flynn?' I ask finally, breaking the unbearable silence.

'Mmm,' he replies, making me wish I could read his mind.

'You didn't answer my question,' I say. 'About my idea …'

'Not … *entirely* crazy.'

'I knew it! I knew I shouldn't have let you—' I wriggle off the bale of hay and snatch the paper from him before storming away. Making my way up the incline, I tear up the paper, letting the wind carry away the pieces.

'Gracie, wait up!' calls Flynn. Twigs snap under his feet as he catches up to me. He reaches for my shoulder. 'I don't want to fight with you over this. I don't want to see you upset like this.'

'Well, I don't think there's anything more to say. You made your thoughts pretty clear,' I say, firing him a look.

'It's not a stupid idea—that's not what I meant. It's just that … what you want to do here—it's a massive job. It means you'll be staying here for I don't know how long. And everything in your life is so …'

'Don't you think I *know* that? I'm trying the best I can,' I say, my voice uneven. 'I want to stay here, Flynn. This is the only place I know that feels like home. Most of the time, I feel like I don't belong in my own life. Have you any idea how that feels? To not recognise the person staring back at you in the mirror? To not know what lights you up, or what makes you sad, or what you care deeply about, or what you're lukewarm about? I spend most of my days trying to work out all the stuff that you take for granted. I don't know if I was happy. I have to trust someone to tell me I was happy. But what if I was faking happy? What if I was secretly miserable? What if I had doubts about my wedding? How would I even know if he is … was … the right guy for me? I don't know anything for sure. I'm still learning how to tie my shoelaces, cook a proper meal, do basic math calculations. I can't even do my own grocery shopping without having a list and it takes me an hour to write that list. I read books and some words are familiar and some aren't. Sometimes, I have to read the same page over twice, three times, or more just for it to make sense. And all I want from my life right now is for it to make sense.' I pause to take a breath. Flynn is looking at me wide-eyed. 'I'm different now, and I don't know who I was before, but I have been desperately trying to work out who I am today.

And I'm close to finding out. Really close. So, excuse me if I want to stay and do that, because I don't really have a choice. If I can't make the repayments here, the bank will take Summerhill away from me or I'll have to sell. Either way, I don't think I can bear to lose it.' I take a staccato breath. 'Do you understand?'

He chews the inside of his lip. 'I understand,' he says, nodding. 'I just don't want to see you fail at the one thing you want to succeed so badly at,' he says, his voice flat.

'Thanks for the vote of confidence.'

'I can't sit back and watch you do it tougher than you already are. If you do this, I want to be one hundred per cent behind you.'

'I'm not your responsibility. I'm not asking you to commit to physically doing this. I know you have your own life and career. I'm just asking for a bit of support.'

Flynn sighs, running his hands through his hair.

'This is a big deal, Gracie. It's a huge commitment, and you know as well as I do that things could go wrong.'

'Then don't let me fail. Help me work out how I'm going to do this. Because I could really do with your help. Especially since I just tore my notes to shreds and they took me about forever.' We look at the grass behind us, dotted with tiny pieces of paper. 'Please?' I say, my bottom lip protruding.

Flynn chuckles and shakes his head, closing his eyes in defeat. 'I'm pretty good with a calculator. Let me see what I can do.' He gives me a squeeze, and reassuringly kisses the top of my head, but as I gaze into his blue eyes, I can't help noticing the obvious worry in them.

Despite Flynn's reservations about me reviving Summerhill, a few days later, I finally muster up the courage to visit a local wholesale gardening supplier. Mason, the burly sales attendant, leads me to a large shed shrouded in an earthy smell of hay mixed with manure. His leather boots leave a trail of dirt behind as he leads me to the vast shelving that houses all the farming supplies I could possibly need: seed packets, gloves, tools, fertilisers and bags of compost. I have spent the previous days making lists: what flowers to plant, their blooming windows, their growing habits. With my neck stretched as I scan the shelves, I'm wondering how many details I might have overlooked. Nonetheless, I tell Mason about my plans for Summerhill, showing him my rough sketches of the fields, while he listens with a careful ear.

'I'm hearing you, but what you're saying if I'm hearing right, you're telling me that you want to have most of your field space working for you in time for a summer harvest, is that so?'

'Uh, yes, I think so.'

His brow creases. 'Big job. But I'm guessing you already know that,' he says, as he gives me one small nod.

'Ah, yep,' I reply.

Callused fingers rub the salt-and-pepper stubble on his face. 'And you haven't done anything like this before?'

I shift my weight from one leg to another. 'Uh, nope. So, I guess I need all the help I can get.'

'Hmm. You going to install a hoop house?'

'Uh, I don't know,' I reply, shrugging my shoulders. 'Do you think I should?'

'Well, if you want to start seedlings throughout in the cooler months, you'll need one.'

He slides a pencil into his hand from behind his ear. 'Right, so tell me again, how many acres have you got there at Summerhill?'

'Around five.'

'What are you thinking of growing?'

'Well, I've got a decent number of roses, one peony field, and there's another of dahlias. But I was thinking of adding some sweet peas, gladioli, and whatever seeds I can sow now for summer flowering.'

'Did you dig up the tubers yet?'

'The tubers?'

'The dahlias you have in the ground—you dug them up already, right? They're in storage?'

A hot flush of panic overtakes me. 'Uh, no.'

His face wrinkles. 'They should have been dug up ages ago. It's too late in the season, now. I think you'll be hard-pressed to bank on a successful crop if you haven't dug them up. They hate wet feet, the dahlias, and if they've rotted, well, then I think you might have lost them. But then again, you might be lucky and see some bloom for you.'

'So, what do you suggest?'

'If you're thinking commercial, you'd best replant some new ones, that way you'll get an early and late flowering crop.'

He gestures for me to follow him. We enter a room stacked with crates of bulbs, tubers and corms.

'You take your pick, sweetheart,' he says. 'Anything this side of the wall you can plant in early spring and you should see some good results.'

I scan my eyes over the labels on the crates. I reach for one of the onion-shaped corms and rest it in my palm, turning over the possibilities.

'Gladdies—they're showy bloomers. Perfect for late spring and summer crops,' says Mason, looking at my hand.

'Stagger the planting over a few weeks and you'll have a steady supply of flowers in around ninety days.'

'When's the earliest you could deliver the supplies?'

He gives me a wink. 'Just say the word and I'll have the truck out there.'

'Great,' I say, nodding.

Mason reaches into the pocket of his shirt, produces a business card and hands me a pricelist.

I wait outside for a cab, a field of possibility swirling through my head, a copy of *Floral Designs* under my left arm, and a bag of birdseed in the other.

The following morning, I don't meet Flynn at the field gate for a run. Instead, I start tidying things up in the barn: clearing cobwebs, cleaning windows, rearranging tables, sweeping the floor. The list of things to do if I do take on this task seems endless, and includes things like preparing windbreaks, checking the soil pH, and preparing the soil for planting. I'll need to get seedlings started in the barn, and at some point I'll need to think of how to implement an irrigation system. If I go ahead with this, I'll have to decide whether to use raised beds or simply plant in the ground, but before I can put anything in motion, I still need to work out whether it's possible to make an income, the kind of income I'll need to stay here. As the figures blur once again, and my head fills with confusion, I can't help thinking that maybe Flynn's right. Maybe this is too big a task, and maybe a neat little cottage garden is a better, more practical option. However, that wouldn't resolve the bank problem.

I'd hoped Flynn might come past this morning with news regarding the figures, but as the clock ticks by, I become impatient. Grabbing my notebook and calculator, I close the front door behind me and head over to his place. I knock once and Flynn calls out for me to enter. I follow the sound of his voice to the kitchen, and that's when I notice two uncleared breakfast plates on the table. Just then, the floral scent of perfume wafts into the kitchen as a woman steps into the room. She's wheeling an overnight suitcase and is wearing a cashmere turtleneck jumper over a pair of tight-fitting pants, and a pair of leather boots. Her ash-blonde hair is swept into a high ponytail.

My heart leaps into my throat. Suddenly, I have no words. I watch Flynn step down from the ladder he's standing on, with a spent lightbulb in hand, before my attention turns back to this woman. This *beautiful* woman. She exchanges a nervous glance with Flynn, the kind of glance that shows me there's something between them that I'm not a part of, and my skin pricks with heat.

'Sorry, I didn't realise you had company,' I say, turning to Flynn.

'Gracie, uh, this is …'

The woman smiles warmly at me.

'I'm Olivia,' she says, extending a hand. Her voice, smooth like velvet, matches her sophisticated demeanour.

'Gracie,' I say, tight-lipped. My heart is racing, my cheeks already burning, and I'm sure they've noticed my embarrassment. I take a step backwards, my hip clumsily bumping into a chair. I extend my arms to stop it falling. 'I didn't mean to come over unannounced like this. I wondered if you'd … I might … come back later, or just …' I turn to Flynn, tears starting behind my eyes '… see you round.'

I head for the front door. Parrot scampers after me, wanting to follow. Flynn trails behind him.

'Gracie, wait,' he whispers.

'No, Parrot,' I say firmly, ignoring his owner. 'Stay. Do not come after me.'

'You don't need to go,' says Flynn. 'It's not what you think.'

I wave my calculator at him to be quiet, as I start crumbling apart from the inside.

The most logical place to go is home. But instead, I run for the willow tree. And there I sit with my back leaning against the trunk, engulfed by the echo of my sobs, for what feels like hours, as I try to calculate why on earth I'm feeling this way.

Just like the figures, the answers don't come.

TWENTY

Now that spring is nearing, the days start to stretch a little longer than they usually do. This evening I'm curled up on the sofa, desperate for a distraction, but there's nothing on TV that interests me. I tuck my feet under the covers of a chunky throw blanket, and draw my knees closer to me, where I rest a plate of honey on toast and mindlessly spend the next hour flicking from one channel to another. I've tried calling Scarlett, but she isn't answering her phone. I lower the volume when I hear the front gate squeak open and the pitter-patter of steps, telling me it's Flynn with Parrot. Anticipation sweeps through me, and I hold my breath.

Flynn knocks the same way he always does, four taps in quick succession, and the door groans open. 'Gracie,' he calls softly.

Exhaling, I call out to him, 'In here!' I pull the blanket up towards my chin as he lets himself in.

Parrot jumps onto the sofa and rests his head on my lap, a welcome source of comfort.

'You shouldn't have come here,' I say.

He sits down beside me, but not close enough that we're touching. 'I know you're upset … but the thing is—I could never stay away from you.' He tilts his neck and searches my face for a reaction.

I don't respond.

'I mean that, Gracie. And I know what you're thinking and I know what it looks like, but you're—'

I stick my fingers in my ears, which is possibly the most childish reaction I could have to this, but I don't want to hear it. I don't want to hear Flynn making excuses about why he's been with another woman.

'Save it, Flynn. It's none of my business. You and her are none of my business.' I slide my plate of toast onto the coffee table and go to stand up, but Flynn moves closer towards me.

'Gracie,' he whispers, extending a hand to stroke my face. 'I care about you … a lot.' He reaches for my hand and closes his fingers around mine.

'I don't know how you can say that when she stayed the night.' I pull my hand away, stand up and head to the kitchen for a glass of water, so I don't have to maintain eye contact with him. He follows me. I lean against the sink, trying to push the image of Flynn and Olivia out of my mind.

'It's really not what you think.'

I turn around to face him. 'It doesn't matter anyway. It's not like we're dating or in love or …' My words catch.

'The thing is, it does matter. Because *you* matter. So, let me tell you about Olivia.'

'I don't really want to talk about her … it … any of it. Like I said before, it's really none of my business.' I reach for a glass and pour myself a water, trying to steady my hand.

'It is your business. I want my life to be your business.'

'Well, here's the thing. You can't be my business. So, whatever that was, whoever she was … it doesn't really matter.' I try to sound convincing. I try to push aside the feelings I shouldn't be feeling. I try to sound indifferent. I fail at all these things.

'I came to tell you that Olivia is my sister,' he says, his voice low and reassuring. 'She's studying art restoration in Paris and booked an impromptu flight to Melbourne to visit my parents and she wanted to surprise me before going back. I hadn't seen her in a few months.'

My insides pinch. I take a deep breath as my hand wraps around my glass, the water still running over my hands. His *sister*? My words catch in my throat. 'What? But I thought …'

'I know what you thought. You might want to switch off the tap,' he says, a boyish smile forming on his lips.

Relief slides over me, but I still feel unsettled.

Flynn leans across, turns off the tap and places his hand over mine as he pries the glass from my hand. He's standing so close to me now I can smell his aftershave and feel the warmth of his body. He stares intently at me.

'Your sister,' I say.

He nods. 'You care.'

I bite my lip and nod quietly, unable to admit it out loud. 'I didn't come here to complicate my life. I came here to find out who I really am, so I could find a way back to my fiancé. And I really wish that I'd organised the electricity

217

in advance, but you showed up and now you're here, and I know barely anything about him, but I feel like I know you. I wish that I'd met you in a previous life because maybe then we could find a way to …'

Flynn squeezes his eyes closed. 'Stop,' he says. He moves a strand of hair from my face. 'Just stop. This—all of it, is going to work itself out, I promise.'

'The bank called again this morning.'

Flynn reaches for my calculator and notebook on the table. He motions to the living room. 'Come, I want to show you something,' he says, taking my hand.

I join him on the couch.

'I know you're upset with me about my reaction to your plans.'

'I'm not upset with you,' I say, as I move my plate onto the coffee table. I dab my finger onto the sticky crumbs and then proceed to lick it. 'I just … I think I wanted you to tell me it would be easy … or at least *easier*.' Noticing a sticky patch on my chin, I wipe over it but miss a spot, because Flynn then licks his finger and mops up the rest of the honey. As I watch him concentrating on rubbing my chin clean, I fight the urge to move closer to him.

'Yeah, so about this idea. I think it's great, but …' He shifts back.

'But what?'

'I don't know if this is the best solution for you.'

'You don't think I can do this, you mean?'

'It's not that, I think that you should maybe consider that you have a life in the city that you might want to go back to some day, and before you commit to something like this, you need to be sure of what you want.'

'But I know what I want.'

He sits there, considering me. 'I think you're very confused right now.'

'You're making me feel like I'm incapable of making my own decisions,' I say hotly. 'Why all of a sudden is me staying or going an issue for you? I want to be able to spend some time doing what I love, what I know, right? That's what you said I should do.'

'Yes, but …'

I question Flynn with my eyes.

He shakes his head. 'What you want to do involves a lot of physical work. You're on your own here and there's only so much Charlie will be able to help you with. Maybe you could wait a few months and reassess things then.'

'Going back to my old life isn't an option.' The rush of heat scalds my cheeks. 'I have to find a way to do this, because I might never remember the past. I need a reason to wake up in the morning. If I don't give this a try, then how will I ever know where I'm meant to be? If you don't help me, then maybe I'll just have to find someone who will.' I cross my arms and without intending to, pout.

Ugh, I can't believe I'm pouting.

'You're pouting,' says Flynn.

'You're upsetting me.'

Flynn shakes his head and smiles. 'I'm just trying to look out for you. This isn't a job for just one person.'

'I don't just want to do this, Flynn. I *need* Summerhill to be a working farm this spring, with blooms to sell. If I can't make the repayments, I lose it.'

'Sorry I can't tell you what you want to hear, but I care about you.'

'You barely even know me,' I whisper, mostly to myself.

Flynn shifts closer and puts his hand on my waist, encouraging my body to move towards his. He looks at me the way someone looks at you when they can't live without you. And when Flynn moves his face close to mine, my heart beats fast as if it's jumping hurdles to be with him. I close my eyes as he brings his lips to mine. It's impossible to not surrender. Flynn's hand reaches for the back of my neck, sending a flutter of warmth through my body. His hands run through my hair as he deepens the kiss. My body softens, my worries momentarily fall away. Everything feels perfect.

Except for the fact that this isn't Blake, when it should be Blake.

My eyes flick open as I pull away, breathless. I rest my hands on Flynn's chest for a second, trying to regain my equilibrium.

'I can't. I know we did once, and I don't mean to lead you on, but … this is wrong.'

He closes his eyes, as if he doesn't want to hear what I'm saying, and then runs his hand through his hair as he moves his body away from mine.

'I'm sorry,' I say, tears blurring my vision. 'I'm so sorry.'

He clears his throat. 'So am I.'

He gathers his coat and heads for the door.

'Wait. Don't go. You don't have to go.'

'I'll see you tomorrow,' he says flatly. His jaw is clenched and he's avoiding my gaze.

'Flynn, look at me. Please. I don't want to hurt you.'

He looks up. 'I know. I understand. I wish it didn't have to be like this. It's just bad timing. Too soon.'

'No, it's not that. It's just … who you aren't. You're not him … you're not … *Blake*.'

Flynn opens his mouth to speak only to close it once more. 'I really better go,' he says, turning away from me.

'I'll see you round?'

'Yep,' he replies, without looking at me, before turning his back and heading for the front door. I glance over my shoulder, stealing a glimpse of him through the fog of tears. I can almost swear his eyes are damp too.

The door clicks shut and I'm left in a bubble of silence, wishing for him to turn around and come back. So much is riding on the decisions I need to make about my new life. Choosing Flynn over Blake, Summerhill over Melbourne. There is so much that could go wrong. And despite all my reading, I still don't know the first thing about irrigation or compost tea.

The following morning, I'm sitting on a bale of hay in the far corner of the barn, listening to the constant chatter of cockatoos and parrots outside. My hands are still wrapped around a mug of coffee that has grown lukewarm when Flynn shows up, hands in the pockets of his jeans. He hasn't shaved, but I like this look on him.

'You didn't show up for our run,' he says. He looks thoughtfully at me, maintaining some distance. I almost wish it wasn't so, yet the further apart he stands from me, the closer I want him to be.

I shuffle off the bale of hay. 'I went on my own. Needed to clear my head.'

'I know what it's like to want something so badly that you can't afford for it not to work. To have everything on the line for this one thing, that if it doesn't work, you're going to be left doubting what the point of anything in your life is.' He pauses. 'So, if this is what you really want to do, then maybe you should at least give it a try. And who am I to stop you?' From behind his back he hands me a notebook, a gentle smile forming on his face.

Between the pages are sketches of the fields. I flick through the subsequent pages, and there they are staring back at me. The calculations I've been trying to figure out. How many dahlia tubers to plant, how many gladioli corms to purchase, how many peonies I can estimate might bloom. Everything I need is here, within these pages. And on the last page, finally, an estimate of how much profit I might make over the next six months if this plan is to work out.

'You really do think this is possible, then?' I ask, looking up at Flynn, who's smiling at me.

He briefly closes his eyes in reassurance. 'Yes, I think this is possible,' he says. 'It's not going to be easy, but I'll do whatever I can to help you. You won't lose it, Gracie. I won't let you lose the farm.'

I stare at him in surprise. 'You don't have to help me beyond this point, Flynn. This is enough,' I say, holding up the notebook.

'You jump in, I jump with you,' he says.

'You're the best kind of friend. And … I'm sorry about last night.'

He pinches his nose. 'I understand. Don't worry about it,' he says. 'I need to take care of a few things today, but why don't we talk about it over dinner tonight?' His gaze rests gently on me, waiting for me to respond. I sigh, unsure of whether this is a good idea. 'It doesn't have to be anything more than dinner if you don't want it to be,' he adds, sensing my hesitation.

'Let me guess. You know a great spot.'

He winks at me. 'Now it looks like you're getting to know me,' he jokes.

I stand up and give Flynn a hug. 'This means a lot to me,' I say, patting the notebook.

'I know it does.' Then, without a word, he crouches down and ties my shoelaces.

'You really don't have to do this,' I say, staring up at the ceiling, embarrassed.

'I want to,' he says, standing up. He holds back a smile. 'There's still so much you can do, still so much you can be, Gracie. Even if you can't tie your own shoelaces as quickly as the rest of us.'

'I want things to go back to normal,' I murmur.

'They will. We've just got to give it time.' He wraps his arm around my shoulder and presses his lips against the top of my head. 'See you tonight,' he says, letting go of me.

Before I can contemplate the fact that he said *we*, or the fact that I almost wish he never let go, he's halfway down the driveway.

Flynn shows up just before seven, freshly shaven and showered, wearing a pair of leather lace-ups, dark jeans and a shirt underneath a blue V-neck jumper that accentuates the sapphire of his eyes as well as the muscular tone of his body.

'I think I might be a bit underdressed,' I say, looking down at my jeans and plain top. My face is bare of makeup, and I haven't had a chance to properly style my hair. I'd brought a straightener with me, but I gave up on trying to use it weeks ago. 'I thought you might have been thinking somewhere casual.'

'You look fine to me.' He pauses, eyes brightening. 'Perfect, actually.'

My cheeks flush as I turn my back and make my way into the kitchen. 'Wait right there, I won't be a sec,' I call. I grab a bottle of wine from the cupboard, pour two glasses, and carry them out to Flynn, who is waiting for me in the living room. 'I won't be long.' I hand him the TV remote and walk away once more. 'Where are we going?' I call out from my bedroom, as I try to find some decent clothes. I'd mainly only brought casual clothes with me from Melbourne, but I manage to find a white chiffon blouse with large black dots and a peter pan collar that would look okay with jeans. Deciding it'll have to do, I slip it on and run a comb through my hair before wrapping it into a high bun. Earrings. Did I bring a pair of earrings with me? I check the dresser drawer, and find a box filled with jewellery. My fingers brush over a necklace with a heart-shaped pendant. Engraved on the back are the words, *Love, Blake.* I take out a pair of silver hoop earrings, and rest the pendant gently back in the box, taking a deep breath as it snaps shut.

'Wow,' says Flynn, a smile stretching across his face as I enter the living room. 'I was only thinking the local pub, but now I've got somewhere better in mind.'

We're barely past the driveway when Flynn declares he wants to show me the Central Springs Reserve. 'I think you'll love it,' he says. 'It's one of the nicest spots around here.'

He drives as far as he can, parks the car and we walk towards a picturesque picnic spot, where signs point towards the various mineral springs and walking tracks that can be taken. We stroll past the spillway, where water majestically cascades from the lake into the reserve. We're the only ones here, aside from a man walking his dog. He smiles at us and his dog, a Scottish terrier wearing a hand-knitted jumper, pulls on the lead towards Flynn, who bends down to shower him with affection. 'Hey, boy,' he says, ruffling the fur on his head. 'What's his name?' he asks, looking up at the man.

'Butters,' says the man, smiling with fondness at his pet. 'Loves making new friends, but he won't stop pulling on the lead.'

'Really?' says Flynn, his interest piqued.

'Yeah, going for a walk is like a tug-of-war,' he replies.

Flynn stands up and observes Butters for a few seconds. 'First up, try changing his lead to a harness style. These ones here aren't great for their necks.'

The man nods.

'Do you happen to have any treats with you?'

The man produces a small paper bag from his pocket as Flynn reaches into his for a clicker, which is attached to his keys.

'I could show you how to train him if you like,' says Flynn. 'Do you mind?' he says, reaching for the lead.

'Go for it,' says the man, stepping aside.

I stand back as Flynn works with Butters, demonstrating how to train him to heel. Flynn glances at me and winks, and as I watch him go through the motions, I become aware of how generous, and kind, and warm-hearted and attractive, Flynn really is. He's in his element, smiling effervescently when, after a few tries, Butters responds by doing exactly what he's supposed to.

'You're a quick learner, Butters,' says Flynn, patting him affectionately, as the dog jumps up to lick him. Flynn hands the lead back to the man. 'Work with him like this once or twice a day and he'll be cooperating in no time. He's a smart dog.'

The man nods in gratitude, as Flynn gives Butters a final caress. 'You did good, boy,' he says.

We say goodbye and continue strolling along the waterway.

'Do you miss your job as a vet?' I ask thoughtfully.

'A little. Things are just on hold for now. I'll go back to it eventually.'

'You were amazing,' I say, a hint of shyness in my voice.

Flynn shrugs, and doesn't answer straightaway. 'You think I'm amazing?' he says, teasing me. He glances over at me, waiting for me to reply.

'You were amazing with the dog. And … sometimes you're also amazing when you're not around dogs, too.'

He chews the inside of his lip in amusement. We continue walking until we reach a small stone bridge. Flynn sits down and lets his legs hang over the edge. I sit down beside him. 'Look at all this,' he says, motioning to our surroundings.

'It's so lovely here. If it's this beautiful at the end of winter, imagine how beautiful it must be in spring,' I say, stopping to take in the surroundings, the bubbling water trickling away below us. Watching it is almost magical. Mesmerised by the flow of something so simple yet beautiful, we're drawn into a moment where time seems to have come to a standstill, and I can't help feeling like I've been here before. My belly flutters with hope. I will a memory to surface, but even I should know by now that memories can't be forced.

'They say this is one of the most romantic spots in Daylesford,' Flynn tells me. We are sitting so close to each other that our shoulders are almost touching. The back of Flynn's hand brushes mine, and a rush of anticipation courses through me at the mere thought of his fingers intertwining with mine. This street, the stroll, the crisp air, the way flowers are starting to blossom—the total charm of this place makes it impossible to disagree with him. But the thing that perhaps makes it even more romantic, is the fact that I'm sitting here with him.

There's something I want to ask Flynn, something I've desperately been wanting to know the answer to since I left the hospital and found out I was … *am* … engaged.

'What's it like? You know … to fall in love? What does it feel like?' I ask, staring into the distance.

Flynn shifts his body closer to mine and looks earnestly at me. 'Well, for some people it happens quickly—in an instant, like the flash of a camera, where the world lights up in a new and different way, and you just know. But for others, it can happen slowly, where you wake up and realise that you've met the person in your life that you want to spend every waking moment with. It's like your heart becomes one with someone else without being able to explain it. When you laugh, she laughs, and when she cries, you feel like something in you has broken too. But the falling part? The falling part's the best.'

'I don't think you can force it,' I reply, fiddling with a eucalyptus branch. I twirl it between my fingers, tearing away each leaf as it becomes the focus of our attention. 'You can't really help who it is you fall in love with, can you?' I say.

'No, you can't force it. But you can help it along.'

I loosen my grip on a handful of leaves I've collected and watch them drift into the water, where they're swept away. Finally, I look up at Flynn. 'So, how do you know for sure?'

'When you know, you know.' He blinks at me slowly, deliberately.

I nod silently and turn my body towards the stream. Sitting there, side by side, as we watch the ducks swim from one bank to the other, Flynn's hand reaches for mine, closing over it as I let out a gasp, my mind immediately wandering to Blake. We sit in silence for what feels like minutes, as the ever-growing sense of guilt hovers in the air, weighing itself down on my shoulders like a tightly knitted blanket I can't seem to shrug off. In the seconds that pass, I contemplate things as I try to put a lid on the sense of anguish that's lodged itself in the pit of my stomach. If I don't pull away, if I don't stop this, I might lose everything I ever had, everything I ever wanted. But if I do stop this, I might lose everything I never knew I wanted. I inhale deeply and squeeze. Flynn squeezes back.

I clear my throat. 'You're holding my hand.' My voice is shaky.

'Uh, yep.' He turns his body towards mine. Slowly, a smile stretches across his face, the kind of smile that matches the gaze in his eyes—a gaze that draws me in, deeply, purposefully, totally. I bite down on my lip, firmly placing a lid on those volatile feelings. I know if I say something, anything, it'll ruin this moment, a moment that I never planned and never could have anticipated, yet can't seem to walk away from. Flynn's deliberate gaze draws me in further, reassuring me. I let my eyes meet his, allowing the unspoken words between us to hover. And the moment Flynn leans in closer, cupping my cheek in his hand and placing his lips on mine, something crumbles away. His tongue searches for mine, and as I return the kiss, unshackling myself from a past I don't recognise, I surrender myself to something that seems so wrong, yet completely right.

Back in the car, Flynn reaches for my hand. 'You okay?' he asks as he turns on the ignition.

'I'm okay,' I reply, staring out the window as we make our way to a restaurant out of town. Flynn leaves his hand on mine, with the other on the wheel, lifting it only to shift gears. My free hand reaches for my neckline—the place where Blake's necklace might have been. I can't help thinking about how he might react if he knew I was doing this—kissing and dining with and ... *falling* for another man. All the sensations make sense. The flutters, the dizziness, the anticipation. The inability to concentrate on other things when he's in the same room. It's not something forced and it's definitely not something I've chosen. But I still don't know if that makes it okay.

'If only I could read your mind,' says Flynn, slowing down as we take one of the curves that leads us towards the restaurant.

'I'm just thinking ... about how complicated things are.'

Flynn comes to a stop at an intersection and looks at me.

'You made a choice to leave the city. When you made that choice, you didn't know what you would find here. But something led you here and now, maybe you should focus on what's keeping you here.'

I swallow hard and try to avoid Flynn's gaze.

'Because there's one thing keeping me here. And that's you,' he says softly.

My cheeks flush and I let the window down to allow in some air. I exhale a long breath. 'I'm *attached* to someone, Flynn.'

He places his hand over mine. 'I know that,' he says, glancing over at me. 'But I'm okay with it.'

I frown. 'But you should not be okay with this. What if I wake up one day and remember him? Then what?'

'Then we'll figure things out,' he says reassuringly, like it's not a problem that there's another man out there—a man who is suffering because of me, a man who loves me, wants to be with me, is waiting for me.

'How can you say that? Like it doesn't bother you one bit.'

We reach another set of lights and Flynn locks his eyes with mine. 'So why aren't you with him, Gracie?'

'I *can't* be with him. It just … doesn't feel right.' But *this* feels right. Being with Flynn feels unexplainably right. I let out another sigh, and rub my forehead, trying to make sense of things. 'Being with you like this, means cheating on him,' I whisper because I don't want to admit it out loud. I don't know what kind of person this makes me.

'Does it? If you don't remember him at all?'

I don't have a chance to respond, because an impatient driver toots his horn from behind us, disrupting our conversation, forcing us past that stop sign, over a line that I don't think we can go back to without our lives being more complicated than they were before dinner.

Portobello's, the upmarket restaurant located on the main street in Kyneton, is a renovated historic brick building with white bay windows and a black-and-white sign hanging from above the doorframe. Beside the sign, an old-fashioned lantern lights up the doorway, like a spotlight. Flynn holds open the heavy wooden door for me as I step inside to the deliciously warm dining area. Here, the room is lit up with the soft glow of tea-light candles that are burning on the wall sconces, and the dim lights from the low-hanging drum chandelier wrapped in a black organza. The crackling fire provides a comforting warmth to the moderately sized room, where the cadence of voices is overshadowed by the laidback jazz riffs in the background. A waitress shows us the way to a table in the corner of the restaurant. Flynn pulls out one of the high-backed chairs for me before sitting down. It's upholstered in a decadent shade of chocolate velvet and feels lush. From here we have a view of the quiet main street of the town that, like every other town around here, sparks no recollection of my former life. The waitress lights a thick pillar candle on the centre of the table before handing us our menus and telling us she'll be back in a few minutes.

'What are you thinking?' asks Flynn as I stare out to the antique store across the street. 'I know you're worried about us … this.'

I shake my head. 'It's not that. I mean, yes, I am worried about that, but I'm sure I've been here before. The reserve … this restaurant … I can't really explain it—it's more like a feeling, not a memory,' I say, glancing around. 'Never mind. I shouldn't think about any of that. If I grew up around here, obviously at some point I've been here, and maybe instead of desperately trying to remember old ones, I should just focus on creating new memories, right?'

'Actually, I've been thinking about that. I think we've established that you prefer apple cider over pear, and Lancashire hot pot over duck liver parfait, and a career with flowers over some soul-destroying job as a stylist, but there's more you want to know, isn't there?'

'Mmm … I think so,' I reply cautiously. 'Where are you going with this?'

'Now that you've committed to getting things happening with the farm, I think that just for a while, you should give this new life of yours a chance. Your interests, your preferences … and us.'

The waitress returns with a stainless-steel jug and fills our glasses with water, and then pulls a small notepad from the front of her black apron, disrupting our conversation.

I reach for my water and gulp it down in one go. The waitress throws me a curious look over her notepad before speaking.

'Can I get you a drink? Wine?' she asks.

'Wine would be great, thanks,' says Flynn, glancing over at me.

I set down my glass, my thoughts flicking back to Flynn's suggestion.

'Red or white?' she asks.

Flynn raises an eyebrow.

A hint of a smile crosses my lips.

Just for a while.

Just for a while I'm going to let myself forget.

'Gracie?' asks Flynn, locking his gaze with mine.

I clear my throat and straighten up in my chair. Without looking at the waitress I reply, 'I'm not really sure whether I prefer the red or white. So we'll try both.'

Flynn grins at me and points to the menu, selecting two bottles.

'Okay,' says the waitress, raising her eyebrows as she tucks away her pad and moves to the next table.

Flynn leans forward. 'You said you couldn't remember what it feels like to fall in love.'

'And?'

'I could show you. What I'm trying to say is, I'd like you to give me the chance to show you what it's really like … to fall in love … with me.'

My breath catches in my chest. The thing that Flynn isn't aware of is the possibility that I already might be. He reaches across the table for my hand.

'I know you're in this weird place right now where everything feels like it's a mess. Everything is unresolved and you feel like you don't know how it will turn out,' he says.

I nod.

'You were going to give things until the end of spring, right? Until you would go back home and work out what to do next.'

I nod again.

'So, here's what I think you should do. Forget about the one thing you're so desperate to remember, and for now, don't feel guilty. Let me help you find all the stuff that makes you weak at the knees, the stuff that makes you smile, the things that you love about life and the things that you don't, regardless of before. And in the meantime, let me fall in love with you, because I'm crazy about you, Gracie Ashcroft.'

'But what about him? What if I happen to wake up one day and remember him? Where would that leave you … or …' I inhale deeply, '*us*?'

'Then that's going to be a good day for you. But like all things, don't you want to push aside the what-ifs and go with what now? Because at the end of the day, what if you don't?'

Flynn has a point, but I still think what he's saying is absurd.

'How could you possibly be okay with that?' I ask, shaking my head. The real problem, however, might not be whether Flynn's okay with that, but whether I'm okay with this. I pour myself another water as the waitress sets two extra glasses on the table and delivers the two bottles of wine. Flynn pours wine from each bottle into four separate glasses and circles back to our conversation. 'I think there are going to be risks. And there's a strong chance I could lose you, but I'm willing to take the risk ... Are you?' he says.

I hold back a splutter, the water washing down my throat the wrong way. It dawns on me that I could potentially lose both Flynn and Blake. But maybe Flynn's right. Maybe it is the time for me to ask myself 'what now'.

Flynn waggles his eyebrows at me from behind his wineglass.

'I think so,' I reply, still not quite believing the words that have just spilled from my mouth. 'But we need to go slow,' I add.

Flynn nods, and slides two wineglasses across the table: one red, one white.

For a moment, I forget about yesterday. I forget about Blake's letters. I forget that the past feels distant and the future feels scary. And for now, I choose the red wine, and try to forget that the wedding I cancelled is less than a month away.

TWENTY-ONE

Charlie meets me at the field gate at the agreed time, wearing a pair of loose-fitting jeans and a checked shirt rolled up to his elbows. He runs his thumbs under his braces before tipping his hat at me as I approach him.

'Gracie,' he says. He pulls a piece of paper from his pocket. 'I was talking to some passers-by yesterday—locals. I was telling them about your plans here, about what you're hoping to do. And I hope you don't mind, but I got you some orders.' He unfolds the sheet and starts reading. 'Ollie Sanders—his mother's in a nursing home, and there's nothing she loves more than peonies in spring, so he'll take a bunch a week through blooming season. Meredith Hollingsworth—she hosts a dinner party a week and will take whatever arrangement you can give her, as long as it's bright and bold—no pastels for her. Mae from the bakery would love some for out front on Sunday mornings. And Dr Greenfield—she'll take a regular bunch for the practice—says flowers always have a way of cheering up the patients. Lillian Bosworth says flowers remind her of her late husband, and since nobody ever buys her flowers anymore, she'd like to buy her own. So, there you go … hope you don't mind, but I couldn't help spreading the word. And, well, Tilly may have had a part in that, too,' he admits, nodding thoughtfully.

'What do you mean?'

'Well, she can't go on selling flowers forever, can she? Somebody's going to need to take the reins at some point. Let's just say, she's been helping spread the word about the future of Summerhill in her own way. She has the highest hopes for you.'

I take the piece of paper from Charlie, deciding I should visit Tilly to see exactly what she's been up to as soon as I have a chance. 'Thanks,' I say, scanning the page, which includes the phone numbers of each future customer. I tuck it into my pocket, one small part of me hoping I won't let them down. My attention turns to the fields. I open up my notebook in readiness for the work Charlie and I have planned for the day. 'Should we start by measuring the fields?'

Charlie nods and we make our way up the rise. 'What are you planning on growing?'

I tell him, pointing out each field. We discuss more plans—composting, windbreaks, soil conditioning and management.

In the fields, the earliest hints of spring have appeared. We make the invigorating walk across the grass-lined slopes, and through a delicate blanket of nodding wildflowers and dandelions that skirt around the trees and line the borders of the field.

Charlie and I are measuring the last field when Flynn joins us from the other side, with Parrot trailing behind him. Parrot starts running around in circles, excited to see me.

'Hey, Parrot,' I say, bending down to let him snuggle into my arms.

'Charlie!' says Flynn, beaming at him as he extends a hand. He turns his attention to me and I can't help feeling a little awkward. 'Gracie.' He smiles down at me, piercing me with his eyes and I can feel myself blushing. 'All ready to start your own little flower renaissance?'

'I think so,' I reply, feeling positive about things. 'Charlie was just telling me we should reserve some space here for some green manure—we're thinking mustard.' I point to the far corner of the field. 'And over there, we'll get a compost heap going. But before any of that, we need to prepare the soil. That's our first job.'

Charlie winks at Flynn. 'I've got the job of sourcing the manure. I'll aim to get it delivered here by mid-next week. And on that note, I best leave you both to it,' he says, checking his watch before leaving Flynn and me to contemplate how we're going to move forward with things.

'Where did you want to start?' asks Flynn, rolling up his sleeves.

'So, we're really doing this?' I clap my hands together.

'Yes, Gracie, we are really doing this. Whatever it takes.'

'Whatever it takes?'

He shrugs. 'It might help bring back your memory.'

'But what if I …' Flynn raises his eyebrows, waiting for me to continue. 'Never mind,' I say, pushing aside these thoughts. I open up my notebook. Flynn moves an arm around my shoulder. 'Okay, so here's my list.' I point to the list Flynn made for me under FIELD PREPARATION. *Mowing. Tilling. Compost.* 'We can't do it manually though, so we'll need to figure out how to hire the equipment we need.'

Flynn closes the book with his free hand. 'You're adorable,' he says.

I roll my eyes. 'You're trying too hard,' I reply, teasing him.

'Even more adorable.'

'Get to the point,' I say, tilting my head in amusement.

He laughs. 'Well, I don't think that a wagon and a wheelbarrow are quite going to cut it,' he says playfully. 'Not if we're going to get serious about this.' He looks out towards his property. 'I think it's time I introduce you to Polly.'

'Polly?'

'One of the most amazing women I know.' He nods towards a red tractor in the distance, parked right outside the barn on his property next door.

'Now that's an expectation to live up to.'

'She's all ready to go,' he says, pulling a set of keys out of his pocket. 'Borrowed her from a friend. Come on,' he says, nodding towards his place. 'I'll race you there.'

Polly does an almost perfect job of mowing down the spent sweet peas.

'You're a pro,' he says through his teeth. He's chewing on a piece of dry grass. I turn my head to give him a smile and he leans over and grabs hold of the steering wheel. 'Whoa there! Eyes on the patch, yeah?'

I laugh and push away his hand. 'What do we do after this?'

'We move onto the next field,' he replies, pointing to the field reserved for the dahlias.

'This is fun,' I say, over the loud thrum of the tractor.

'Knew you'd love it,' says Flynn, moving his hand onto the wheel to steady it as we make our way into the next field. Polly makes her way through them all, until the vibrant green layer of grass is stripped from the earth, and the fertile soil below becomes exposed. I turn off the ignition. Flynn jumps out the side of the tractor and extends a hand to help me down.

'We did it,' he says, a satisfied look on his face.

'Yep,' I reply, wiping my sweaty hands on my jeans. 'We're one step closer to where we need to be. Should we measure out the spaces for the weed mats?'

Flynn takes a long sip of water. 'No, I think we should call it a day and have something to eat. I'm starving.'

'Oh, of course. Sorry, I shouldn't expect you to stay back and help with that, too.' Flynn's standing there with a smirk on his face, as if he's waiting for something, so I feel like I have to continue. 'Thanks. For today. For helping me work out what we need to do here. It's … nice of you. To be here for me.'

'You done? Can we go eat now?'

'We?'

'Uh, yeah. I already told you I'm starving.'

'Well, I've still got a lot of work to do. I'm guessing I can fit in half an hour before it starts to get dark.' I toss him the keys to Polly. He lifts one hand and catches them without looking away from me.

He takes a step forward and wraps an arm around my waist. He smiles as he leans forward to kiss me. 'I'm heading home for a shower. I'll come past later.' He lets go of me and starts to walk away, an irresistible smirk on his face.

'Okay, so … I guess I'll see you round,' I say. I glance over my shoulder at him. 'Tonight, after my long, hot shower.'

Now I'm the one smirking, and blushing, and trying to stifle back a laugh. I throw my head back and look up at the pink sky that seems to stretch forever.

The sky is blushing too.

Flynn's timing is impeccable, arriving as I step out of the shower, which turned out to be more of a quick dash under the water before it even had a proper chance to heat up. I'd become sidetracked in the kitchen.

'Let yourself in!' I call. I wrap myself in a towel and pull the shower cap off my head, my hair falling down my shoulders.

'Are you cooking something?' he calls. 'I can smell something—is that smoke?'

'Oh my God!' I call, racing out of the bathroom. I've completely forgotten about the roast I had in the oven. Water trails behind me and onto the floorboards as I patter into the kitchen, almost slipping as I race towards the oven. Flynn reaches out a hand to steady me.

The roast is already on the sink, plumes of smoke emanating from the charred block of meat. I stand there, staring at it, stunned.

'Oops,' I mouth, cringing as I turn to look at Flynn. And that's when I notice that my towel has slipped and Flynn is staring at the naked flesh of my thigh that has become exposed. His hand is still on my upper arm.

'I think this is more proof that I really am a terrible cook.'

'Looks that way,' he says, releasing his grip. His eyes are still on my naked thigh. I pull my towel across to cover the bare flesh, and blink at him.

'So, uh, should we order in?' I say sheepishly.

'No need,' he says coolly.

'Honey on toast?' I shrug.

Flynn chuckles. 'Sounds perfect.'

I go to move forward, but Flynn's standing in front of me. I move right as he moves left, and we bump into each other. Heat rises to my cheeks.

'Oops, sorry,' he says. Now his body is so close to mine, I can smell the mint on his breath and the scent of his aftershave— a fresh, sharp, masculine blend which is impossibly distracting, despite the acrid scent of smoke in the kitchen.

I gaze up at him, as he dips his head slowly, moving closer to kiss me, his hand skimming over the naked flesh of my back. I might have just got out of the shower, but my body has no trouble keeping warm. Everything tingles as Flynn's kiss ignites something in me, and before I know it I'm returning the kiss. He pulls away slowly and smiles lazily at me. My hands grip the towel in front of my chest. 'I really should get changed,' I whisper.

'Or not,' he whispers back. He cups the back of my head with one hand, his fingers trailing through my hair, as his other travels to my hands, which are still gripping the towel. He gently pries my fingers away, one by one, without releasing me from his embrace. His mouth presses against mine more firmly as the towel drops to the floor, exposing me completely. My heart is hammering in my chest and I'm almost out of breath. I tear myself away, a gasp escaping me.

'I don't think it's right to do this ...'

'Shh,' he whispers, guiding my hands to the hem of his t-shirt. 'I promise you it'll be okay.' With his hands over mine, he guides it up over his head, exposing his torso.

'But I think—'

He takes my hands again and this time wraps them around his neck. 'You think too much. Don't think.' He kisses my neck, slowly, purposefully. I inhale deeply, a series of staccato breaths. As much as I want this, I can't seem to find a way to relax.

'You're still thinking,' he murmurs.

I flick my eyes open and laugh nervously, my brow creasing slightly. 'Sorry, I just …'

'Close your eyes.'

I close my eyes, and surrender to the anticipation and excitement. Our lips meet again. Flynn's tongue searches for mine, and I'm suddenly weak at the knees, all thoughts and doubts falling away entirely.

'Hold on,' he says, lifting me up in one quick motion. My legs wrap around his waist. 'Do you trust me?'

I open my eyes and nod. My heart feels like it might explode. Flynn smiles back, his eyes looking at me in a way that makes it impossible to not bring my lips back to his.

Yes, I trust you. I totally, utterly, completely trust you. But not only that. I think I love you.

Morning comes too soon, light streaming through the shutters in the bedroom, nudging me awake. My body is enveloped by another's, which doesn't belong to my fiancé. I blink my eyes into focus as my cheek rests against Flynn's naked chest. I lie there, savouring the moment, watching the rise and fall as my hands lightly skim the bare skin of his torso. He stirs gently and rolls his body to face mine as his hand glides over the curves of my waist. I resist the urge to nestle my body closer to his and instead, I wait a minute or so before wriggling away. Taking a deep breath, I sit on the edge of the bed, pulling the sheets over me. Blake's t-shirt is lying on the floor beside Flynn's jeans. I bend over and pick it up, bringing it to my face, feeling the softness of the cotton against my skin. 'I'm sorry,' I whisper. 'I'm so, so sorry.'

Flynn starts to stir.

'Gracie?' he says, sitting up. I glance over my shoulder at him, unable to hide the streaks of tears that are gliding down my face. His eyes travel to the t-shirt I'm holding in my hand. It hangs limply, void of life force.

Flynn rubs his temples and runs a hand through his messy hair. He stands up and pulls on a pair of boxer shorts.

I close my eyes, feeling the sting of tears. I hang my head, taking a moment to think of something to say. But what is there to say?

'I'm sorry. I thought I'd feel differently, I thought I'd be able to give you and I a chance, but I don't know if I can.'

Flynn sits down beside me and brushes the loose strands away from my face.

'Do you feel anything for him?' asks Flynn, pinning me with his gaze.

I feel myself grimacing. 'No,' I say.

'Okay,' he says, reaching for my hand. He strokes my face. 'Do you feel anything for me?'

I try to hold back the swell of emotions. 'Yes. I do. But I …' I take a deep breath. The only way I can make peace with this is if I tell Blake the truth, hoping that somehow he'll find a way to understand.

'I think it might be better if we put things on hold … until I get a chance to speak to him. I don't think this is fair on you, either.'

He places a finger against my lips. 'You don't need to feel bad about this—or us. Let's enjoy this while we can. So, no thinking this morning. Just …' He plants a kiss on my mouth. 'Relax.' He smiles. 'Okay?'

I take a deep breath, feeling the weight of his body against mine as he guides me back onto the bed. I nod. 'Okay,' I say. 'I totally want to relax with you this morning.'

His mouth twists into a satisfied grin. 'Good,' he says, lifting the quilt over our heads. 'Because I'm totally not in the mood for a run this morning.'

TWENTY-TWO

Mason is stepping me through the entire process of what's going to be involved in bringing the farm back to life. He gives me a quote on the irrigation system, at which I gasp and try not to appear as shocked as I actually am.

Then there are the smaller expenses, but expenses nonetheless. Like the buckets, and flower conditioners, and paper sleeves, wires, tools and twine. Those items alone total several hundred dollars. After I dip into my savings, I won't have much left for living expenses.

We reach the barn, where we gather to discuss the first supplies. I take a deep breath and reel off my order: 'Five hundred dahlia tubers, three hundred gladioli corms and a variety of seeds—California poppies, zinnias …' I finish relaying it, snap my notebook shut and smile nervously at Mason, who tucks his pen behind his ear and tells me he'll deliver the seeds and raising mix later today so I can start propagating them, and will arrange a truck to deliver the tubers and corms in a few weeks. In the meantime, Flynn, Charlie and I will need to prepare the fields so they're ready for planting.

Mason hands me a copy of the order form before leaving. He drives away, his truck rattling down the driveway as I lean against the barn door and wonder: *How on earth am I going to pay for them?*

On the day I'm supposed to be getting married, I oversleep. Rolling out of bed feels like too much hard work, so I lay there for several minutes, tucked under the sheets, staring out of the bedroom window, light streaming through the slits in the shutters. It bounces off the walls, casting tiny rainbows on the ceiling. Over the past three weeks, Summerhill has undergone a transformation. Thanks to Flynn and Charlie, the majority of the flower beds are prepared, the soil is conditioned and the barn is filled with masses of seedlings all waiting to be planted out.

I shower and dress and make my way into the kitchen when the phone rings. It's Scarlett, calling to check on me.

'I'm fine,' I tell her, not really sure of what else there is to say. I don't really want to broach the topic of Flynn with her. 'How are you? All okay with the pregnancy?' I ask, as I place two slices of bread in the toaster.

Scarlett rambles on about already suffering from interrupted sleep due to bathroom visits, her ever-expanding waistline and the condition of her hair and skin, but my attention is focused on the mailman outside, who's carrying a delivery of flowers. I open the front door before he has the chance to knock.

'Delivery for Gracie Ashcroft,' he says, handing me the bunch and pulling out a consignment note. I sign for the delivery and bring the flowers inside, where I set them on the kitchen table.

'Gracie, are you there, did you even hear a word I said?' asks Scarlett, still on the phone.

'Uh, yeah, pregnancy sounds like it's treating you well,' I say, tugging at the card that's wedged between the cream and soft-pink roses—David Austins—that are emitting the loveliest scent into the room. Wedgwoods or alnwicks? I press my nose to one of the cupped blooms. *Heavenly.* Definitely alnwicks with those delicious raspberry notes.

'I just told you I don't want any more children if I have to go through any of this again.'

I stifle a laugh. 'Sorry, it's just that a delivery arrived for me.'

'Let me guess—bulbs and seeds.'

'Nope,' I reply, pulling the card from the envelope. 'Flowers from Blake.'

Goosebumps appear on my skin, but I try to ignore the prickly sensation, listening to Scarlett's reassuring words about how all the gardening I'm doing will be a great distraction for me.

We say our goodbyes and I turn my attention to the stove and watch the butter coat itself across the frying pan, the scent of animal fat infiltrating the kitchen. I crack two eggs and watch them turn white, before flipping them onto a plate. I open the note. The eggs grow cold as I begin to read.

Dear Gracie,

Today's going to be a hard day—at least it will be for me.

I've been doing some thinking, and I want you to know a few things. I spoke to Scarlett the other week after she visited for the weekend and she told me how you were feeling. The last thing I want you to feel is guilt. None of what happened is your fault. I know it must be hard for you to feel anything for me except a sense of obligation to feel something for me. So, I've been thinking … how about we make a deal? For the time being, trust yourself enough to see where life takes you. I'm going to stop writing for a little while, until you can figure out where you want life to lead you.

However you end up spending today, know that every-thing is going to work itself out. It always does.

Love,

Blake

If Scarlett has been talking to Blake, she obviously hasn't mentioned anything about my *friendship* with Flynn. I fold his note and tuck it back into the envelope.

I'm scraping my cold breakfast into the bin when there's a knock on the door. It's Flynn. I know this because I recognise the way he knocks.

'Come in,' I call.

'Hey there,' he says softly, joining me in the kitchen.

'Hey,' I reply, glancing over my shoulder at him. He looks tired this morning. He hasn't shaved, and he's wearing the same shirt he had on last night.

'Hard night?' I ask, frowning at his dishevelled state.

He offers me a warm smile, but it doesn't light up his face in the way it usually does.

'You don't look so crash hot yourself,' he says.

I run my hands through my hair, trying to tame it. 'Gee, thanks. You really know how to make a girl feel like a million dollars. Want a juice?'

'You still look like a million dollars,' he says, his voice low. He looks at me so intensely, and holds my gaze until I have to lower my eyelids. 'You're always beautiful to me.'

The way he says it makes me want to burst into tears. 'Today is supposed to be my wedding day,' I blurt.

Flynn glances at the flowers on the table and gives a small nod that lets me know he understands.

He pulls me into his arms and I can't help throwing my arms around him, too. He holds me close, before delivering a kiss on the top of my head, where his face remains, nuzzled into my messy, uncombed hair.

'I know it's hard,' he whispers. 'I'm sorry this is so hard on you.'

'I wish things weren't like this. It's not fair on you,' I say, my words muffled against his chest.

'Don't worry about that right now. You don't need to worry about me.'

I pull myself away from him.

'I'm thinking that today's the kind of day you want to spend wallowing in the hurt so that you can get up tomorrow and face the day,' he says.

I nod, and bite my lip, swallowing back more tears. As strange as this entire situation is, I'm grateful that Flynn gets it.

'So, instead of laying those last weed mats out there, maybe we should stay in, watch movies and eat chocolate?'

I start laughing through my tears. 'I don't even know what my favourite movie is.'

'Does it even matter?'

'It matters to me. I don't know what I would have wanted before the accident. How do I know if the choices I'm making today are the right ones?'

'Don't you feel like things are right when you're out there in the field? I can see it the moment the sunlight hits your face—you're there, in your element. It's like you're a totally different person.'

'Compared to?'

'Who you were.'

'But you don't know who I was.'

'All I know is that whatever you're doing here is making you happy. It doesn't take a genius to see that.'

'What if I was happier before?'

'Does it matter if you were? Doesn't it only matter if you're happy now? This is your life now, isn't it?'

Maybe Flynn's right. Maybe the past is the past and the only thing that matters is the life I'm creating for myself today.

He takes a long sip of juice before setting down his glass. 'I'm going to find some DVDs.'

'Jerry Lewis,' I blurt.

He turns around and narrows his eyes. 'What did you say?'

'*The Bellboy*.'

He cocks his head, looking curiously at me, an expression of amusement on his face.

'My favourite movie … is *The Bellboy*.' I have no idea how I know this, but I can't help grinning at this random fact.

He lifts his eyebrows and grins at me. '*The Bellboy* it is, then.'

Flynn comes back an hour later with not one Jerry Lewis film, but what seems like an entire collection. He lets himself inside, carrying the stack of DVDs in the crook of his arm, balancing precariously on top of each other, keeping them in place with his chin.

'Did you bring chocolate?' I ask, reaching for the paper bag he's holding. He lifts it up out of my reach.

'Oh, come on. You can't do that. What did you get?' I reach for the bag again.

The DVDs tumble to the floor. I raise my eyebrows and mouth 'sorry' before laughing. We both crouch down to pick them up, bumping heads on the way, which makes me laugh even harder. We gather the DVDs, before leaning back into the comfortable folds of the sofa. Flynn's hand reaches into the bag to pull out a chocolate bar, which he hands to me without dropping his focus from the movie. I snatch it up and open it.

'Don't forget to share,' he murmurs.

I break the chocolate in half and hand him the larger portion. He looks down, opens his palm, grabs mine and swaps them.

'I can't make you happy today, but I can let you have the biggest piece.'

He slides an arm around me and draws me closer to him. I watch the rest of the movie nestled against him, chocolate melting in my mouth, mourning the wedding that never happened in what couldn't be a more unexpected way.

TWENTY-THREE

'I get you all set up and then you drop off the face of the earth!' says Tilly, nudging past me with a bucket of flowers in hand. She rests it on her cart and places her hands on her waist. 'Well, then?' she says, demanding answers.

'I've been busy,' I say, following her behind the cart. 'You should see the fields, Tilly, we've been working crazy hours getting them prepped. I've pinched out the tops of the sweet peas and they'll be ready to plant out in the field in no time.'

An array of colourful ribbons is lined up on a wooden dowel, positioned underneath the roof of the cart like a horizontal rainbow. She starts pulling a length of cherry-red grosgrain from a roll. She hands me a pair of scissors.

'Snip,' she commands, pointing at the place where I need to sever.

I do as I'm told and help her arrange the flowers she has with her today into single bouquets.

'You haven't seen busy,' she scoffs. 'You wait and see come harvest time.'

'That's actually one of the reasons I wanted to see you,' I say. I tie the ribbon into a bow and lift up the flower arrangement, adjusting the stems before handing it to her. 'I'd like some training, you see. In arranging. I've got a few customers already, and I need to know how to work with the flowers—how to cut and condition them, the best way to store them, what fillers to use …'

'Fine,' she says. 'We'll meet twice a week, every Tuesday and every Friday afternoon until harvest. But I don't think you'll need me as much as you think you will.'

Summerhill is almost ready for planting. We've tilled in all the rows, amended the soil with compost, and laid down irrigation lines. While Flynn finishes setting down the last weed mats, I'm trying my hand at brewing a different kind of tea—compost tea.

My boots squelch into the ground as I haul the last two buckets of water to the barrel Charlie has provided for me. The nearest tap isn't as close as what we need it to be, and I grumble under my breath when I almost trip and lose some of the contents of one of my buckets. Now that the barrel is full, it's time for me to add the compost. Having an ongoing supply of organic matter to feed the soil is going to be crucial to keep our farming sustainable, the plants healthy, and costs down, so we've started a heap in the corner, too, the less-than-glamorous but essential part of farming. Charlie hands me a shovel and raises his eyebrows. 'And now comes the fun part,' he says as he drives his shovel into the heap. He tips the contents of the shovel into the barrel and that's when I know I shouldn't have been standing so close. The water hits my face and I suck in a breath, half shocked, but mostly disgusted. Charlie lets out a roar of laughter as I go to wipe my eyes and then my face. I look down at my top, the murky liquid seeping through the fabric of my red checked shirt.

If only Scarlett could see me now.

'I'm sorry, love,' he says, trying to hold back his laughter.

I try to appear annoyed and fail. I burst out laughing too, until tears run down my face and my belly starts to ache.

'I haven't laughed like this in … well … I'm not sure. But that doesn't matter.' Grabbing my shovel, I scoop up some manure and heap it into the barrel. 'And I thought this job was just going to be about pretty flowers and happy clients,' I mutter, shaking my head.

'It's good to see you smiling, love,' says Charlie.

I consider his words. Is that the way Charlie sees me? Overly serious? Unhappy?

'I've been doing a lot of that lately. And I intend on doing a lot more. Everything here—everything I have in my life right now, makes me very, very happy.'

He smiles back warmly. 'As life should be.' He lifts his shovel. 'I'd take a step back now if I were you.'

We both start laughing again, just as Flynn approaches us. 'Looks like I'm missing out on all the fun,' he says, wrapping an arm around my shoulder. 'You don't smell so good,' he says, peering at my clothes. 'What's that in your hair?' he asks, furrowing his brow. 'Don't tell me …'

'Mmm-hmm,' I reply, nodding. 'It's exactly what you think it is. Still find me as attractive as you did this morning?'

I rise up on my toes to kiss him.

'Oh no you don't,' he says, right before my lips meet his.

I press gently against him. 'Oh yes, I do.'

Every muscle in my body aches, or at least it feels that way by the time Flynn and I finish up in the fields. I arch my back and stretch up to the sky, a gelato of varying shades of blue. We've spent the last few hours making some final adjustments to the sweet-pea beds: driving in stakes, fitting in the netting, and ascertaining the best way to tackle the problem of windbreaks, given the fields here are mostly bare of any trees or hedges. I circle my shoulders and reach for the hammer, driving in the last stake before calling it a day.

'All ready for planting out now,' I say, wiping the beads of perspiration from my brow.

Flynn licks his thumb and rubs my cheek. 'You've got some dirt ...' He pokes out his tongue. 'Right here,' he says. I gaze upwards at the same time he gazes down at me. Before I can blink, his lips are on mine.

'That was ... unexpected,' I say, trying to centre myself.

'Was it?' he asks quietly. 'I could do it again, if you like.' He smiles to himself before turning over a crate for each of us to sit on.

'I think this deserves a beer.'

'The kiss?' he says, laughing.

I roll my eyes as I start pulling off my gloves, my clammy fingers exposed to the cool air.

'You know, Summerhill really does feel like home to me, now.'

'That's good,' he says, wiping his hands on his jeans.

'And since I feel this way, maybe I should go see Blake. I mean, sooner or later I'm going to need to face him, right?

Sooner or later my memory is either going to come back, or it isn't, but at some point I'm going to need to see him, aren't I? Especially if we—'

'Is that what you want?' asks Flynn in an even tone, which is so straight to the point it takes me by surprise.

'I think it's what I should do, and maybe that's the *right* thing to do.'

'But is it what you *want* to do?' He looks straight-faced at me.

I stare blankly back at him and shrug. 'Forget it,' I whisper, regretting my decision to bring it up in the first place. I know it can't be easy for Flynn to hear me talking about Blake like this.

'Once you've decided, let me know.' He walks right past me and heads out of the barn. I follow him, but he's quick to jump onto Polly. He turns on the ignition before throwing me a look that tells me I shouldn't call after him or follow him.

'I'm sorry, but I told you things aren't straightforward. This is exactly why—'

'I understand where you're at, Gracie. I don't blame you for any of it, and I know this is hard.'

'You don't have to go. Stay and we'll talk. Figure out a way for me to right this.'

'I don't really feel like talking about this at the moment. I've got some things I need to sort out.'

'Things? What kinds of things?' I say, frowning.

He clenches his jaw. 'I don't want to lose you.'

He moves the tractor into gear and I'm left watching the wheels turn over the murky path.

'But maybe I'm not really yours to lose,' I whisper.

I'm sure he hasn't heard me over the hum of the motor, and then I think to myself that maybe that's a relief, because deep down, I'm thinking the most honest thought of all. I'm thinking that I wish I was.

TWENTY-FOUR

After Flynn left yesterday, I didn't see him for the rest of the day. That didn't stop me thinking about him, or Blake, or how I really should consider confronting Blake. What would I say? 'Sorry, but we need to call off whatever we had because I think I'm falling in love with another man?' Scarlett had warned me that the way I wanted to go about things wasn't exactly what she considered the 'right way'. After all, it would have made more sense for me to stay, meet him, assess my feelings and *then* leave. But what's done is done and now I'm going to need to face the consequences of my decision.

Deciding that I owe him some degree of honesty, I write him a letter, the last letter I'll write until I finally muster up the courage to face him.

Dear Blake,
  I couldn't sleep last night and it wasn't because I was thinking about the accident, or my life before. It was

because I was thinking of the road ahead. I love it here in Summerhill. I wish I could describe to you how much I love it. It's like life is at my fingertips, like I'm about to witness the world come to life with every growing flower.

I don't know how to make this any easier for you, but I'll come to see you soon and that's when I'll explain everything.

Gracie

I fold the letter and place it in the back pocket of my jeans before heading out to the field to meet Flynn. I place two straws into a couple of mason jars where fresh lemonade bubbles away, and place them on a tray. With my spare hand, I grab my hat and pull the door closed behind me. Although it's crisp outside, the sun's out. It blurs my vision, but I don't have a free hand to shield my eyes so I squint, trying to work out where Flynn is.

'Hey! Over here,' he calls, as I approach the field. Flynn's standing there, shirtless, and several feet in front of him is the newly constructed frame of a hoop house.

'What's this?' I say, surprised. A polytunnel will make all the difference to our blooming windows, allowing me to extend the growing seasons. If Flynn's still upset about yesterday, he's definitely not showing it today.

'A hoop house,' he says, grinning. He tucks a screwdriver into his back pocket.

'I know what it is, but … you're building this for me?' I ask, still holding onto the tray. The glasses wobble as I set them down on the wagon. 'I don't have the money to—'

'It's taken care of. This is going to make life a lot easier for you, and I figured you deserved life to be a little bit easier for you right now. I know how much all of this means to you.'

'I'm glad you came into my life,' I say, looking down at my feet. 'I don't know why you did, or why things are turning out this way, but I'm glad you're here.'

Flynn wipes his face with his discarded shirt. 'I want you to know that I'm really sorry about yesterday, and I want to be able to right this.'

'Really, this isn't your fault. If anyone's to blame for this entire situation, it's me. I'm the one who's complicating things, not you.'

'I know we've been working really hard, but I'm going to find the time to go see him before the peony harvest,' I say decidedly.

He bites his lip. 'Okay,' he murmurs, nodding.

'So, we have a bit more time—to see if what we have is … worth risking everything else for.'

Flynn swallows hard. 'You're worth the risk.'

Now that everything is prepped, the gladioli are ready for planting. Flynn and I are in the barn, sipping on cider while Flynn's trying to figure out the quickest way for us to plant the hundreds of corms that are on tomorrow's list of things to do. I'm poring over a mail-order catalogue lusting over the ranunculi, those quirky long-stemmed flowers that sit upright but not stiffly, delicate like poppies and beautifully cupped like roses. I'd chosen the double-bloom varieties in a range of pastel colours, thinking they'd be more popular with brides, thanks to Tilly's sage advice. I've been meeting her twice weekly, learning how to handle flowers, create posies and garlands and centrepieces. She has taught me to always have a rose-thorn stripper handy, to always snip stems on an angle, and to always keep harmony and balance in mind. When I'm with her and with the flowers, time seems to stand still and I always go home feeling like my heart is open a little wider. Yesterday, I came home with two things. A bouquet of roses and gerberas, and a flower crown, which I'd somehow remembered how to make without Tilly showing me. I was so delighted with the outcome, I brought home fresh flowers to experiment with that evening. Now, I have four crowns on the barn workbench that could do with finding someone to wear them.

I try one on for size.

'How do I look?' I say, turning to Flynn.

He doesn't hear me. He's got a pensive look on his face as he sorts through the crates. I pretend to cough to catch his attention. He looks up at me, caught off guard for a second as he blinks musingly at me.

'What's the matter?'

'Nothing,' he replies. 'You just reminded me of something.'

'Is that a good thing?' I ask, fiddling with the crown.

He sets down his cider on the bench and approaches me. He steals a kiss, pressing his tangy lips against mine. I close my eyes and let my hands run through the hair on the back of his head. He deepens the kiss before lifting me onto the bench.

'We've got work to do today,' I whisper, my lips pressed against his ear.

'Mmm-hmm,' he replies.

'And that's exactly why we can't waste any more time,' I say, pulling away. I place my hands on Flynn's chest and wriggle off the bench. 'I was thinking you might like to read to me tonight, though.' I reach for my tool belt. 'That's if you're not busy. I could use a hand falling asleep.'

'Only if I get to choose the book.'

'Okay,' I say, raising my eyebrows. 'I'll let you choose the book, as long as you bring the chocolate.'

He laughs. 'Done.'

The gladdie corms resemble little onions. It's hard to believe that in ninety days, hundreds of these will be brightening up the farm in a spray of pink, cream and peach.

'Ready to go?' asks Flynn, carrying a crate load of corms. A rush of excitement fills me as he sets them down on one of the wagons.

We place the corms into each of the tilled rows, one by one, around fifteen centimetres apart. As each row fills with the promise of beauty, of life, of nature's precious blessings, a sense of peace overcomes me. Any worries I've had about the past or the future, of my memory returning or not, seem insignificant now, as if none of it really matters at all. I breathe in the crisp air, feeling the sun caress my skin, enveloping me into a sense of belonging.

Flynn and I work at this for another hour, until we decide to take a rest. He helps me up, my knees stiff and my back feeling even stiffer. I stretch myself out, trying to relieve the tightness in my body.

'Almost done,' says Flynn, assessing things.

'We're only a quarter way through,' I say, feeling a little discouraged.

'Well, it's a big field,' he replies.

'We should keep going,' I say, pulling at the handle of the wagon.

Flynn reaches for my arm. 'You don't want to burn out.'

'I'm fine,' I reply.

Flynn keeps his eyes trained on me.

'Seriously, I'm fine. I just want to get this done.'

'Fine,' says Flynn, adjusting his hat. 'Another hour and then we'll break.'

We end up working way longer than an hour. It's late afternoon by the time we drop the last corm into the ground. I hobble to the wagon and unfasten my tool belt, depositing it in there. Flynn slides his arms around my waist and rests his head against my forehead.

'I don't think you'll need me to read to you tonight,' he says, smiling. 'So maybe I'll just tuck you in and kiss you goodnight.'

'Sounds like a plan.'

He lifts me up and hauls me over his shoulder. I squeal, kicking my legs, but he doesn't let go. We reach the bottom of the hill, my stomach aching from laughter, and the pain in my back not as apparent as it was before.

Inside, I rinse my face, wash my hands and head into the living room, where Flynn is standing, two steaming cups in hand. He hands me a hot chocolate and in one long exhale, my body sags into the sofa. I drink the delicious liquid and he drinks his, and when I wake up there's a blanket tucked around me, and Flynn is nowhere to be seen. But I really wish he wasn't gone.

TWENTY-FIVE

Flynn and I spend the next week planting and sowing seeds from the early hours of the morning when the sun isn't yet stretched across the sky, to the late afternoons when the breeze flirts with us, numbing our fingers and pinching our cheeks. Charlie has been coming to help twice a week with jobs like weeding, general maintenance and the odd errand.

We're dropping in the last dahlia tubers today. Soon I'll have to start thinking about how I'm actually going to sell these flowers once they bloom.

Mason was right about the dahlia tubers needing to be dug out, so we'll see what comes of the crop that's been left to overwinter, hoping at least some of it will be commercially viable. Once autumn arrives, it'll take around two months to dig up all the tubers, hose them down, separate and dry them, and finally pack them into crates for the winter for replanting again next spring.

I've resorted to keeping track of everything on the random sheets of butcher's paper plastered on the barn walls, a place that is in desperate need of organisation before the first flush of flowers. Flynn was right. All of this is a huge job and even though I won't admit it, I'm starting to get tired.

I place another dahlia tuber into the soil and close my eyes, feeling the intense ache travel up my back to my shoulders.

'You okay?' asks Flynn, creasing his brow. He wipes his hands on his jeans and walks over to me.

'I'm fine.' I wipe the perspiration from my forehead and bring myself to stand. 'How are we going to manage to get this all done?' I say, letting out an enormous sigh as I rub my lower back. My eyes hone in on the row of fertile soil that stretches to the edge of the field and looks like it extends for kilometres.

'Have a rest,' says Flynn, guiding me to the two wooden stools we'd set up under an umbrella. He twists open a bottle of water for me and sits beside me.

'I can't afford to have a rest. Look at this!' I say, pointing at the crates filled with hundreds of the tubers we still need to plant.

'We've been up since five o'clock this morning, we've taken only two short breaks, you barely ate a thing at lunch, and we've been going at it like this for weeks. You're tired.'

Flynn keeps his eyes trained on mine.

I lower my voice. 'All right. You win. I am tired.'

'Okay, that's it,' says Flynn, springing up from his chair. He pulls off his gloves and tosses them into one of the barrows. He winks at me. 'We're taking the rest of the afternoon off. Let's go.' He extends a hand and pulls me up from the stool.

'We can't, Flynn, there's too much to do.'

'Exactly, so no burning out now.'

I hesitate. 'But …'

'We'll get it all done in time, I promise,' he says, reassuring me. 'You watch. It'll all come together.'

'How can you be so sure?'

He shrugs. 'Because it has to.'

Flynn and I are sitting together on the small patch of grass under the willow tree, my fingers curled around a bottle of ginger beer as I leaf through my notebook.

'This really is the best thinking spot ever,' I say, squinting at the sky through the canopy of green leaves above us. 'We should take afternoons off more often,' I joke. I inhale deeply, feeling the muscles in my body relax.

'Yep,' agrees Flynn.

'I think I'm ready,' I murmur, gazing up at him. He's sitting with his back against the tree, and I'm leaning against his body, his arms around me.

'What for?'

'For Scarlett to tell me a bit more about my life before. I think it'll be easier for us both—if I start to understand who I was. Now that I know who I am at this moment, I think I'm finally ready to know more.'

Flynn's body stiffens. He shifts his weight back. I turn my body to face him.

'I'm happy with my life. I've found myself and this is my life now, irrespective of who I was or what I was doing before. You have nothing to worry about. I've made my decision—about Blake, and I know this will hurt him, but … I can't help the way I feel about you.' I place my hands on his cheeks. 'I think I want you to read me to sleep every night,' I say, smiling at him.

'If that's what keeps you happy, I'd say that's completely doable,' he replies, stroking my hair.

'Well, actually, I've been meaning to tell you that I think I'm … I think I finally know what it feels like to be in love.' I lean forward to kiss him, when he places his hands on mine and moves them away.

'Gracie, there's something I should talk to you about …' he whispers. 'About you not remembering part of your life before. I know you're aware that you could …'

I reach across and put a finger to his mouth. 'Shhh. I know I could wake up tomorrow remembering things. But don't ruin it. Don't ruin the moment.'

His arm slips around me, pulling my body closer to his.

'Because I was just about to tell you, I love you.'

There are at least one hundred seed packets sprawled out on the barn bench: larkspur, lupins, zinnias and snapdragons. I'm trying to squeeze in as many varieties of cut flowers as possible to fit on every spare inch of the land we can manage to utilise. I've been selective with the seeds I've chosen, opting for some of the rarer varieties of blooms. With any luck, my investment will pay off. Not only will I be selling the freshest and most locally grown blooms in the area, as opposed to flowers that often are imported, but I'll be selling varieties that not everybody will be able to easily get their hands on. If all goes to plan, we should see a delicious bounty of colour pop in the field beginning with the peonies next month. We've already seen the first flush of roses, which Tilly has gladly taken off my hands.

The sweet-pea seedlings I'd started in trays weeks ago are coming along nicely, and are ready for planting out in the field. Flynn enters the barn with a couple of bottles of cider, which he pops open. He presses a finger against my nose, winks and hands me a bottle before clinking it against mine. 'These ready to go?' he says, motioning to one of the plastic trays.

'Yep, all set.'

He smiles and flashes me a wink before starting to line them up in the wagons.

'We're really doing it,' I say in wonder. With almost everything done to prepare the fields, I can't help feeling excited about the possibilities.

Flynn reaches for my hand, the warm clasp of his fingers intertwining through mine.

'Told you we'd get it all done,' he says. 'And now, we wait to see what blooms.'

Two days later, Flynn leads me into the barn with his hands over my eyes. 'No peeking,' he says, whispering into my ear. I place my hands over his when we stop walking and he pulls his hands away. I open my eyes and gasp.

Flynn has completely transformed the barn space. Two large chalkboards are mounted on the back wall for keeping tabs on the day's work ahead, daily harvests and orders. There's a wooden sign above them: *From Seed to Centrepiece*, a business name we'd come up with together when working in the field a couple of weeks ago.

Flynn has installed a new workbench for me, as well as some practical storage spaces for buckets, floristry supplies and watering cans.

'And … wait for this—the best part of all!' He pulls down a sheet that's suspended from the ceiling to reveal an enormous refrigerator.

'No way!' I say, bringing my hands to my mouth. 'I can't believe you did this. I was only gone a few hours yesterday. Did you do this while I was at Tilly's?'

He nods. 'You deserve it.'

Another letter arrived from the bank two days ago. I'd spent over an hour on the phone yesterday trying to convince the manager to extend the due date of the repayments since the bill for the seedlings, tubers and bulbs arrived that morning. As kind as Flynn's gesture is, there's no way I can accept this from him as a gift.

'I'll need to cover your expenses. Leave the receipts for me and I'll—'

'No need,' he says, interrupting me.

'But …'

He steps closer to me. 'Seriously. No need.'

'Thanks, but for the record I plan on paying you back every cent. Wait until I tell Scarlett about this. I can't wait to show her everything we've been doing.'

'Show her?'

'Yeah, I'm going to invite her over. She's due to have the baby next month, so I should probably get onto that sooner rather than later.' Ever since she came to visit, Scarlett and I seem to skim the topic of Blake (or Flynn), but I get the impression she thinks I'll come home for good soon. I don't blame her—I haven't exactly told her about the extent of my work here on the farm.

Flynn stacks a few buckets on top of each other and carries them over to the corner where the others are.

'Flynn? Did you hear me?'

He looks up. 'Oh, yeah. Scarlett. Can't wait to see her.'

I frown, sensing something's off. 'You seem distracted.'

'I forgot to turn on the timer for the irrigation,' he says. He plants a soft kiss on my forehead before brushing past me.

'But I already did,' I reply, rubbing the space on my head where he just kissed me. He doesn't answer.

I follow Flynn to the fields, where he's halfway up the incline, Parrot by his side.

'Flynn!' I call. 'Wait up!'

He slows his pace before turning around. I jog up the hill and meet him.

'What's wrong?' I ask, raising a hand above my eyes to shield them from the sun.

'Nothing,' he says.

'You were acting a bit weird when I mentioned Scarlett and when she was here you—'

'Drop it, Gracie. It's nothing.' He says this with a firmness in his voice that makes me want to question him, but he's already striding up the hill again.

'Would you tell me … if there was a problem?' I ask, following him. 'Is it because Scarlett's a part of my life before? That you're worried about Blake, somehow? Is that it?'

He doesn't reply. I reach for his arm. 'Flynn,' I say, the firmness in my own voice now apparent. 'Tell me what you're thinking.'

'I told you, Gracie. There's nothing to tell you right now. Just let it go.'

'I think it's because you're worried that I might remember him. I keep saying I'm going to talk to him. Maybe I should go to Melbourne next weekend and get it over with. Would that make things easier?'

Flynn stops mid-stride to look at me. He swallows, his Adam's apple bobbing up and down. His fingers run over his mouth and over the stubble on his face. He goes to speak but holds back.

'No? Yes?' I search his eyes for answers; he gives me nothing.

Finally, Flynn shrugs.

'What is it, Flynn? Tell me what I should do. I don't want to make this harder for you.'

'I don't know what to do, Gracie. That's the problem.' He rubs his temples.

'Even if I remember him, in the near or distant future, I want you to know that I've made my decision. To be with you.'

He nods silently, not meeting my gaze. Somehow, I don't think he believes me.

TWENTY-SIX

The fields are coming to life now—the peonies have formed perfectly tight round buds, tiny ants marching over them as they enjoy a taste of nectar, the sweet peas are starting to reach for the sky, their tendrils curling around the stakes, and the buttery green tulip stems are growing taller every day. Rosebuds are forming on the David Austins surrounding the fields, and the seedlings I started in the barn have been planted out in the polytunnel under its protective cover. A few more weeks and the field will be bursting with colour. There's still no sign of my memory returning, aside from minor flashes of *knowing* things to be true and jolts of deja vu, but strangely enough, I've started drinking tea again.

Flynn's outside tinkering with Charlie's ute, whistling to old classics, oblivious to me watching him. He checks his watch and wipes his brow, and then moves to the barn, emerging a minute later with a container of oil in hand. He works on changing the oil, rubs his hands together and presses down on the bonnet before looking up towards the cottage, where I'm sitting on the bench.

Flynn wipes his hands on his jeans and joins me. 'What have you got there?' he asks, looking at the wooden box between us.

'Photos of my mother,' I reply, opening it to show him. 'Tilly gave them to me.'

Flynn's arm slips around me and I show him the photos. 'I don't remember a lot about her. But I remember enough to know she loved me and I loved her back. And I feel close to her when I'm here on the farm. The flowers remind me of her. Does that make sense?'

'It makes sense. I don't think you need to remember everything in order to know the way someone loved you.' He checks his watch. 'We should get going,' he says, beginning to stand. 'I should get cleaned up.'

We step inside the cottage and Flynn enters the bathroom while I get changed into some fresh clothes. Flynn hovers in the doorway, watching me while I try to choose a top. 'I'm going to go clothes shopping as soon as the harvest is over,' I say, lifting another top from a drawer and holding it against my body in the mirror. 'I'm going to fill the closet with pink and lemon and maybe the odd shade of navy.'

Flynn makes a point of looking at his watch again.

'Oh, I know, I know! This old thing will have to do,' I say, reaching for a green-and-black shirt. I wriggle out of my top, managing to somehow get it stuck around my head in the process, thanks to forgetting to unbutton it. 'Would you mind?' I call. A moment later, Flynn's hands are on my waist as he peers down at me through the gap between me and my shirt.

'I wouldn't mind at all,' he says, his hands on the top button of my jeans. A laugh escapes me as I try to squirm away. He lifts me up and onto the bed as I continue to try to wriggle out of my top. 'Hold still,' he says, reaching for my button. I raise my arms and he slides it up over my head. He hovers over me, greeting me with his luminous smile before leaning over and kissing me. 'We could always stay in, you know. Since I'll be in the city for the weekend, we could make tonight unforgettable, just to be sure you remember me,' he jokes. 'Would you mind looking after Parrot while I'm away?'

'Uh, yeah … sure. You're going to Melbourne this weekend, though? As in tomorrow?'

'Yeah, I thought I told you. I need to take care of some things.'

'You didn't tell me.'

I'd been planning on visiting Melbourne myself this weekend, but I decide not to bring it up, and that I'll go the following weekend. Bringing up my confrontation with Blake has been awkward enough lately. So, hopefully, by the time next weekend rolls around, the door that I want closed will close, and I can leave the past that I don't remember completely behind me.

We don't end up staying in, but we do arrive at The Old Mill much later than we'd planned to. As expected, Flynn is starving. We order a range of different plates, after which I declare that I hate the taste of rabbit, find risotto overly filling, but could eat loads of asparagus and pumpkin if you'd let me. Especially if they come in a pie. As far as dessert is concerned, I could easily pass on banoffee pie, let myself go wild over pavlova, but prefer to steer clear of anything resembling a panna cotta.

With our bellies full, and an early morning ahead of us, we loop arms and walk down the gentle curving road to the car, which we've purposely parked about a kilometre down the road.

Maybe it's the wine, or the fact that I mixed wine with cider, but as we walk to the car, I find myself thinking about Flynn and the future—our future. I've been so focused on the harvest, on getting Summerhill to the point where I can stay, that the topic of Flynn and how long he might be planning on staying here hasn't really crossed my mind until now.

'Do you plan on going?' I blurt without meaning to.

'Going where?' asks Flynn, looking strangely at me.

'Leaving Summerhill. Going back to your old life.' Now that I've started speaking, I can't seem to stop. 'You have a clinic, which you barely ever talk about, and now that the harvest is coming up, I just wondered what your plans were. Are you planning on moving back to the city?'

Flynn stops in the middle of the street and looks up at the stars. 'I don't want to leave. But I might have to.'

My breath catches in my chest. 'You're leaving?' I say, not quite sure that I've heard him properly. I didn't expect him to have this answer at the ready.

'I didn't say that. It's just that I've got a life back in Melbourne that I need to—'

'What do you mean by that? A life?'

'You know I've got a business in the city, Gracie,' he says, his voice uneven. Flynn seems unusually on edge, giving me reason to think he's given more thought to this than I have.

'Is that it? *Just* a business,' I say, the scepticism in my voice obvious.

'God, what do you think? Of course, just a business. A lease that's almost run out. Friends. Some family. But nobody else, if that's what you're wondering.'

I bite the inside of my lip. I don't know what to think. 'Then why don't any of your so-called friends or family come to visit? Aside from Olivia?'

He doesn't answer me. Instead, we both look up to the sky as the thunder rolls in, and make a run for the car.

When I wind down the window and the earthy smell infuses the car, I know the storm is going to be a bad one.

'We're going to finish that conversation,' I say, crossing my arms.

'You're looking too much into things, Gracie.'

My attention turns to the trees we're passing, that are wavering in the howling wind, bending and stretching in ways they shouldn't be. My body stiffens, bracing itself for the worst. Flynn and I never got a chance to finish setting up the windbreaks.

'I didn't check the weather report,' I say flatly.

'We'll be home by the time it hits,' says Flynn, his eyes on the road. It's pelting down now, and the wipers are struggling to keep the window clear from the wet.

'Can't you go any faster?' I ask, trying to keep my voice level.

'I can barely see what's in front of us,' he says, braking.

I let out a sigh and grip my seat, unable to think of anything but the fields.

After what feels like hours but in reality is only a few short minutes, Flynn pulls up the driveway and says, 'Hold on, I'll get an umbrella,' only it's too late. I'm already out of the car, the heavy rain splattering against me. He calls out to me, but I don't hear him properly because I'm making a run for the fields.

My jacket catches on a nail on one of the wooden posts, ripping as I forge ahead through the wind and rain. Eventually, I reach the first field of peonies. It's the sweet peas I'm mostly worried about; in this tender infant stage, they're way too fragile and in too much of an exposed position to be able to survive this kind of weather. I sprint across the field until I reach them. Stakes are down, netting dislodged. All that work … A moan escapes me and all I can do is sink to my knees, joining the flattened mess in front of me.

'No!' I call out into the night.

Nobody hears me but Flynn.

'Gracie,' he says, his hands pressing against my shoulders. He crouches down beside me, a soggy carpet of mud beneath us. 'It's going to be okay,' he says, framing my face with his hands. I can barely make out his face in the rain like this, but he pulls my body towards his, so I'm resting my cheek against his shoulder. And we sit there, in the rain, watching the world around us turn sour, until the rain relents, and all that is left is one big mess we'll have to clean up in the morning. 'Everything's going to work out,' he whispers. And despite the disaster of the evening, in that moment of being held, of feeling his heart beating against me, I want to believe him, but I don't quite know if I do.

That night, I bring myself to call Scarlett.

'Sorry to be calling so late. I couldn't sleep.' My fingers rub the neckline of Blake's t-shirt.

'Talk to me,' she says, her voice groggy.

'We've had a bad storm and I've been working on the garden lately. I think there might be a lot of damage to the flowers I've planted,' I say, without going into too much detail about the farm.

'Chin up—you can always replant things,' she replies.

'Mmm, it's more complicated than that,' I murmur.

'Something else on your mind?'

'How can you possibly know that?'

'I'm your best friend. It's my job to know that,' she says playfully.

'I'm in love with him.'

'Who are you in love with, Gracie?' she asks, sounding more awake.

'Flynn. You know—my *neighbour*.'

'Flynn?'

'The guy you met when you were here. The guy you were acting so weirdly around …'

'I know who he is,' she says, her tone serious.

'Right. Well, it felt right. Like we somehow fit together. And as annoying as he can be, there's something about him that makes me feel the way I do even if I can't pinpoint why, and I think I'm—'

'Oh my God. You're in love with him,' she repeats, disbelief apparent in her voice.

'I didn't mean for this to happen, it just did and now I'm worried that I'm going to lose him—that he plans on moving back to the city.'

'Unbelievable,' she whispers. 'This isn't right.'

A rush of panic sweeps through me. Telling Scarlett about my feelings possibly isn't the best move.

'I know, but I can't help it. When I'm with him, I feel like myself. I like being with him. *Love* being with him.'

'That's not what I mean.' She pauses. 'He's not who you think he is,' she says finally.

'What do you mean?' I say in shock as her words sink in. 'Is this why you were acting strangely around him when you were here?'

'No. I mean, yes, it's just …' She lets out a loud sigh.

'Just what, Scarlett? Who is he? Do you know him? Is that it?'

There's silence on the line.

'Where do you know him from?'

Still no answer.

'Scarlett!' I say, more assertively now. 'You know him, don't you? How do you know him?' Goosebumps spread across my arms.

'Gracie, please … just leave it.'

'Is he an ex-boyfriend? A friend of Blake's? What?'

'You should not be asking me this. I don't want to lie to you.'

'Then don't.'

'It's not my place to tell you—you're going to need to talk to your neighbour.'

A sinking feeling stirs in the pit of my stomach.

The last thing I want is to be lied to.

The spring sky is moody, mirroring the way I'm feeling about life today. Even the sky seems confused. Sunbeams poke through masses of thick clouds before disappearing, lighting up the world for a split second before fading away as the horizon darkens with strokes of smudged graphite.

'It won't be as bad as you think,' says Charlie as we make our way to the fields.

Only it is worse. It's much worse.

'What's the damage?' he asks, directing his question to Flynn, who is already in the field, stepping over the fallen stakes, trying to assess things.

'We lost half the sweet peas,' he says, shaking his head.

I stand under the umbrella in a state of disbelief, the plump drops of rain falling around us, my eyes travelling over the fallen stakes, where vines that were filled with hope are now limp and lifeless.

'We'll be able to salvage some of them,' says Flynn, noticing me. 'We'll start re-staking them today,' he says, trying to reassure me.

Charlie looks up at the sky, a palette of dark greys. 'If we're going to do it, we need to get a move on.'

The morning passes in the blink of an eye. Flynn, Charlie and I have been re-staking the damaged vines, trying to save as many plants as possible. As much as I've wanted to talk to Flynn about the conversation I had with Scarlett, Charlie's presence made that discussion impossible, until now. We're finally alone, packing things up in the barn, and at last I have the chance to broach the subject with him.

'I spoke to Scarlett last night,' I begin, as I close the barn door. 'Your name came up and she made it sound like you're hiding something from me … that you aren't who I think you are.' I am trying to sound as casual as possible, although the strain in my voice is apparent.

Flynn swallows, his jaw clenched. He holds my gaze for a heartbeat, before looking away. He fumbles with the keys in his pocket.

I stare at him, my eyes demanding answers. 'I can't possibly imagine how she'd know that. Do you?'

'I'm not ready to tell you more right now, Gracie.' He massages the stubble on his chin. 'I need to get going. I'm leaving for Melbourne in an hour and I'm already late.'

'What does that mean?' Dread anchors itself in the pit of my stomach. 'What is it you're not telling me?'

I hold my breath, waiting for an answer that doesn't come. A beat of silence passes.

'You go back to the city some weekends and sometimes during the week. What exactly do you do there?' My heart starts hammering in my chest. Something isn't right. Flynn isn't looking at me. Instead, he's completely ignoring me by staring at his shoes.

Seconds pass.

'Flynn?'

Still no response.

'Flynn,' I say, trying not to let my voice rise.

His eyes flick up at me. 'Not the right time, Gracie.' He leans in and kisses me on the cheek. 'It's nothing you need to worry about. I'll call you from the city and as soon as I get back, we'll sit down and talk.' He turns around and starts walking away.

I start following him. 'Wait! You can't just leave like this! Is there someone else? Is that it?'

I stop in my tracks, holding my breath as I wait for an answer.

'No, Gracie. There's no-one else but you.'

'Then what …' My voice fades into the distance as Flynn takes another step forward, leaving me completely dumbfounded.

The sky opens up again, and I'm left standing in the rain, breathing in the scent of something that doesn't smell quite right.

TWENTY-SEVEN

After a restless night, I try calling Flynn to no avail. His phone goes straight to voicemail. I text him in the hope he'll see my message, asking him to meet me in the afternoon at the Royal Botanic Gardens in Melbourne. Before I meet him, though, I plan on finally confronting Blake.

I call a cab, throw whatever I can into my suitcase, lock up the cottage, drop Parrot off to Charlie's, and head to the city.

From Flinders Street station, I fumble my way through Melbourne's hurried streets that thrust me into the wildest change of pace. If there's one thing I've learned since moving to Summerhill, it's that the slow pace, the way the flowers have the chance to leisurely yawn and stretch without the pressure of having to rush, is the most beautiful way to live a life. At the first sign of a cab at the far end of the street, I start waving. It stops for me, the water from the gutter spraying against me as it comes to a halt.

I tell the driver the address of the apartment, hoping I might find Blake at home. The thought of seeing him sends the most intensely nauseating feeling through me. As we make our way through streets I don't recognise, my phone rings. It's Scarlett.

'Hey there,' I respond.

'I know you're ages away, but I'm in the hospital.'

'Oh my God, are you in labour already?'

'No, but my blood pressure's through the roof, and they're saying it's pre-eclampsia. They're monitoring me and I'm waiting for the doctors to tell me whether I'll need to deliver early. I was hoping you might be able to come? I'd like you here.'

'Of course. I'm on my way.'

Scarlett gives me the details of the hospital and I hang up the phone as the cab driver comes to a stop outside the apartment.

'There's been a change of plans. Frances Perry House, please.'

At the reception desk of the hospital, I ask for directions to Scarlett's room. I pass by the kiosk, selling imported flowers that look so stiff, almost fake in how perfect looking they are, but I buy a bunch of them anyway—a spray of lisianthus that I'm almost certain won't last more than a day or two in the vase.

I take the lift to the second floor of the hospital and ask for directions at the nurse's station.

'I'm here to see Scarlett O'Conner. How is she doing?'

'We're monitoring her. The doctor should be doing another round any minute. Just head on down the hall and to your left, love,' says a nurse.

I knock on the door once before entering. There's a man sitting by her bedside, a man who from the back looks alarmingly familiar. He frames her face with his hands as he gently leans in to kiss her. Pulling away, he strokes her cheek and pulls her into an embrace.

'Gracie,' says Scarlett, noticing me as she looks up from over his shoulder. She's propped up against several pillows, tucked under a white thermal blanket over a pale-pink sheet. She looks as puffy as the pillows she's resting against, but more beautiful than ever, a curve from her enlarged belly visible from under the blanket. 'How did you get here so quickly?' She sounds as tired as she looks, but my eyes aren't on her. They're on the man who's just turned to face me. There's a wedding ring on his left hand. He lets go of Scarlett's hand and goes to stand up.

I freeze, hovering in the doorway. My legs feel shaky and I reach out for the doorframe to steady myself. This doesn't make sense.

My eyes narrow as I watch him move. I can't seem to catch my breath.

'Flynn?' I say, my voice barely audible. 'You and Scarlett? *This* is what you've been hiding from me?' He clears his throat and looks at Scarlett, whose eyes are wide open.

Hot tears fill my eyes. She was supposed to be my friend— my best friend. Our eyes lock for a second, hers filled with the deepest kind of sorrow that matches the level of hurt in mine. My eyes dart back to Flynn, where I look him up and down, not quite believing that this could be the man I placed my trust in, the man I fell in love with, completely and wholly, while I effectively let another man, a man who loves and adores me, who thought he'd spend the rest of his life with me, go.

A split second passes before Scarlett speaks. 'Gracie, there's no need to panic. This is Noah,' she says, a calmness in her voice.

My eyes widen. 'What?!'

I shake my head in disbelief and I can't tell whether it's relief or anger causing my body to shake like this. 'Brothers?'

'Twins, actually,' says Noah, stepping forward. 'Missed you, Gracie.' He smiles at me, a smile that's almost identical to Flynn's. My eyes meet his and travel over the features of his face, where a tiny scar resides above his left eyebrow, above eyes that are a shade darker than Flynn's. He's wearing a t-shirt with a print design. Flynn only ever wears plain t-shirts, more tight-fitting than this one. The edges of a tattoo are visible from under his right sleeve, a tattoo that Flynn doesn't have. I go to speak but my words catch. I try again. 'I'm sorry, but I don't remember you.'

He nods in sympathy.

'I don't understand. How can Flynn be your brother? I mean, what are the chances of him moving in next door and being your brother?' My head feels heavy. Too much information to take in at once. So many unanswered questions.

I turn to Scarlett, who appears paler than she did before. 'I wanted to tell you. It's just … it wasn't my place to tell you—it's not my place to tell you.'

I blink at her, trying to take it all in. Was I that adamant I didn't want to know details about my life that she'd respect that wish, even under these circumstances?

I rub my temples and pace back and forth, trying to work this out. 'So, if you're Flynn's brother, then it's likely I knew Flynn before the accident?'

Noah purses his lips and glances at the wall, avoiding eye contact. Scarlett doesn't reply.

The world around me suddenly feels bigger and scarier than ever.

Scarlett's doctor steps in between us all, breaking the silence, and I can't do anything but turn around and head for the door to escape.

Outside the hospital, I wave down another cab, and give him the apartment address. By now it's already mid-morning, and I'm praying Blake isn't at work.

The streets are moderately trafficked and the cab driver, clearly impatient, begins to accelerate at any chance he can get, before braking suddenly when he comes closer to the car in front. I clasp my seatbelt tighter to stop the jolting. At the next set of lights, he speeds up again, and I want to tell him to be careful, to slow down, and the instant he slams on the brakes again, and the screech pierces my ears, I regret staying quiet. We've hit something.

I open the door and stumble out of the car.

'How could you?' I say, crouching down in the middle of the road, the limp body of a small terrier lying on the asphalt. She whimpers in pain, her eyes drifting open and closed as her limp body barely moves, aside from the gentle rise and fall of her chest. Car horns toot as the traffic weaves in and around us. The driver has a desperate look on his face. 'How could you be so careless?!' I scoop the dog into my arms and place her in the back seat of the cab.

'What are you doing, lady?' he says, standing there, looking horrified.

'You're taking me to the closest animal hospital before this poor dog dies,' I demand through gritted teeth.

I can tell he wants to argue with me, but I slam the door closed and fasten my seatbelt before lifting the dog onto my lap. 'You'll be fine,' I whisper, stroking her honey-coloured fur. 'What's your name?' I ask, checking her collar. 'Dottie,' I say, reading her name tag. A few minutes later we've reached the nearest vet clinic. The cab driver hauls out my suitcase, and I glare at him before awkwardly dragging the case inside, while carrying Dottie against my chest.

A vet nurse greets me at reception. 'She's been hit by a car and I don't think she's in very good shape.' She nods and takes a clipboard. 'She's not mine,' I say, feeling her weight in my arms. She's beginning to feel more limp by the minute. She's now closed her eyes. 'We've only got one vet working today's shift, but I'll call him out right away and we'll take a look.' She takes Dottie from my arms and carries her into one of the rooms. 'You're welcome to stay to see how she is, or you can call to check on her later. Would you mind leaving your details so we know where to contact you if we have any questions about what happened?'

I accept a piece of paper from her. 'Sure,' I say, taking a pen. I fill out my details and her attention turns to the person waiting behind me. Unsure whether to stay or go, I opt to stay. I huddle in a corner, beside a woman with her cat, while the sterile scent of antiseptic filters through the air. The nurse eventually calls the woman with the cat into a room, telling her the vet is almost ready to see her. I check the time. I've been here for almost an hour.

Deciding I should go and make a phone call to the hospital to check on Scarlett, I rise from my chair and head for the door. 'Here's our number so you can check on her later,' says the nurse, handing me a business card.

'Thanks,' I reply, accepting it from her. I head for the door, glancing down briefly at the card, when the vet calls out. 'Let her know that Dottie's going to be okay.'

There's a familiarity in his voice that I can't quite pin. My eyes read over the card in my hands.

Dr Blake Beaumont.

Windsor Veterinary Hospital.

I freeze, my heart thumping against my chest as if it's trying to leap out.

'Oh my God. *Gracie?*' says a male voice from behind me.

I slowly turn around to face him.

'Flynn?' I say, feeling confused. He and Flynn are *colleagues?* This is what he was hiding from me?

I feel the colour drain from my face. I look around, conscious that Blake might emerge from one of the surgery doors at any moment.

Flynn shakes his head and steps towards me, the rubber soles of his shoes squeaking on the linoleum floor.

My eyes travel to his name badge.

Blake.

I rush out of the clinic door, and start gasping for air in the middle of the street.

'Say something. Say anything,' pleads Flynn, who has followed me outside. His face is smothered with an unbearable look of desperation. I can't seem to let out any words. Craning my neck, I try to spot a cab.

'Gracie,' he repeats, more firmly this time. 'Please. Look at me. Give me a chance to explain.' He reaches for my hand, but I shake him away. My entire body is trembling with anger.

'How could you?' I say, hot tears pricking my eyes. I'm frantically trying to hold myself together, but the moment Flynn bites his lip, a frown forming on his brow, tears forming in his eyes, his heart breaking right before me, I lose it.

'I can't believe you did this,' I croak, my voice fracturing with the realisation that Blake and Flynn are one and the same man. I shake my head and look up at the sky, trying to draw strength from above, trying to convince myself that this isn't true. It can't possibly be true. *Can it?*

The chestnuts being knocked from my hand at Charlie's stand.

Our morning jogs.

The Wild Wombat. The bridge in the Central Springs Reserve. Portobello's. All places that seemed familiar because they were familiar, because I've no doubt been to these places with Flynn—no, *Blake*—before.

'I wanted to tell you. I wanted to find the right time to tell you.' Flynn shakes his head, his eyes damp and full of sorrow.

The sinking feeling becomes heavier, weighted with the joyful memories of the past few months at Summerhill. Precious moments that slip through my mind like a movie being played over, and over, and over again.

Losing someone hurts like hell, doesn't it?

God, he was talking about me, about how he felt when he lost *me*.

A cab makes its way down the road towards us and I step onto the kerb to wave it down.

'Wait, where are you going?' says Flynn.

I ignore him, fling open the cab door, take a seat, slam the door closed, and look straight ahead. 'You had a chance to tell me—so many chances to tell me, and you didn't! I think it's a bit too late now, don't you?'

'No!' he calls. He bangs his palm against the driver's window and tells him to wait, before running in front of the cab and opening the other passenger door. He slips into the seat beside me and closes the door.

'Gracie,' he pleads, catching his breath.

I scrunch my eyes closed. I don't want to hear it. I don't want to hear what he has to say. All I can think of is the fact that he lied to me.

'Where to?' the cab driver asks stiffly, glancing in the rear-view mirror as he pulls out into the traffic. Whether I like it or not, wherever we're going, Flynn is coming with me. He glances nervously at me, before reeling off an address. The address to o*ur* apartment. The place *we* once called home.

I turn my body away from him and rest my face against the glass. And as the droplets from a fresh shower of Melbourne rain trickle down the window, tears of hurt and betrayal and disappointment slide down my face.

We arrive outside the white stucco building after twelve minutes of excruciating silence, aside from my intermittent sniffling. I've managed to use every single tissue in my possession. I blow my nose, stuff the large wad of scrunched tissues down my bra and search my bag for my wallet to pay the taxi driver. Flynn beats me to it, digging into his pocket and producing a fifty-dollar note. The driver fishes for some change, Flynn tells him to keep it, before exiting the car and opening my door.

I cross my arms, still unable to look at him. I reach for the door to try to close it, but he holds it open. I exit the cab, tugging my suitcase out from the back seat. Flynn takes it from me and I follow him inside, the echo of our footsteps making me wonder how many times we might have entered and exited this building, hand in hand, arm in arm. Flynn slides a key into the lock and holds the door open for me. His jaw is clenched, his brow creased. He appears so uncomfortable, that as angry and hurt as I am, something in me aches for him and what he's been through in all of this. To him, I'm his *fiancée*—the fiancée that he lost the day he lost control of a steering wheel on a drive that turned our lives completely upside down and destroyed everything.

The photo frames on the side table that I turned down after arriving home from the hospital with Scarlett have been turned the right way up. I slowly step down the hallway, pausing to check the photos, to make sure this is actually true. My fingers sweep over the glass, over pictures of us frozen in time—moments I don't remember. Like the time we sat in this particular tree, went to this particular restaurant, or sailed on that particular boat, or spent time in that particular … field of peonies. My hand covers my mouth as I pick up another frame containing a collage of photos of Flynn and I in Summerhill. The two of us kissing under the willow tree, holding up a sign saying, WE'RE GETTING HITCHED!, the two of us standing in the peony field, Flynn's arms around my waist as I throw my head back in laughter, the two of us riding Polly. It's all so unfathomable. Finally, I run my fingers over the black-and-white photo of the two of us, the one I saw after my return from hospital. Flynn's hair looks different now—it's longer, the natural waves in his hair more apparent, his jawline is more defined and he's hardly ever clean-shaven like he is in this photo.

'I thought you had dark hair,' I whisper. 'It was short. I thought …' I shake my head. Flynn looks completely different to the impression I had of him from this photo. 'My God, I don't know what I thought.'

Flynn stands next to me, patiently waiting as I take it all in. When I finally look up at him, he swallows hard. 'It's a really old photo. We were a lot younger then.'

I nod silently and rest the frame back down.

'Come,' he says, nodding to the living room. 'Drink?' he asks, waiting for me to sit down. I wedge myself into the corner of the sofa and place a pillow on my lap, which I hug tightly. 'No, thanks,' I reply, sounding as morose as I feel.

Flynn steps into the kitchen anyway, and comes out with a glass of water. He places it on the coffee table, on top of a copy of *Country Dwellings*.

He sits beside me and clears his throat. 'I never meant to hurt you like this. Hurting you is the last thing I wanted to do. I'm sorry. Really sorry. You have no idea how sorry. I just … didn't know how else to …'

'Manipulate me?' I reply hotly.

He cringes. 'I knew that if I let you go—if you left and never came back, I might have lost you forever.'

'You couldn't have possibly known that,' I fire at him.

'You're the most stubborn woman I know. If Scarlett couldn't convince you to stay, then who could?'

'So, instead of turning up at Summerhill and introducing yourself you thought that pretending to be a *stranger* was the better option?'

'You and I both know what would have happened if I had turned up at Summerhill to see you.'

'No we don't actually. Because it never happened.'

Flynn runs his hand through his hair.

'Why didn't Scarlett tell me? She's supposed to be my best friend.'

'I begged her not to. I told her I'd tell you when the timing was right.'

'Well, your timing is bloody awful,' I say through gritted teeth.

He clenches his jaw as his eyes momentarily close.

'She knew all along?' I ask, trying to think back to the way she reacted when she saw Flynn in Summerhill.

'No,' he says. He takes a deep breath. 'I didn't tell her or Noah that I went to Summerhill. And when she did find out—when she saw me there—I made her promise not to say anything to you. Don't blame her, Gracie, I put her in a terrible situation.'

'You didn't have the right to do that. When were you planning on telling me? You kept this whole thing a secret. You kept it from Scarlett and then you made her keep it, too. What were you *thinking*?'

Flynn rubs his temples but doesn't answer.

'You took advantage of me when I was at my most vulnerable, Flynn! Who does that?!'

'I didn't know what else to do,' he says flatly.

I stand up and make my way down the hallway.

Flynn follows me.

'Gracie, please … you need to understand why I did this. I never gave up on you. I never gave up on us. You—'

'Don't you dare!' I yell. 'It's not like I made a conscious decision to forget you!'

'You never even gave me a chance to see you. You left that hospital and you walked out of there and into another life, a life that didn't include me! What was I supposed to do? Just let you go?'

'Yes, Flynn, you were supposed to let me go, so that I could work things out!'

'So you could potentially fall in love with someone else? And lose you completely?'

I feel like I've been slapped. I take a step backwards. 'That's not fair. You manipulated me. You barged straight into my life and …'

'And?'

… *you made me fall in love with you.*

'I loved you. I *trusted* you,' I whisper.

'And I'd do it again, a thousand times over if it meant I could live another day of my life with you in it.'

'You had no right. You had no right to do this.'

'You once told me that you never wanted to live your life without me in it—no matter what. And I know you don't remember that, but every single day I wake up wishing that you would. So that you'd know what we had, and what we lost.'

'Stop.' I place my hands around my ears.

'No. I'm not done yet! I'm not done until I finish telling you how much I love you. Because you have no idea what I lost, the minute the paramedics put you onto that stretcher and wheeled you away. You don't know what it was like for me to walk into this apartment and not find you here. And you sure as hell have no idea what it's been like for me to lie to the most important person in my life, when I spend almost every minute of every day wanting to tell you the truth but I hold back because I never wanted this day to come. Because whatever is happening now, is everything I was afraid would happen. In all of this, I never wanted to lose you, but I figured losing you, knowing I'd tried to at least salvage what we had, was the better option.'

Flynn lets out a long breath and wipes his eyes with his thumb and forefinger.

'I loved you so much,' he whispers. 'And I have no idea if you'll get past this, but for what it's worth—I love who you are now even more than I ever did before.'

I can't respond to that right now, so I bite my lip and turn away, opening the front door, the breeze sending a chill through my body.

'You don't have to go,' he says, but we both know I can't stay.

I turn around before stepping out the door.

'Flynn. Is that a name you just made up?'

'Blake Flynn Beaumont,' he replies flatly.

'I think I prefer Flynn.'

TWENTY-EIGHT

I spend the night in a hotel overlooking the Yarra River, watching the digits of the alarm clock flip over and over until the early hours of the morning, while the last few months of my life play over in my mind. If Flynn—Blake—hadn't come to Summerhill, would I have potentially fallen in love with another man? Would I have come back to Melbourne and slowly allowed Flynn back into my life? Would I have fallen in love with him again with the expectation that I *should* love him hovering over me like a heavy cloud? I don't think I would have. But how can I be sure? I can't possibly be. And that's the thing that weighs on my mind the most—that there's no way of truly knowing. Yet, Flynn, through the very act of hiding who he really was, showed me that maybe, somehow, we do end up with who we're meant to end up with. It doesn't change the fact that he lied to me, and that's something I don't know if I'll be able to forgive. I have no way of knowing if he lied to me before.

I shower and dress and catch a cab to the hospital to see Scarlett. She smiles when she sees me, but her eyes are filled with worry.

'Everything okay with the baby?' I ask, sitting beside her on the bed. 'May I?' I hold my hand above her belly.

Smiling, she nods. 'Of course. The baby is doing okay. They're inducing me in an hour.'

'So soon?'

'They say the baby should be fine.'

I smile with relief. I'm happy for Scarlett.

'Noah said you spoke to Blake.'

The joy dissipates, like a leaf dropping from a flower that has little life force left in it.

'Flynn,' I say, correcting her.

She shakes her head. 'Sorry, yes, well, this is going to be a bit awkward.' She pokes her finger through the hole in her thermal blanket. 'I'm sorry I didn't tell you the truth. I didn't know what to do, to be honest. Which is another reason I didn't call as often as I wanted to. It was all too hard.'

'You're supposed to be my best friend,' I whisper. 'I wish you had told me.'

The colour drains from Scarlett's face. 'He begged me not to tell you and I begged him *to* tell you. He just …' She shrugs and looks at me with earnest eyes. 'He desperately wanted a second chance.'

'Well, he lost it.'

Scarlett's shoulders sag. 'You're angry. Hurt and angry. Which you have every right to be. Even with me.'

'I can't be mad with you, Scarlett, you're about to make me a godmother.'

She offers a half-smile, moving her hand onto her belly. 'Well, I hope the godmother can sort things out with the godfather,' she says. 'Although, technically you're almost an aunty.'

'You didn't tell me about Noah, either.'

'I tried to tell you so many things before you left for Summerhill. You were so adamant you didn't want to know anything.'

She's right. I can't argue with this. It was something I fought so hard for.

'Have you remembered anything about any of us?' she asks.

I shake my head. 'No,' I reply. 'But I'm starting to think that maybe none of that even matters. Maybe what matters is simply how I feel about you all, now.'

Eleven hours later, I'm passing Scarlett ice chips from a plastic cup and mopping her brow with a cool face washer, while she writhes in pain, tiny moans escaping her as she tries to breathe through her contractions.

'Thank God you're here,' whispers Noah between contractions, while Scarlett closes her eyes, trying to find some respite from the pain. 'I knew you'd be better at this than me.' He laughs. It's the kind of laugh you share with someone you know well, the kind of laugh you have when you know the person will laugh back. So I do. I laugh. And then he smiles and we're sharing a moment. A moment that gives me a glimpse of something we might have had before. A friendship. A bond. A relationship. His smile is similar to Flynn's but not quite the same. It's his eyes. They don't look at me the same way Flynn's do. They don't say the same things Flynn's say. Scarlett jolts me from my thoughts by announcing she has to go to the bathroom.

'Right now?' I ask, glancing over at Noah.

'Quickly,' she says, hobbling towards the bathroom.

'Hold on, let me help you,' I say, grabbing her by the elbow.

A midwife, who has just started the evening shift, enters the room and introduces herself as Annalise. 'All right! How are things coming along, petal?'

Noah shrugs. He looks partly terrified by the entire situation.

'Contractions?'

'Um, a minute or so apart,' I tell her.

Noah nods, confirming things.

'She needs to go to the bathroom,' I say.

'Not yet, she doesn't. Back on the bed, Scarlett. Let me check things out,' she says.

'But I really need to go now,' says Scarlett, doubling over in pain as another contraction hits.

Annalise guides her to the bed. 'I think you might be close to meeting your baby,' she says, raising her eyebrows as she looks at Scarlett over the rim of her glasses.

Noah and I turn away as the midwife makes her checks, exchanging sideways glances with each other, while Annalise gives us a commentary of what she's seeing. Finally, she announces, 'You're ready to start pushing, love! Now, this is how you're going to do it …'

Noah and I look at each other in surprise and race back to the bed. 'Okay, what do we need to do?' asks Noah, assuming position beside Scarlett. She rolls her eyes and then squeezes them shut. 'Why do you have to ask such silly questions?!'

'Ice chip?' I ask, extending my cup, which now contains a handful of tiny ice chips in a puddle of cold water. Scarlett ignores me.

'Okay, so this is what we'll do, Scarlett,' says Annalise, taking control. 'We're going to take advantage of gravity.' Noah's eyes widen and I can't help stifling another laugh. Which seems completely inappropriate, but I can't help it. Maybe it's the nerves, the sheer anticipation, or the fact that I wasn't prepared for any of this before I left Summerhill.

Annalise instructs Scarlett to get up, where she assumes a kneeling position with her forehead resting on her arms against the bed. She points for Noah and I to stand beside her.

'You can do this,' I say, rubbing her back.

'I can't do this,' she moans. Annalise provides more instructions. When to breathe. When to push. When to suck on the gas.

'Of course you can,' I say, my cheek almost resting against hers. 'You're about to meet your baby, Scarlett. You're about to become a mother. You're going to have a baby to love and nurture and fill your heart with so much joy you won't be able to describe it.'

She nods, scrunching her eyes closed as she bears down with all her might.

Twenty-six minutes later, Belinda Grace Beaumont mesmerises us with her angelic presence. Scarlett and Noah have become parents. Flynn and I have become godparents. And as I exit the birthing suite, and come face to face with Flynn in the waiting room, I can't help but wonder what else we have become and what the future holds for us.

Flynn stands up from the visitor's chair to greet me the moment our eyes meet.

'It's a girl,' I tell him, before he can say anything.

'Can we talk?' he asks.

'Not the right time,' I say, not meeting his eyes.

There's a group of people still seated beside the chair Flynn was in. Their eyes are on me. I suck in a breath. They recognise me. I look back at the four sets of eyes, gentle yet nervous smiles appearing on their faces. I don't need to be told which couple are Flynn's parents, because Flynn is simply a younger-looking version of his father. His mother, a well-dressed woman around my height, with perfectly accessorised jewellery and short blonde hair, looks as if she's come straight from the local country club. I assume the other couple are Scarlett's parents. Flynn's mother is the first to stand up. She approaches me and extends two manicured hands over mine and squeezes.

'We've missed you, Gracie,' she says. 'I'm Nora.' She envelopes me in a reassuring hug before stroking my face with her hands. She smiles into my eyes and then leans forward and whispers, 'Everything's going to be fine.' Then, she turns her body slightly, towards the rest of the group. 'This is Stuart, Blake's father, and then we have Mara and Seb, Scarlett's parents.'

I nod and smile, unsure of what to say. Thankfully, Noah emerges from the suite, declaring, 'Here she is!' which means the attention quickly turns to him and the baby. Flynn looks anxiously at me, unsure of whether he should move forward.

'I should go,' I whisper. I nod towards Noah. 'You should meet your niece. She couldn't be more beautiful and perfect.'

'Where are you going?' he asks, but I can tell he knows the answer.

My legs feel heavy as my footsteps echo down the corridor. I look straight ahead, resisting the temptation to look back, only I can't. When I turn around and see Flynn holding the baby, and he looks up at me and smiles, I see both the man who lied to me, and the man who might one day be a father. The man who was supposed to become my husband and the man who was meant to be my future.

TWENTY-NINE

Back in Summerhill, the world has turned colourful overnight. The peony buds are smiling at the sky and the world around me looks as if it has burst to life. The green layer of grass is awash with the lush growth of the herbaceous borders, as trees take on their verdant hues. Lorikeets flitter, dipping their beaks into the terracotta plates I've positioned by the bird feeder, shared with the odd butterfly and the occasional bee. The rosebuds, once tightly wrapped, are now unfurling, ready to unleash their heavenly scents into the garden I've so reverently nurtured since my arrival here. Everything is fresh and about to bloom, and during this time where I should be feeling hopeful, I'm as fragile as a withering papery blossom unable to withstand the heat. The life I never knew, and the life I thought I knew, don't seem to be meeting and I can't work out where Flynn fits.

I'm on my way to see Tilly when the mailman arrives, carrying a single letter with him. I accept the envelope, knowing exactly who it's from before it reaches my hand. My finger slides underneath the paper, ripping it open. I take a deep breath and start reading.

Hey ladybug,

You're allowed to be mad, and kick and punch and scream. I knew that there would come a time when you would do all of these things. I'm sorry you found out the truth about things in the way that you did and that's entirely my fault.

I know Summerhill the way you do. My family spent every summer there since I was twelve years old. I fell in love with you under the willow tree. It was your spot and then, over time, it became our spot.

I never wanted to hurt you, Gracie. The thing is, after you left, I knew you would never have let me in. I couldn't bear the thought of living a single day without you, knowing you were hurting just as much as I was, only in a different way.

Not many couples get the chance to fall in love twice. But we did and what we have is special. So, once you're done kicking and punching and screaming, remember our tender moments, but don't hold onto the anger too tightly. You know what happens to roses if they ball. They never open. They never get to see how beautiful life can be when they open their petals and feel the warmth of the sun. You're too special and beautiful for that. Besides, you know better than anyone that roses know how to heal themselves once they've been cut.

I love you, and I'll always love you. And if you give me the chance, I'll tell you all about our life before, and maybe, just maybe, we'll get the chance to fall in love with each other for a third time.

Forever yours,

Blake Flynn Beaumont (but you can call me Flynn)

I fold the note, and sigh. I can't find a way to circle back to Flynn right now. There's too much for me to reconcile. My choices. His choices. Future choices.

As I make my way down the driveway to the street to visit Tilly, local cyclists glide down the footpaths and up the gentle slopes past me. Tourists, with their hiking sticks, head for the nearby walking tracks to explore all the precious gifts from nature this beautiful place has to offer. She doesn't notice me by the stand immediately, but when she does, her face lights up.

'Where have you been?' she asks, her voice demanding answers. 'Storm hits and you disappear? If it weren't for Charlie I'd have sent a search party looking for you.'

'There's been a lot happening. My best friend had a baby and … well, I discovered a friend of mine has been lying to me. And even if I understand why he lied to me, I can't seem to get past the fact that he isn't who I thought he was.'

'He's not just a friend, now, is he?'

I shake my head. 'He's much more than a friend.'

'When you pick a peony, a tight-budded, perfectly rounded ball, you never quite know what you're going to get. But sometimes what you do get is much more than what you expected. A lot more beautiful and special than you ever could have anticipated.'

'You knew? You knew who he was too?' I narrow my eyes.

'Well, not immediately. But I suspected. The way he doted on you, the way he looked at you, the way he finished your sentences for you. Didn't surprise me. Not one bit. Though, I can imagine you'd be feeling a bit bruised and battered. Nobody wants to ever be lied to, Gracie. But I'm going to tell you something. I've told you once, and I'm going to tell you again. It's their unseen beauty that makes the flowers special.' She lowers her voice so she's speaking in a hushed whisper. 'And maybe what you couldn't see is the entire point. Maybe it's the flowers that brought you back to the very place, and the very person you should have been close to all your life.'

I sigh, pulling a bunch of hydrangeas from one of the buckets, the beauty of an abundance of creamy white petals offering some respite from the disappointment I'm feeling. Could Tilly be right?

'A few more weeks and I can stop buying these imported blooms,' she says, pulling a rose from a bucket. She places it under my nose. 'Can you smell it?'

'Hmm, yes and no.'

'Exactly.'

'I lost quite a bit in the storm, Tilly. Almost all the sweet peas.'

'It was considerably brutal,' she admits.

'Which means that I don't know if I can stay after spring. I might need to sell, after all.'

'Rubbish,' she scoffs. 'If you want to make it work, you'll make it work. And if you don't want to make it work, you'll give up. But I'll tell you this—it's never a good idea to give up on the things you love.'

I find Charlie in the fields when I get home. He's carrying out some repairs, re-erecting the remaining stakes in an effort to rescue whatever plants he can.

'I put up a windbreak,' he says, hammering in the last stake. 'Hopefully, it'll prevent any more damage in case another storm hits. The most unpredictable things those storms, the way they sweep through, take you by surprise, jolt things around and then leave a gaping hole at the very core of what your heart's tied to.'

'Do you think we can save them?' I ask, running my fingers along one of the snapped stems.

'Maybe not all of them, but some. You got hit pretty hard out here, and it's going to take some work to get things back into shape. But we'll do what we can, and keep growing some new seedlings while we can. We're just moving into a new phase while we find our footing. No need to despair.'

'Charlie?'

'Yes, love,' he says, looking up at me.

'Thank you.'

'You're welcome,' he says, smiling back at me.

I kneel down beside him, and join him in fastening the stakes to the plants, drifting in and out of conversation as my thoughts flicker to Flynn. I have no idea whether we'll ever find our footing, too.

THIRTY

With the peony harvest now only weeks away, I can't seem to shake the feeling that I need to take a break. Somehow, on the way back from my stroll, I end up at the willow tree. The drooping branches swing gently in the breeze, reminding me of my time here with Flynn. We'd stop under this tree to talk, letting the luxury of time pass us by.

I sit on the grass and pick at some wildflowers, building a daisy chain, losing myself to the hum of a song I can't name, but which seems so familiar. Memories of Flynn and me on our morning jogs and afternoon strolls filter into my consciousness. A bird flutters past me and rests on one of the willow's branches above me, and that's when I notice a string of lights suspended from the tree. I squint, trying to get a better look at them. I'd never noticed them before. I stand up and reach for the switch nestled between the trunk and a branch. They don't turn on, but a memory floats into my mind, and it's enough to take my breath away.

'I think we should get out of here soon,' Blake whispered, his lips brushing my ear ever so slightly. 'There's something I want to show you.'

'Right now?' I asked, my attention focused on the bride and groom dancing their final dance for the night under a canopy of paper lanterns emitting a soft glow in the middle of the barn-turned-wedding-venue. For two weeks, Blake had worked tirelessly to transform this space into something that could cater for a little over a hundred guests for his brother's wedding. For all the hours he put into it, you'd never know that a few short weeks ago this barn was filled with cobwebs and twenty-five bales of hay.

As awkward as Noah was on the dancefloor, there was something endearing about the way he tried, despite his feet not being able to keep up with the rest of him. Scarlett spun around and laughed, her joy palpable. I loved seeing her like this.

'You're going to love it.' Blake plucked the strawberry from his champagne glass and popped it into my mouth. He knew I loved strawberries. He knew everything about me. He knew me better than I knew myself. 'I think we should be next,' he said casually. He finished off his glass of champagne and gave me a side glance, his mouth forming a mischievous smile, like it always did when he was up to something.

I almost choked on my strawberry. I coughed, my eyes watering, and Blake laughed so hard I reached out to slap him across the arm.

'If that's how you're proposing, I'm going to say you need to lift your game in a big way,' I said, clearing my throat as I reached out to a passing waiter for another glass of champagne. The waiter paused next to Blake and he took a glass, too.

'To a future proposal,' said Blake, flashing his perfect smile at me. He looked so handsome in his grey suit and white shirt, a nice change from his usual powder-blue scrubs, even if they did highlight the sapphire in his eyes.

I clinked my glass against his. 'Better make it a good one,' I teased.

He took the champagne glass from my hand, leaned forward and delivered a kiss on my lips, the kind of kiss that took my breath away. The kind of kiss that promised the world and then delivered. Then he rested his cheek against mine for a second or two like he usually did, and I inhaled his scent, a scent I'd never tire of, and never forget. Finally, he whispered in my ear, 'You're my world, ladybug.'

He set down the champagne glasses on the wooden barrel beside us and grabbed my hand. 'Let's go,' he said, his eyes sparkling.

'But we need to say goodbye, I'm the maid of honour! We can't just leave!'

'Half of the people here are too drunk to notice.' He laughed, tugging gently at my arm. I glanced around the room. He was right. Nobody would notice us gone.

Blake squeezed my hand and we made our escape into the moonlight, past the congregation of guests smattered in small groups around the lawn surrounding the barn, empty champagne and cocktail glasses in mismatched arrangements on the wooden barrels serving as tables.

'I can't wait to get out of these shoes,' I said, pausing to slip them off. I carried them in one hand and walked barefoot on the grass. It was a warm night, one of those balmy summer nights that made you forget that winter even existed.

'Okay, so what did you want to show me?' I'd known Blake long enough to recognise he was up to something.

'I'll tell you when we reach the willow.'

The hum of cicadas amplified as we made our way across one of the paddocks on the hill to our tree. A weeping willow positioned at the bottom of the paddocks that separated the property of my childhood home and Blake's summer home. We spent countless hours here as kids, counting the scrapes on our knees and the mosquito bites on our legs, and that continued into adulthood. It was where we shared our first secret, our first kiss, our first fight, and countless other memories over the years. It was our thinking spot, our love spot, our chilling-out-because-we-felt-like-it spot. But the most special part about the willow tree, was that it was ours.

'I don't see anything. It's too dark,' I said, squinting.

'Okay, ladybug, see if this helps,' he said, reaching up to one of the branches.

A second later, the tree lit up, its branches intertwined with dozens of fairy lights, illuminating the space around us.

'No way,' I whispered, looking up at the luminescent canopy of leaves above us that cascaded down the branches like a waterfall of lights.

Blake smiled and faked a cough, while his eyes darted to the tree trunk. My eyes settled on what Blake had brought me here to see. I inhaled sharply and placed a hand on my mouth in amazement. In front of me, hanging from the tree, was a hand-painted sign with the words: *Marry me?*

I stood there blinking and before I knew it, Blake reached for my hand and pulled me close. He rested his forehead against mine, and lowered his voice. 'What do you say?'

I nodded, trying not to cry. Blake was my everything. He always had been. And I'd never imagined a life without him because it was impossible to even remember a day without him in it.

He reached for my hand and slipped a ring on my finger, but I hardly managed to give it a second glance before I wrapped my arms around his neck and lost myself in a kiss.

'Yes?' he asked, when he slowly pulled away.

'Yes,' I replied, a smile forming across my lips that matched the swelling in my chest.

'Thought so. I don't think we should go back to the house tonight. Too many people ...' He slipped a finger under the strap of my dress and started kissing my neck.

'Here? What if someone sees us?'

Without taking his lips off mine, he reached up into the tree and switched off the lights.

'Better?' he murmured.

'Yeah, but isn't it a little uncomfortable?' I felt him smile against my lips.

'There's a blanket in there,' he said, pointing to a small teepee, erected under the tree.

'Pillows?'

'Pillows too,' he said.

'You had this all planned out?' I laughed, peeking at the linen folds exposing the cosy hideaway in the moonlight.

'Practically since the day I met you.'

'Could you turn the lights on one more time?'

Blake shook his head. 'What now?' he said, pretending to be annoyed. He reached up for the switch.

'I just want to see my ring,' I said, holding it up in front of me. I spent a few seconds admiring its detail, the way the centre stone was surrounded by tiny pink diamonds set in rose gold. They reminded me of the petals of a daisy.

I glanced up at him, and smiled. 'Okay. You can turn the—'

Before I finished my sentence, the lights were off and Blake's lips were back on mine. The world was perfect. I never wanted to forget this moment. I'd never felt so happy in my entire life.

My hand drops the switch, leaving it dangling from the tree.

I loved him.

I was happy. *We* were happy.

We had everything. We had each other. We had our whole life ahead of us.

And now we are broken.

THIRTY-ONE

The day of the harvest finally arrives on a spring day that carries the fragrance of fresh flowers on the breeze. Thanks to Tilly and Charlie, I've managed to pre-sell an abundance of flowers. I'm starting with the roses this morning. I was delighted to find that most of the roses turned out to be perfect for bouquets—most of them David Austins, with a few rarer old English varieties Tilly had planted many, many years ago. Charlie has already set to work setting up the empty buckets, filled with water. He'll load them on the back of the ute to take to the chestnut stand, which has been converted to a roadside flower stall. We have weeks of harvesting and filling orders ahead of us.

I stroll through the peony field, a milkshake of colour: light pinks and creamy white buds, some still closed shut, some already stretched open, squishy like marshmallows, ready to open into puffy balls any day. On days where I'd felt tired and unsure of whether I'd have the energy to keep going, Flynn would describe this field to me. And now that I'm here, alone, I can't help wishing he was here to enjoy it with me.

I take the snips from the front of my apron and begin to look for the best blooms to cut. As I make my selections, I'm filled with a sense of purpose so strong, so palpable, that it takes my breath away. I can't imagine a life anywhere else but here.

Charlie toots as he drives the ute loaded with the first bucketfuls of flowers down the incline to the roadside stand. Tilly is already waiting for him, sitting under an umbrella, with Maggie keeping her company. She'll help her manage the flowers in her own special way—by selecting stems for the mixed bouquets.

Just before lunchtime, after filling the last bucket with roses, Charlie heaves it onto the back of the ute. This load will go into the refrigerators in the barn.

'Looks like we're done for the day, Charlie,' I say, pulling off my gloves. After lunch, I'll continue the day's work in the barn, making arrangements for the orders that have come in. This has become one of my favourite parts of flower farming—witnessing the connection between customers and fresh blooms.

'If you don't have any plans tonight, why don't you come over for dinner?' asks Charlie. He's been asking me this every few days, but I've only accepted his offer once or twice.

'It's okay. I just plan on having an early night. There's a movie on TV I've been looking forward to watching.'

'Oh really? What's the name of it?'

'Sorry?'

'The movie?'

'Um … can't remember.'

Charlie tsks. 'Would you just go back and see him?' he says, shaking his head at me.

'What do you mean?'

'Your light's a little dimmer since you came back from Melbourne.'

'I miss him, Charlie. But I don't know that letting him back into my life after what he did is the right thing to do.'

'I can understand that. But have you considered whether not letting him back in is the wrong thing to do? Flynn's a smart man, Gracie. He'd have known what he was doing and what kind of trouble it could have gotten him into. The way I see it, he wasn't going to let you go without a fight. And isn't that the kind of man you want in your life? One that can't bear to live without you?'

I inhale a deep breath. 'Maybe,' I reply.

Charlie tilts his head. 'We're just having quiche and salad—nothing special. But it would mean you wouldn't have to eat alone. What do you say?'

I smile, and shake my head in defeat. 'I'd love to come to dinner.'

Later that evening at Charlie's, Lara says a quick goodbye and lets us know the table's already set and the quiche is in the oven. Maggie doesn't recognise me, but her face lights up when I present her with the flowers—a delicate pink spray of tightly cupped Heritage David Austins tucked away amongst some dusty miller and eucalyptus.

'Should we put them in water?'

She nods, eyes bright.

'Where do we keep the vases, Gerry?' she asks. I look around, but there's nobody in the kitchen except for me and Charlie.

Charlie motions to one of the cupboards and taps it. 'This one, love.'

I question him with my eyes. He shrugs in response, a pang of sadness visible in his expression.

Maggie rummages through the cupboard and turns to me, smiling, as she hands me a coffee mug.

'Oh!' I say, somewhat surprised. 'This vase is just *perfect*.'

Charlie exchanges a grateful look with me, and once I manage to trim the stems to a suitable length, we place the mug of flowers in the middle of the table as a centrepiece.

We sit down to eat and once finished, Maggie rises from her chair, declaring she's ready for bed. 'Is Mum coming tomorrow?' she asks.

Charlie sets down his knife and fork and goes to stand. 'She'll be here bright and early in the morning.'

Maggie smiles and turns away.

'Goodnight, Maggie,' I say as she starts shuffling out of the room.

'Night, dear.'

'I'll be back in a bit,' whispers Charlie. He weaves his arm through hers and helps her down the corridor.

I'm washing up the dishes when he re-enters the kitchen.

'Who's Gerry?' I ask.

'Her brother,' he replies. 'Gone twenty-two years. And her mother's been gone over thirty.'

'You lie to her about her mum coming to visit. Why do you do that?'

Charlie reaches for a tea towel and rubs a plate dry. 'What else am I supposed to do? I do it for the same reason you stuck those flowers in a mug and called it a vase.'

I dry my hands and meet his eyes. 'You lie to her to make her feel safe.'

'Yes. But more than that—I lie to her because I love her.'

'And under these circumstances it makes it okay,' I say.

Charlie keeps his eyes trained on mine. 'Gracie, darling— sometimes when you love someone so deeply, lying is the only option you feel you have. It doesn't always make you a bad person.'

On the drive home, I try to imagine what life might have been like for me if Flynn was the one who lost his memory. Would I have let him go? I can't know for sure, but what I do know is that I fell in love with the same man twice. Charlie drops me off home to my empty cottage, where I flop onto my bed, hold Flynn's t-shirt near me, and in the early hours of the morning, make my final decision. There is no doubt in my mind that Flynn and I were meant to be together. And it's up to me now, to not let him go.

Approaching my apartment, I'm in the back of a cab where the driver, Thomas, tells me about how he made a choice to leave a career in acting for one driving a cab. 'I was miserable. Starving and unhappy, and a real wet bag of sand to be around,' he says brightly. 'See, there's more to cab driving than meets the eye. There's good and bad of course, but we *see* people,' he says, chattering away. 'You can learn a lot about people by the way they behave in the back of a cab,' he says, tittering. 'It makes the day go by, but I feel happy in this job. I like the freedom, and the conversation, and I might never cross paths again with the people I meet, and they might never remember me, but in the time I can get them from Flinders Street station to the Docklands, I bet I'll have found a way to make 'em smile!' he says, pointing his finger in the rear-view mirror as he grins at me. I can't help smiling back.

'You found your purpose.'

'That's right.' He winks. 'And when you're doing something you love, and you're surrounded by the people you love and could never live without, then it's a very good day, and an even better life.'

I glance out the window to the place I used to call my home as Thomas pulls up.

'Thank you, Thomas,' I say, handing him some cash. 'I will remember you.'

Thomas beams at me, before winking. 'That's what they all end up saying.'

Flynn answers the door after what feels like forever. He buzzes me up and Parrot lunges towards me as he opens the door.

'He's always preferred you over me,' he says, shaking his head.

'You took him to Scarlett and Noah's after I got home from hospital?'

Flynn nods. 'There's so much to tell you.' He motions to the living room. 'Come through.'

We make our way into the living room, but neither of us sits.

I clear my throat. 'You stayed away.'

He clenches his jaw and nods.

'I missed you.'

'I did the wrong thing by you,' he says, shoving his hands into the pockets of his jeans.

'I should have given you a chance after the accident.'

'You were scared.'

'You were hurting.' I blink in quick succession, trying to hold back the tears. 'The accident split our lives apart. It must have … it must have been so hard for you. To stay away and then make a decision to come to Summerhill, and you might have lied to me, but I would have *cheated* on you. What kind of person does that make me?'

'Cheating on someone who had become a total stranger to you overnight? You're human, and nobody is going to judge you for any decisions you've made after the accident—least of all me. It was harder for you, Gracie. So much harder for you. You lost everything.'

'Only I didn't. I found you. I found you because you never gave up on me. You never gave up on us.'

Flynn's eyes are damp. 'I shouldn't have done what I did.'

'You fought for me, Flynn. You fought for me, and you fought for our relationship. You knew what you were risking by coming to Summerhill, especially since you were also trying to keep a business afloat, and yes, I'm upset that you lied to me, but you showed me that I could never live without you. And if you didn't do that, I would have spent the rest of my life wondering whether I was meant to end up exactly where I was meant to end up—with you.'

Flynn takes a deep breath. 'You're everything to me, Gracie.'

'I've changed though, haven't I?'

'In some ways you have, but deep down you're still the same person, only you're more real, now. Those things you used to be able to do—like multi-tasking, and cooking fabulous meals, and managing to work long hours on little sleep while achieving more promotions than anyone else in your company—none of that matters. None of that makes you who you are. You're special because you're kind, and caring, and you always choose to see the good things in life. You know how to make people smile. You know how to make people feel things. You always have, only I don't think you knew it.'

'It sounds like I was chasing the wrong things. How am I different now?'

'You've slowed down. It's like you're in rhythm with your own life. You laugh more. You see things differently.' A hint of a smile lights up his face. 'And you struggle to tie your own shoelaces, and you're hopeless at maths, terrible with directions, even worse at cooking. But you know what? I wouldn't trade any of this for the person you were before. Because you are more beautiful and special to me now than you ever could have been. I love you for who you are, and who you could be.'

Flynn sits down on the sofa and motions for me to take a spot beside him.

'After your mum passed away, you threw yourself into work, you were doing these crazy hours and we stopped going to Summerhill on weekends. My place next door? That belongs to my parents—my family would spend entire summers there. Anyway, you put Summerhill on the market the month after the funeral. It's like any memory you had of life there was too painful for you to come closer to. We were happy, Gracie, *really* happy. We had everything to look forward to, but when it came to work, your career—you just couldn't seem to find a way to be happy. You kept chasing promotions, yet you always complained about work.'

'Well, I've got to admit, styling doesn't really seem like an appealing job to me.'

'Took me by surprise the day you accepted that job. I mean, you're talented and smart, and so hard-working, it didn't surprise me they hired you, but you were the one that wanted to move to the city. You thought it would offer us more. More of what, I don't know. But I'd have been happy setting up a practice in Summerhill.'

'There's something I need to know. What caused the accident?'

Flynn trails his fingers through his hair and lets out a breath. His Adam's apple bobs up and down. 'I was driving. We were arguing.'

'Over what?'

'Over Summerhill. You were about to tell me you didn't want to move to Daylesford when we had the accident. It was my fault—I wanted to make the move and was pushing you to give me a final answer. You'd initially agreed to it, but I had a feeling you'd changed your mind.'

'Scarlett told me I moved to the city after you graduated. Why didn't I want to stay in Summerhill?'

'You thought there was more to life than living on a farm. You were tired of the slow pace of life out there and your mum—she had always worked so hard on the farm and she told you once that she wanted more for you. So, I think the move was your way of trying to find something else.'

'Only I didn't find it.'

'No,' he says thoughtfully. 'And with the wedding approaching and the lease coming up on our apartment, we'd come to the decision about moving about a month before the accident. We'd been talking about it for months. I thought it would be good for us to, you know, settle somewhere and start a family in a place that we both spent so much time in and loved so much. You were going to take Summerhill off the market, but you kept putting it off. I knew deep down you weren't happy about the idea.'

'I love Summerhill.'

'Me too. Maybe deep down you just needed more time. You wanted a lot more money for Summerhill than what it's worth. I think that might have been because you didn't really want to let it go.'

'Wow,' I say, taking it all in. 'I can't imagine living anywhere else but there. So … where does that leave us, then? Are you … is it still somewhere you want to move to?'

'Well, about that … you might have to twist my arm,' he says.

'I've still got your toothbrush.'

He grins. 'I think you just earned yourself the last piece of chocolate.'

I wrap my hand around Flynn's. I squeeze. He squeezes back. I squeeze three times.

'I love you too, ladybug.' He pulls me closer to him, and holds me in his arms, drinking me in with his eyes, as he wipes the traces of tears from my cheeks. I close my eyes, inhaling his scent.

'You smell like your grey t-shirt did.'

He laughs. 'I'm wearing my favourite aftershave. I kept that bottle here. You recognise it?'

'Yes,' I say, laughing through the tears.

Flynn smiles back. 'There's so much to tell you, ladybug. So many beautiful things about our life together.'

'I want to know everything I never wanted to forget.'

I lean forward and press my lips against Flynn's, feeling the sense of comfort sweep over me, knowing, finally, that who we end up with, is exactly who we're supposed to end up with.

THIRTY-TWO

/

One month later

'That's the last load,' I say, lifting a bucket of the first flush of dahlias onto the back of the ute, a splash of colour covering every last inch of space. Charlie gives me a thumbs-up sign and turns on the ignition.

'We did it, Flynn,' I say, as his chin nestles into the space between my neck and shoulder. Under the early morning glow, we watch the ute rattle down the driveway. We've worked tirelessly over the past weeks, managing not only to cover the mortgage repayments, but earn a little more to cover living expenses, too. The gladdies should be ready to pick in a couple of weeks, and following that, the sweet peas and the flowers we've grown from seed.

Flynn takes my hand in his. 'Willow tree?' he says.

'Yep,' I reply, squeezing his hand. The willow tree has become a special place where we take time out of each day for Flynn to help me remember.

'I've actually been meaning to tell you that I remember something that happened here,' I say.

'You do?' he says, his eyes brightening.

'Just the proposal.'

'It was a pretty decent proposal,' he says, smiling to himself.

'Well, yeah, it was.'

'Nothing else?'

'Not much else. But we have a lifetime for you to tell me everything.'

'So where do we start today?'

'Wherever you want,' I say, sitting down on a patch of grass. I lie back and Flynn joins me as we peek through the canopy of leaves to the sky above.

'Okay, so I remember the moment I fell in love with you like it was yesterday. You were sitting under this willow tree, and you were humming to this tune, like nobody could hear you, and you were threading a daisy chain, with your tongue poking out of the corner of your mouth—'

'What was the song?'

'I don't remember.'

'Okay, no matter, go on …'

'So, you were threading this daisy chain and—'

'How do you know they weren't dandelions?' I smile, brushing my hand over the ground covering beside me and reach for a dandelion stem.

'I'm pretty sure they were daisies.'

I roll over onto my side and hand him the dandelion. He slips his arm around me, so that I'm nestled close to him.

'Fine. They may have been dandelions. If you want them to be dandelions, we'll call them dandelions.'

'Okay,' I say, a satisfied smile stretching across my lips. 'It doesn't really matter though, does it?'

'No, I guess it doesn't,' says Flynn. 'What matters is what you can see now.'

I look out onto the field, awash with colour, bursting with life and that's when I feel it, the closeness to everything I've ever known and wanted. In those flowers, there is my mother, there is friendship, there is healing, purpose and meaning. And there is Flynn.

In the unseen beauty of the flowers, I see everything, even if I don't remember it.

ACKNOWLEDGEMENTS

I'm filled with much gratitude for the network of people I'm fortunate enough to be surrounded by that made *The Memories Of Us* possible.

To Victoria Oundjian, Sabah Khan and the Avon team, thank you for such a warm welcome to the fold and for embracing *The Memories of Us* in the way that you have. Your enthusiasm and excitement about this book means so very much to me.

To my editor, Alexandra Nahlous, we have a much stronger book thanks to your brilliant insight and wonderful suggestions. Thank you.

To my agent, Cassie Hanjian, I'm so grateful for all your support and effort. I truly appreciate all that you do to guide me to shape my work into the best it can possibly be. Many thanks also to the wonderful Rachel Clements for championing this novel in the UK.

I'm surrounded by a wonderfully supportive network of writers who I am blessed to have in my life. Looking at you, Alli Sinclair, Josephine Moon, Kirsty Manning, Lisa Ireland, Sally Hepworth and Tess Woods.

To my early readers, Bella Ellwood-Clayton, Mary Lovelien and Natasha Lester—thank you for your honest feedback, helpful suggestions, ongoing support, encouragement, and precious time. Each one of you in your own special way has helped me make this into a better book.

To Amanda Wooding for the brainstorming session in Tuscany. I don't know that I could have reached *The End* in quite the same way without you.

Mara Novembre, your unwavering faith in me does not go unnoticed. Thank you, always.

I also owe thanks to Jenny Parish of Country Dahlias, who not only runs one of the most heart-stoppingly beautiful dahlia farms in Victoria, Australia, but so generously afforded me her time and answered the many questions I had about flower farming. Any gardening-related errors are entirely my own.

Since writing this book, I've had the pleasure of connecting with artisan flower growers and members of the floral community not only in Australia, but worldwide. I'd like to thank them for their commitment to the growing "Slow Flower" movement which means we all get to know the pleasure of locally grown and sustainable flowers within our communities. Thank you for making the world a happier, more beautiful place by bringing us fresh blooms to enjoy.

Infinite love and thanks to Mum, who is always there for me (I really am the luckiest daughter in the world), and all my family and friends.

And to Fabio, Christian and Alessia—thank you not only for bringing immeasurable levels of joy and love into my life on a daily basis, but also for being the best people in the world to make new memories with.